the hours
between us

the hours between us

A Novel

CAROL GRAF

Mill City Press, Minneapolis

Copyright © 2016 by Carol Graf

Mill City Press, Inc.
322 First Avenue N, 5th floor
Minneapolis, MN 55401
612.455.2293
www.millcitypublishing.com

Events Described Are Based on Dr. Graf's memory of combined, real world situations. However, the names of all patients discussed in this book, composite or otherwise, have been changed. In addition, in each of the medical cases described, identifying details, such as patients' ages, genders, ethnicities, professions, familial relationships, places of residence, medical history and diagnosis have been changed. With a few exceptions, Dr. Graf's colleagues, friends, and treating physicians have also been changed. Any resemblance to persons living or dead resulting from changes to names or identifying details is entirely coincidental and unintentional.

ISBN-13: 978-1-63505-176-6
LCCN: 2016913108

Edited by Jane O'Boyle
Photography by Rudmer Zwerver/Shutterstock
Cover Design by C. Tramell
Typeset by Mary Ross

Printed in the United States of America

For Christian and Erin,

children of my heart

and Abby and Thomas,

gifts of love

Author's Note

From the beginning of my medical residency until the end of a thirty-year private practice of psychiatry, I have spent thousands of hours with patients. Over time, I realized that their unique and compelling stories had not only touched me, but changed me. For as surely as I had become a character in their life stories, some of my patients became one in mine. It was the reality of this experience in my life as a psychiatrist that led to the telling of this story. While much of the content is based on truth, I have taken writer's liberties to cloak and protect the privacy and identity of all patients and family members, including the creation of composite characters which synthesize a number of patients and symbolize them all.

Because my book is so fundamentally grounded in truth, yet modified by a storyteller's freedoms, I have chosen to call *The Hours Between Us* a real-life novel.

Carol Graf, M.D.
September 2016

Chapter One

My secret name for my grandmother was Dumpling. I first met her when I was five years old on a blazing July day in Muskogee, Oklahoma. I was hanging upside down from the lowest limb of the giant cottonwood tree in our front yard when an old dark blue Chevrolet, covered in dust, pulled into our driveway. Out of the passenger side door stepped a round woman, almost as wide as she was tall, with a long black braid woven with many strands of gray. It turned out that she was my mother's mother, a stranger from South Carolina.

Grandmother was clearly on her best behavior for that trip. I do believe she smiled during those days in our Oklahoma house, even though the dark shadow of her mental illness was carefully veiled behind those smiles. She was a constrained, benevolent dumpling on a mission to retrieve her only daughter and return her to South Carolina. To do this, she had enlisted my grandfather, not only as a driver, but to provide my father a job in his successful company. Grandfather was ready to retire and let his youngest son, Uncle B.B., and my father run his textile mill in Boykin, South Carolina. I was not privy to all the machinations employed by my grandparents, but their timing was impeccable. My father was ready for a change. He was spending more and more time away from his family flying oil executives all over the southwest and he had concerns about the safety of the aging corporate aircraft of the 70s.

The one thing I had always known about my grandmother was that she was part Cherokee. Her great grandmother was a full-blooded Cherokee. My mother told me repeatedly that our high, wide cheek bones and black hair had come from her mother's ancestors. I had identified with those Indians because I, too, had their blood and they lived all over Oklahoma.

Like the unsuspecting Cherokee Indians who freely roamed the eastern lands of the Great White Spirit, I was as innocent and blind to the coming of Dumpling, as they were to the white man. I had had an idyllic childhood, years of stability and security, while my parents had been cloistered away from their families. They had been happy in Oklahoma and their joy fell on us as surely as a warm rain nurtures the earth.

The Dumpling's mission succeeded. My parents packed up and headed east, back to the home of their own childhoods. In school, I later learned about the fate of the great Cherokee nations of North Carolina and South Carolina. They embarked on their infamous Trail of Tears in 1838 when they were forced to walk a thousand miles in freezing rain and snow to Oklahoma. They buried four thousand of their loved ones along the way. Like my ancestors, I would soon bury my unfettered childhood, as well as my father's happiness and my mother's peace of mind. If I had known, I would have thrown a tantrum and had to be dragged to the car kicking and screaming.

We drove the reverse route of the Cherokee, leaving Oklahoma, passing through Arkansas, Tennessee, and North Carolina and into South Carolina. I wonder now how many bones of the Cherokee lay forgotten in the ground under the asphalt and our rolling tires. I unknowingly followed that hallowed pathway back to their homeland, but I didn't cry at the time.

My first clear memory of my grandmother after our move back to South Carolina was what I, from the distance and safety of age, still refer to as the "shotgun incident." After our arrival in the small town of Boykin, we lived with my grandparents while my grandfather had a house built for us in town. That house must have sweetened Dumpling's original deal. Dumpling never recovered her Oklahoma smile. I never witnessed that smile while we lived in her lair. It vanished for the rest of my life with her. I think I used the nickname I had given her like a talisman to lessen the impact of her ominous demeanor.

Every day of the two weeks we lived with her, Dumpling made my mother cry. My father would leave for the mill with Grandfather, dropping Mark off at school. The rest of us stayed home. Mother would try to help her mother with the cooking and cleaning. Everything she did was wrong and the slightest things seemed to set her mother off. Dumpling was prone to rage. Her normal voice bordered on shrill but would escalate into a shriek and elongate into a rant when she was upset. My mother's childhood was being reenacted and I was drawn into the drama.

"Eva! For God's sake, can't you do anything right?" became the mantra for almost every new day.

Finally, my mother broke down. In a desperate attempt to protect her, I stepped between her and a raging Dumpling. Probably, the earliest seeds of my experience with mental illness were planted deep inside me that day. Over the years to come, they were watered with tears, cultivated with bravado, and harvested when I became a medical resident in Psychiatry. But, at the time I faced my grandmother, I felt helpless and unable to protect my mother or myself.

Once, as I led my mother away from another emotional blow up, Dumpling yelled down the hall, "Go ahead, Eva, go with that *wild child*. Just leave me!" It was the first time she called me by that name. Mama explained, "She just thinks you're a tomboy. That generation thinks all girls should be more feminine." I snorted. *Feminine and crazy, like her*, I thought. But I *was* a tomboy and that was the first time it sounded like a bad thing. One day, the inevitable breaking point was reached.

When my father came home around dusk, I tattled on my grandmother. I wanted him to know what was happening while he was gone because he had the power to do something. My grandfather never came home until after my bedtime.

"Daddy, Grandma's been yelling at Mommy again. She's been crying in her bed all day. Can't we go back home to Oklahoma? That woman is mean, Daddy. Mommy needs help."

What I meant was that I needed help, too.

"Start packing," Dad said in a general announcement to everybody, "we're leaving. We'll go to Uncle Ed's boarding house until our place is finished." Uncle Ed was my grandfather's brother.

Dumpling screamed and howled as she raced from room to room, following my mother, imploring her not to leave home again. I was one scared five-year-old girl. I had tattled, but didn't expect this.

"Let's go pack," I said, herding my nine-year-old brother Mark and eighteen-month-old Jamey to the room we shared. I started throwing clothes, toys, games, and even snacks into suitcases. I was unsure if the boarding house would have provisions. Lugging the bags to the back door, Mark took them out to the car. I held Jamey's hand as I dragged him through the den towards the back door. In my other hand, I clutched my beloved ragged cloth bunny, Ninny. My father ushered my mother and a huge suitcase along the central hall.

As we all approached, there stood my grandmother blocking the back door holding a double barrel shotgun leveled at my father. Now, I *knew* about that shotgun. My grandmother kept it in a corner of the rear entryway in plain sight of all us grandchildren. She said she needed it "ready in case of emergencies." My curiosity grew exponentially every time I passed that gun. Finally, my father caught me handling it. He carefully explained what a shotgun was and what it could do. He opened the breech and showed me the shells tucked into the two barrels. He put the fear of God into me about ever touching it again. He must have forced Dumpling to hide it, because it had disappeared. Until now.

My father was over six feet tall, while Dumpling barely edged above five feet. I wanted to shrink Jamey and me to the size of gerbils so we could duck around Dumpling's legs and out the door. But I was frozen to the spot five feet away from a shotgun-toting Dumpling. Jamey sucked his thumb and whimpered. I thought Dumpling was going to kill my father in some insane, distorted attempt to save my mother. At that close range, it was even possible that the buckshot would hit my mother, too. I was flooded with terror. Primal, deep, and paralyzing, it marked me for life. The frozen tableau fragmented as my Grandmother began to wail.

"If you take my baby away again, I'll kill myself."

She slowly rotated the shotgun so that the barrel touched the underside of her chin. Could she even reach the trigger? My father never lost his composure, even when the gun was pointed at him. He closed the gap between himself and Dumpling like an avenging angel, dragging my mother behind him. Without breaking stride, he scooped up Jamey, handing him off to my mother as she made her escape through the back door. He lifted me in his strong arms, cradling me and Ninny from the emotional volcanic eruptions threatening us both. He became my safe place at that moment and for many years afterward.

"Tiffany, do the world a favor, go ahead and pull the trigger," my father dared as he swept past my grandmother.

As we descended the steps, I listened for the click of the trigger and the loud shotgun discharging, but there was only silence.

Chapter Two

I have often wondered if the repeated childhood traumas I experienced with my grandmother created a kind of homing signal deep within my psyche that guided me into the profession of psychiatry. Perhaps destiny predetermined my final pathway. Whatever the truth of the matter, I am a psychiatrist and have worked with adults and children for twenty years. I love what I do, thriving in this most wonderful and difficult profession.

Ironically, the linchpin of my humanity seems to lie in the wounds of my inner five-year-old wild child…wounds which taught me about empathy and compassion so vital in my work. I am particularly fond of and susceptible to five-year-olds who need help. I try never to underestimate what they know and feel, for it is still true that they know the language of the heart far better than the adults in their lives, far better than most psychiatrists, including me.

Today, it was a five-year-old little girl dressed in a pink ballerina outfit. Ally was the baby of the family sitting in a ring of chairs in my office. We were here so Ally's parents could "tell the children" that their marriage had failed and they were going to separate. Although I had seen Lauren and Alan for some months in couple's therapy, I had never met their three children.

It is especially difficult for children to come into a psychiatrist's office blindly and I had spent the first half of the family session getting to know them, hoping to develop some trust as we edged towards painful disclosures. The ten-year-old twin sisters were clearly the stars of the family and impressed me with their accomplishments. Gentle attempts on my part to lead them into discussing family issues were deftly avoided. As they talked, I kept glancing at Ally. She was wedged between her older siblings on the loveseat, tapping the heels of her soft, pink ballet shoes on the wooden frame. In my twenty years of private practice I had never had a child, or adult, for that matter, wear a costume to my office, even on Halloween. It fascinated me and I wondered if it was simple childhood fancy or her version of armor.

"Ally, I love your ballerina outfit. Is there a special reason you wore it today?" I asked.

"I am a ballerina and I am very beautiful when I dance. Would you like to see me?"

Both siblings rolled their eyes and their mother vigorously shook her head in my direction.

"Yes, Ally, I would like to see you dance," I encouraged as I purposefully quieted her mother. Her father was actually smiling.

Ally stood and curtsied, her blond curls creating a halo around her smiling face. She began to dance and twirl in delicate, light steps around the middle of the room as we all watched. Ally became the first person ever to dance in my office. She finished with another curtsy and I clapped in delight. Her sisters visibly relaxed, as did her father. Not so her mother.

"I really don't think we have time to waste like this," she said, her voice on edge. The family dynamics were replaying: Mom with an obsessive need to control, passive-avoidant Dad, twin over-achievers who denied negative emotions and a five-year-old who watched it all.

"Dr. Ingersohn, the children have no idea why they are here," Lauren rushed on. "Alan and I have kept everything away from them…."

In the midst of her mother's words, Ally raised her hand, politely asking for permission to speak. The tap-tap-tapping of her shoes beat a steady rhythm on the small couch.

Her mother pointedly ignored her and continued, "We felt that keeping a united front was in the children's best interest…."

Now, Ally started waving her small hand back and forth like a flag, clearly annoying everyone in her family.

Her mother's anxiety turned to vitriol as she targeted Ally in a furious voice, "Please *stop* kicking that couch, Ally, and don't interrupt. You *always* interrupt!"

Immediately, I came to the child's defense.

"Ally," I called her name hoping she would look up from the floor where shame had taken her, "do you have something important to say?"

She looked straight at me, "Are Mommy and Daddy getting a divorce?"

Her words were like a lightning strike that rendered everyone in the room mute. Even I was caught unaware.

I leaned towards Ally, "Tell me why you're asking that."

"Because Mommy and Daddy don't love each other anymore. Their eyes can't even see each other at all."

Ally spoke the unadulterated language of her heart. Her parents had no idea that their youngest child knew the truth about their problems. Their denial had, indeed, blinded them, just as Ally said.

Lauren dropped to her knees in front of her daughter, "Oh, Ally, I'm so sorry, so very sorry." The family closed the spaces between them, creating a huddle on the floor where they cried and clung to one another. Their work together had finally begun.

I watched them quietly, full of hope for their difficult journey ahead. It was moments like these that sustained me as a psychiatrist. There were really very few of them in the vast number of hours a therapist spends with patients. Therapy is hard work. People don't come in to have fun. They are propelled by fear, anger, anxiety, hurt and depression. Suffering. Certainly there are light moments and even humorous ones. Occasionally, time is wasted simply to provide relief. And then, like today, there is a breakthrough moment, when psychological defenses tumble down and love is stronger than fear. These kinds of moments are unrehearsed, spontaneous, powerful. My job is to make it safe enough for them to happen. At times they carry a certain risk for therapists, because they evoke our own past history and, sometimes, *our* ongoing emotional issues. They expose our humanity.

As I continued to watch the family, I remembered my own separation and divorce. Images of my two young children from seven years ago appeared superimposed over Ally and her siblings. God, my daughter had only been six back then, one year older than Ally. Like a kaleidoscope, my own Gracen and Ally's images juxtaposed, swirling as they aged, becoming teenagers... spiral after spiral of emotional pain, growth and healing. I saw and knew then that Ally would be all right. It was just going to take time. My ongoing job would be to help Ally's parents *see* their children's needs as well as their own.

The family therapy hour was my last of the day. I was tired and felt uncharacteristically restless as I ushered the family out. I needed to get home to my *own* children. Stopping at the desk of my secretary, Sarah, I found the only thing standing in the way of my escape: a revolving caddy holding four pink telephone message slips. Three were routine and could wait until tomorrow. One was from Dr. Rob Gellman. I recognized his personal cell phone number. His message read: "Important referral...call ASAP...no matter how late, Kai! Rob." It was printed in Sarah's precise, perfectly printed handwriting.

Rob was an old medical school classmate who practiced hematology/oncology at Hollings Cancer Center at the Medical University of South Carolina. He specialized in cancer of the blood and lymphatic systems. Referrals from him were always serious. There was a time when I wouldn't accept a patient with acute leukemia or lymphoma from anybody. I am still very selective and cautious in that arena.

"I am just too tired to talk to Rob Gellman right now," I muttered to myself. It was mental fatigue, not physical, that I was feeling. I needed to run five miles to shed the heavy energy accumulation of the day. "I'll call him tomorrow." I wasn't sure if I really would.

I packed my briefcase with the few files I needed to finish that night and slipped out the back door, leaving Sarah to close the office. I felt almost desperate to get to my children, to hold them in my arms, look them in the eye and really, really see them.

Chapter Three

I sat cross-legged on my dock, watching the early morning mist rise over the tidal creek before me. Lingering warm air from the preceding hot, humid summer day had touched the marsh waters cooled by the night. I had stolen from my warm bed at dawn to cloak myself in the fine condensation, becoming invisible to all but the spirit world, hearing only the soft susurrations of the incoming tide. I could see only the faint outlines of Boone Hall Plantation's main house across the water, brushed by the ghostly limbs and canopies of the live oaks. Boone Hall was the last of her kind on this eastern side of Charleston.

I closed my eyes as the sun began to burn away the mist and start its climb. Unbidden, Ally in her pink tutu appeared in my mind's eye. I watched her slowly dance and twirl her grief away. At some point, I *became* Ally, watching myself dance, feeling the release of movement.

When I'd returned home from work the night before, Gracen and Andrew were munching pizza and watching television. Wednesday was pizza night and they were teenagers. I was so disappointed; having supper together was the time we "rounded up" and relaxed. I hadn't seen them since our sixty-second breakfast. They were riveted to *NCIS*. When they finally looked my way, there was minimal guilt. I pointed to the kitchen table. Sullenly, they relocated. Taking a slice of pepperoni and mushroom out of the box, I said, "Let me ask you both a question," I took a deep breath, "how do you think you're doing now? It's been seven years since the divorce."

They looked at me like I was speaking Swahili.

Gracen asked, "Mom, are you *okay*? Did something happen at the office today?"

"Am I that transparent?" I should have known I couldn't hide anything from her.

She shot her brother a look before answering, "When you come in hang dog and grabbing pizza, you're pretty easy to read."

"I'm sorry if I was abrupt. A family came in today so the parents could tell their three children they were getting a divorce."

"Like what happened to us, huh?" Andrew's mouth was full.

"Amazingly similar. Painful for them all. Painful for me, too," I slipped in.

"That pain goes away, Mom. Andrew and I are doing fine. You and Dad are *so* different; we just can't understand why you ever got married. *And* we wonder whether either one of you will ever marry again." Gracen didn't mince words.

"A little girl in the family reminded me that when we stop seeing each other, it's the beginning of the end of love relationships. I don't ever want to stop seeing you two. I really, really love you," my voice quavered.

"You're not gonna cry, are you, Mom?" Andrew stopped mid-bite.

I shook my head as the tears started.

"Mama, we're okay, really," Andrew did not like to see me cry.

I tried not to show emotion in front of him. After the divorce, I had always tried to be strong for them, but right now, I felt very vulnerable.

"We love you, too, Mom." Gracen leaned over and brushed a kiss over my wet cheek and cuddled my arm as she laid her head on my shoulder. That kid always knew the right thing to say. When she innocently took the last slice of pizza, I laughed.

The smell of freshly brewed coffee wafting down to the dock brought me back to the present. Thank God for coffee pots with timers. I inhaled deeply. Heavenly hazelnut Brazilian ground coffee. Too bad I didn't like to drink it. I am probably the only person in the world who brews coffee for the smell, but doesn't drink the stuff. It tastes bitter, no matter how much cream and sugar I add. I tried to drink coffee in medical school, hoping the caffeine would keep me awake while studying in the evenings and during endless nights on call. Couldn't stand the stuff, so now I toss the coffee after the aroma gets me out of bed. I smiled, remembering some of the teasing from the other residents during my psychiatry residency about the sniff-but-don't-drink-coffee thing.

"Mom, pancakes are ready and Gracen isn't up yet," Andrew shouted down the slope of the grassy back yard. My eyes popped open to a blaze of bright green marsh grass...and reality. I had no idea what time it was, but if breakfast was served, it must be close to departure time for school. Andrew drove and if his sister wasn't ready when he backed out of the driveway, I would have to take her.

As I headed up the steps to the deck that wrapped around the back of the house, Andrew was walking out of the kitchen to the weathered wooden table on the screened porch. He had a huge stack of blueberry pancakes from Aunt Jemima's frozen section. The kid was the king of the microwave ovens. He drove, he cooked, he was an honor student and he had the privileged place of being my first born. It was Andrew who taught me how to be a mother. Everything we did together that first year had been new, exciting, and even a little scary. All in all, it was pure discovery. By the end of his first year, I earned the stripes of motherhood. With each succeeding phase of his life, I added to my experience. Even now, at sixteen, he still amazes me on a regular basis. He never had the adolescent "sleeping sickness," unlike thirteen-year-old Gracen. As a baby, we called her Rip Van Gracen when she started sleeping twelve hours a night at three weeks old. As she aged, she slept through alarm clocks, rock music on the clock radio, and very loud voices.

"Andy-San," I used his pet name, "did you let Poochie-Ching and Tallulah out yet?" Our golden labs were aging and had occasional accidents if they didn't get outside early enough.

"Out and back in. I put some bacon on their dog food. Mom, seriously, I am not waiting on the sleep freak. If she's not ready, I'm going to leave her," he warned.

"I'll have her down in ten minutes. How about wrapping a pancake around some bacon for her?"

I got a look of disgust that only a sixteen-year-old boy could manage.

On the way up the stairs, I remembered I had a drug rep to see before my first patient at 8:30. I was going to be rushed. The alarm clock was blaring as sleeping beauty slumbered on. All I could see was a mass of tangled red hair spilling over the tropical-weight down comforter. I turned off the alarm and sat on the edge of her canopy bed. I stroked her beautiful curly hair, then gave it a yank! Groans of protest were muffled under the covers.

I whispered in her ear, "Up in three or I call in Creepy Mouse."

"Mom, *puh-leeze*. I'm a little old for that," she complained.

Listen, little girl, I thought to myself, *Creepy Mouse will not go into moth balls just because you're a teenager. I am not ready for you to leave all your childhood behind yet.* Maybe I was saying I wasn't ready for her to leave me either.

It was only a ten-minute drive to my office. I pulled around back and parked, walking the pathway that wound through leafy dogwoods and summer perennials to the back porch of my office. As I unlocked the door, I entered my professional world. I could almost hear the door to motherhood close behind me as I started my daily work ritual. I walked across to the mahogany desk against the wall and turned on a small bronze lamp. I tossed my briefcase and purse on the textured pale green wingback chair flanking the desk and sat down to read the mail, making notes to Sarah. It was Wednesday. I was halfway through my work week. Thirty something hours a week straight hourly therapy was about all any psychiatrist could do. Most of the time, I worked three ten-hour days. Often there was spillover to a fourth. I glanced at a plaque sitting on the back of my desk: "Life is an adventure; be ready." It had been a gift from a patient. I stared at it and felt a little tingle of anticipation or was it anxiety? Was I ready? Ready for what? I had no idea if I was ready or not. Sarah buzzed me on the intercom to tell me the Prozac rep had arrived. I liked Brad. He was funny. It was a good way to start the day.

I saw three patients and the morning passed quickly. At the 11:50 break, I decided to return the call to Dr. Gellman. My ambivalence had been raging all morning. He and I had been in the same medical class twenty years before. He had been the class lady killer, a handsome free spirit who liked to chide my seriousness. I could almost hear his voice from long ago: "*Kai, lighten up! You're too damn serious.*" Well, I always wanted to be prepared and that did translate into responsibility, didn't it? Even back then, I was hiding my own vulnerability.

I glanced at the clock: only six minutes before my next appointment. Did I have time to call? Who came up with this fifty-minute hour schedule for patients? It only allowed a ten-minute break to stretch, transition from the last patient to the next and touch base with the front desk secretaries. Something deep inside urged me to call.

"Pick up, Rob," I spoke to the phone. If he didn't answer now, I might not try again today.

"Kai, how's my favorite shrink?"

"Pretty shrunk and pressed for time. What's up, Hunk?" I teased him with the nickname bestowed upon him by the young hospital floor nurses in our junior year.

"Hunk," he laughed. "Tell that to the missing-in-action hair and the too-many-cafeteria-meals pot gut. No one would recognize this *chunk.*"

I laughed, but I heard his fatigue. His work took its toll day after day, year after year. Cancer doctors lose so many of their patients. They don't do this kind of work just for money.

"Kai, I've got a special referral for you," Rob said, "and don't give me that trash about my referring to someone else. This one has 'you' written all over it."

"Tell me," I said, matching his tone of seriousness.

"I've got a twenty-six-year-old girl who graduated *cum laude* from Princeton; recently finished her second year of a doctoral program from the University of Chicago. Get this," he breathed in a funny way that sounded like the exhale of cigarette smoke, "a PhD in Metaphysics and Religious Studies in Chicago. I don't even know what a degree in metaphysics means! She's beautiful, too. Looks like a refugee from a modeling agency. Doesn't seem to know it though."

"What's wrong with her, Rob?"

"Acute myelogenous leukemia - AML. As you know, it's one of the most difficult kinds to cure. She waited way too long to seek treatment. She was in summer school in Switzerland and damned near died trying to get back to the U.S. They stabilized her at Sloan Kettering in New York City. She and her family decided to transfer her care down here to MUSC. She insisted on being close to home.

She's got a good chance of going into full remission after more intense chemotherapy. We've learned a lot since med

21

school when so many of our leukemia patients died. But AML is still a bitch to treat: it won't stay in remission. Sloan Kettering's been having the best long term results with stem cell transplants in AML cases. A five year survival rate is only about twenty percent after transplant. She's not ready for transplant yet."

He fell silent. I felt a sense of dread in the pit of my stomach. I wasn't sure I was ready to take on a hopeless leukemia patient.

"Is she willing to see a psychiatrist?" I asked.

"She asked for it!"

"She asked to see a psychiatrist?"

"I told you this one had your name on it. I'm not even sure *you* can handle it. This girl is really unusual. When she was tentatively diagnosed in Zurich, she went to the Internet, learning all she could about leukemia. When Sloan Kettering clarified that she had AML, she accumulated a two-inch folder of information which she shared with me. We discussed it like a case presentation we would have made in medical school. She knows it's an acute case and time is of the essence. She told me I had to be up front and not treat her like a kid. She said she wanted a partnership with me as the head of her team, to include 'a cutting-edge oncology pharmacologist, an acupuncturist and a holistic psychiatrist.'"

"Tell me again why she transferred her treatment down here."

"She grew up here. Graduated from Ashley Hall. Her parents are both professors at the College of Charleston. She's too sick to go back to school and says she'll make her stand here, where the marsh and salt water can hold her. Where her family can be with her. If it comes down to bone marrow transplant, she'll go back to Sloan Kettering. One of my old residency buddies is a specialist in AML treatment up there. We're still in the initial push for remission. I think she's come home to die, if she loses the battle. And, Kai, just to keep it interesting, her grandfather is Dr. Stephen Edinger."

"*The* Stephen Edinger?" I echoed.

"One and the same." The ex-governor of South Carolina and currently the president of MUSC. Rob knew he had just brought in the heavy artillery.

"Okay, Rob. I'll have to find a spot to fit her in. How much time do I have?"

"She wants to interview you before she makes a commitment."

I laughed. "Interview me? That's a change. I hope I measure up," I said only half-jokingly. "By the way, what's her name?"

"Stephanie. Stephanie Edinger."

"Tell her to call and make an appointment." I hung up and glanced at the shell clock across the room.

"Damn." I was ten minutes late for my next patient. As I walked down the hall to the waiting room, my thoughts were still on Stephanie Edinger. "She's making her stand here where the marsh and salt water can hold her," Rob's words reverberated in my mind. I could understand why this sick graduate student wanted to come home to be treated in Charleston. There was no way that Rob Gellman or Stephanie Edinger could have known that every day the marsh and tide gave me sustenance, washed away the debris and sorrow of my work and renewed my own spiritual energy. I heard a deep, intuitive "click" of hope. I knew I had to see her. Question to myself: *was I ready?*

Chapter Four

My first impression of Stephanie was that she was a caged tigress, relentlessly pacing the confines of my small waiting room. As I walked into the secretarial reception area to speak to Sarah about a prescription call to a pharmacy, I glanced up through the small sliding glass window to the waiting room and saw her. She was tall and thin, moving with a feline grace that couldn't conceal a tightly confined, almost frenetic energy within. She wore a light blue warm-up suit and white tennis shoes, their winged symbol splashed across the jacket's pocket and sides of the shoes. Her long, blond hair was pulled into a ponytail and laced through the back of a white baseball cap with the matching Nike logo front and center. She was alone in the waiting area. It was five o'clock and she was my last patient of the day. She had asked for a two-hour session and I had conceded to ninety minutes, which was the ideal time for an evaluation.

As my gaze lingered, she turned presciently and our eyes locked. She strode to the window and motioned Sarah to open it, her bright green eyes holding mine.

"Dr. Ingersohn," it almost sounded like a challenge.

"Yes," I replied. "Stephanie?"

"The one and only," and we both smiled.

Her beauty was radiant, natural. She wore no makeup. Freckles sprinkled across her nose and high-boned cheeks saved her from perfection. She certainly didn't look like she had almost died several weeks ago.

"I'll be with you in a moment," I spoke reassuringly and turned back to Sarah for final instructions.

I experienced a small feeling of anticipation as I walked back into the hallway leading to the waiting room door.

When Stephanie entered my inner office, she stood in the middle of the room and inspected it like a prospective buyer. I waited in the doorway for her to finish her appraisal. Most patients head for the peach loveseat along the wall to the left of the doorway, or one of the pale green wing chairs flanking the single window on the other wall. French doors stood at the end of the room and opened onto a deck. Above the doors was a large, lighted exit sign, a strict requirement of the Charleston County Fire Department. Its large red lettering certainly marked the way *out* in case of an emergency. I always considered it a rude contrast to the soft and tranquil décor.

Stephanie turned to face the light flooding in through the French doors.

"Doesn't look like what I envisioned for a psychiatrist's office," she said. "I like the light. I'm not sure I could have stayed if it had been dark in here."

"Do you feel you can stay, then?" I asked.

She looked over her shoulder at me without answering and stepped closer to a large painting over the loveseat. It was a still life of a fine porcelain pitcher filled with pale pink blooming azaleas, with matching antique tea cups and saucers set on a round, white, chipped wooden table. She stared at it intently. "Does this painting have a name?" she asked softly.

"It's called, 'My Mother's House is a Fragile Place'."

"Did one of your patients paint it for you?"

I was surprised that she would ask that. "Yes. She painted it for me in response to the work we had done together. We traded her therapy for it."

When patients sat on the loveseat, the painting was a backdrop that always reminded me of the incredible journey of the artist, a former patient who progressed from alcoholism and depression back to creative freedom and wellness.

Stephanie continued to gaze at it.

"Is the painting speaking to you?" I asked.

"Did her mother love her?" She almost breathed the question.

This time, I was shocked.

"No," I replied. "Her mother's fragility and wounds kept her from being able to love...even her daughter. That core wound was the primary focus of her therapy."

Stephanie reached out and gently traced the outline of the cream-colored Victorian tea cup. Just at that moment, she stood in silhouette as the late afternoon sun streamed around her. It could have been a still frame of "now" reaching across some timeless divide between past brokenness and healing, from despair to hope. Stephanie broke the spell by turning around and plopping into the wing chair that happened to have my yellow writing pad in it.

"I'm sorry," I said, "That is my chair. I'm happy to offer you its twin, or the loveseat, or even the desk chair." She laughed and moved to the matching chair kicking off her shoes. We both settled in and Stephanie tucked her long legs up under her.

"I guess Dr. Gellman told you about my problem."

"Very briefly. He said you were assembling a team of specialists to help you with your treatment. He said you wanted to interview me as a prospective member of your team." I said it with a hint of a smile.

"Your name came up from several sources. Dr. Gellman and my parents' rector at Grace Episcopal spoke of you. They both called you Dr. Kai. I had lunch with the Right Reverend McKenna last week. He told me you were old friends from the annual Medicine and Ministry of the Whole Person conference. He seemed to think you might fit the bill of what I am looking for in a psychiatrist. The good reverend came to Grace Episcopal the year I went to Princeton, so I've only known him peripherally. My mother sent some of his sermons on tape to me when she feared for my salvation. She calls the Ivy League schools 'dens of iniquity'. You know, all those years in the Episcopal Church have hardly dented the Catholic in her. Anyway, one of the sermons she sent last Easter was called 'Eternal Life', sort of based on Hans Küng's book. You know any of Küng's work?"

"Ironically, I was given one of his books by a patient last Christmas." He had been diagnosed with Lou Gehrig's disease and felt Küng's writing helped him cope with his progressive debilitation and pending death.

"Did you read it?"

"I did. It's deep. It covers medical, philosophical and theological aspects of actual death, dying and afterlife. Fascinating...and heavy!"

"Did Dr. Gellman tell you I'm in graduate school at the University of Chicago? This is what I am studying. I mean metaphysics and spiritual beliefs."

I nodded that I knew she was in that field.

"I don't profess to understand everything Küng says, but it challenges me to stay open and keep learning," I responded.

Stephanie looked piercingly at me. "That's what I need from you, Dr. Ingersohn. I need you to stay open and walk along with me. I want a straight, honest relationship with you.

When I ask you a question, I don't want you to turn it around on me and say, 'Now, how do *you* feel about that?' We need a set of guidelines that work for me, so I took the liberty of writing some of them down."

She reached into her blue backpack with the ever-present Nike/Mercury symbol, and pulled out a folded piece of white paper. She scanned it quickly, and then handed it over to me. It read:

1) We are equals. I defer to your training in medicine and psychiatry and you defer to my knowing my own truth.

2) No psychobabble. Straight talk only, and honesty. Always honesty.

3) You agree to share some of your life as I share mine. (I know this is different, but a must for me.)

4) No religious dogma. I will quit if you try to push religion down my throat. I'm pretty confused and angry with God. I think I still believe in God, but that's all I can say right now.

5) Help me integrate my mind and emotions with my physical body and my spirituality.

6) Help me try to live.

I read her contract. It was obviously done on a computer, with lines at the bottom for both of us to sign.

I looked at Stephanie.

"We are equals and I will always respect your truth as preeminent," I said. "That must always be at the core of therapy. That, and trust. We must both learn to trust each other. Without that, we won't be able to work together.

As for number two, I may lapse into psychobabble. Just tell me when I do and I'll try to use words that don't block your understanding. And I will tell you when I think you are avoiding or being dishonest with either one of us."

"Number three, I can share some of my life, particularly if I think it can help you. I have ups and downs just like everybody. But, you are here as the 'patient.' You're not paying me to tell you my problems."

"Stop right here, Doc," she said. "I know you must have your problems. If I can't see your problems, I won't be able to trust you. If you come off like some know-it-all guru, I will just discredit you."

"You may discredit me anyway, Stephanie. You sound like you're fully capable of discrediting anybody you want to discredit. I'm not perfect. Please don't ask me to be. If I say something or do something you don't like, then you will need to tell me. Not just quit. So, may we add number seven to this contract— that we will honestly confront differences and decide together if one of us needs to quit therapy?"

"You mean *you* quit therapy with a patient?" she retorted.

"I have," I answered.

"Like when?"

I immediately thought of a case many years before when I could not continue therapy with a patient who had survived advanced ovarian cancer. I began telling the story to Stephanie, purposefully cloaking it.

"I had worked with her for a year, even bringing in her husband for couples work. She was *committed* to unhappiness. She had actually survived surgery and chemo for one of the most lethal cancers in existence and had been *cured*. But, she had *no* gratitude for it. She was angry, cruei and miserable, but not depressed, which her oncologist thought when he referred her to me years after the initial diagnosis. I had never had a patient, before or since, so committed to playing the role of victim. I tried everything, finally confronting what I saw. She admitted it. She came to therapy to complain and blame and saw no reason to fundamentally change. She hated her husband, but didn't believe in divorce. She never had children and didn't want them. She had no intention of returning to the work she had once enjoyed. She was 'hostilely dependent' on those who supported her, including her parents and siblings. Finally, I quit. We talked it out and she was able to leave by blaming me. And I *had* failed her by being unable to help her break out of the neurotic lock of blame, anger and judgment. Paradoxically, I would have failed myself just as much by being an ongoing repository for her venom with no hope of healing."

The story seemed to give Stephanie a lift.

"You know, I think you are the right 'shrink' for me."

"Because I can quit?"

"Because I think you're strong enough for me. The last psychiatrist I saw in high school was a wimp. My mother made me go so she could tell him what he had to do to fix me, which meant making me do things her way." Her lip almost curled as she was talking. "She even wanted me to take drugs to make me more compliant. That mealy-mouthed shrink tried to get me to take lithium. He gave everybody lithium, and, get this, he ultimately put *her* on it." She laughed out loud at the memory, straightening her legs out in front of her and visibly relaxing. "So, can we sign the contract?"

"One more thing," I interjected. "Number four, about religious dogma. Stephanie, it will never be my job to force you into any kind of boxes, psychological or spiritual. My job is to help you do your own healing – not only your body, but your heart, mind and spirit. To walk along with you and help you stay on the pathway, to be a guide."

"So, you will be my guide in the dark," she whispered.

Her words hung between us like a promise received. It was a good place to close. I switched gears back to the practical. "How often do you want to see me?"

"Every week for now," Stephanie replied.

I wondered where in my crowded schedule I would find another hour a week. "I may have to work you into cancellations until a regular time opens up."

"I only have time right now, and you *will* find time for me," she said resolutely.

I underlined "No religious dogma" under item four of her contract, added item seven governing "quitting," and signed my name to the bottom: Dr. Katherine Ann Ingersohn, Guide. Stephanie did the same, playfully adding Guide-ee alongside her name.

It was 6:45 p.m. and time to stop. Stephanie stood and reached up in a full body stretch, then bent over and put both hands flat on the carpeted floor. I watched with envy as I could not remember the last time I had been that limber. She straightened, turned and shook my hand. She paused by a small, square, mahogany table placed at the end of the loveseat, beside the door to the hall.

The tabletop was covered with a variety of miniature swan figurines: a wooden puzzle swan and a bronze bell with its long swan neck gracefully curving into a handle. An ivory enamel swan with its wings spread stood near the rim ready for flight. Some of the swans had the area between their folded wings hollowed to hold potpourri or small seashells. A cut crystal swan reflected prismatic colors from the lamp light above it. An artfully woven straw swan had a pink ribbon around its neck.

"What's with all the swans?" she asked as she knelt down to look at the display at eye level.

"When one of my patients really begins their deeper work in therapy, they can choose a swan from the table to take home to keep as a visual symbol of the inner work they are doing. Some do early on, some never take one. I only ask that, one day, they bring a new swan to leave on the table for someone else to choose."

"Can I take one now?" she asked tentatively. "Even though I'm only beginning?"

"If it feels right."

In answer, she picked up the ivory enamel swan, poised for flight.

"This one's for me." She lifted it possessively and wrapped it in Kleenex from the box on my desk. Then she tucked it into her purse.

She led the way out of the office and I followed, watching her ponytail swish as we walked down the hall to the check-out desk where Sarah sat waiting.

We had never even said the word leukemia. I had taken no history; hadn't heard but one thing about her childhood and adolescence. But we had accomplished a supportive framework for our work together. The beginning itself is often an indicator of how a therapy will proceed. Who was this young, beautiful Joan of Arc, clad in her Nike armor, gathering an army to do battle with leukemia? Why did I sense so strongly a fragile little girl being asked to face her terrors in the dark?

Sarah and I chatted quietly for a few minutes as we went through the rituals of closing the office. I loved leaving my office at the end of the day in broad daylight. When Daylight Savings reverted to Eastern Standard Time, darkness descended by 6:00 p.m. Every year, I always had to readjust to ending my day in the dark. I was a card-carrying, bona fide sufferer of S.A.D., seasonal affective disorder. When summer light began to wane, my body's light sensors went into red level alert. I learned years ago that a trip to the Caribbean for a blast of light in late January would get me through the winter. It was a splurge and in my health budget. I glanced out at the bright light to reassure myself that I had several more months of summer illumination to carry me home, and sighed.

"That Stephanie is a ball of fire," Sarah said. "She came out here and told me to put her on the schedule every week *and* she wanted the first cancellation."

"This case will be extremely challenging and you know exactly what I mean, Sarah."

"Is she a model? She's so striking. It's the way she carries herself, I think."

"No," I replied, "an exceptionally bright grad student who's come home to battle a dragon."

Sarah straightened up the stack of magazines on the waiting room coffee table and turned off the lights and music. I set the alarm and we walked out together, closing the door on the day.

Chapter Five

I was in deep dream sleep. My "dream self" was watching as my eyelids fluttered erratically like a wounded butterfly touching down on its final flight.

I dreamed I was at my office, sitting with an old woman. I began the interview, "Now, tell me why you are here."

Abruptly, the woman stood up and walked to me. Taking me by the hand, she led me to the single window behind my chair. Tired eyes suddenly shone with fervor.

She soundlessly pointed out the window to a large live oak tree. One of its gnarled old limbs dipped so close that it nearly touched the window. There was a beautiful, bright red cardinal sitting on the limb. I was riveted. The bird appeared to be watching us both. Suddenly, it turned into a small brown barn owl and left its perch, flying towards the window with such force that it made me shrink back. I chided myself as I looked at the solid glass barrier; then noticed the upper casement of the window was actually open! The small owl's wings batted furiously at the screen and broke through the open window!

I threw up a hand in an instinctive gesture of protection, palm out, fingers splayed. The owl's beak hooked into the palm of my outstretched right hand, embedding itself deeply. I cried out in pain and surprise. I slapped at the owl with my left hand and tried to shake it loose, but it seemed to hold on tighter.

I turned to the old crone, begging, "Please, help me." She only smiled.

I was forced to help myself. Gently, with my left hand, I began stroking the owl's feathers over and over, speaking in soft, imploring tones. The bird calmed.

Finally, it released me and flew to sit on the old woman's shoulder. Now she seemed like the goddess Athena with her wisdom owl that stared unblinkingly at me. I looked at my hand which didn't hurt at all. I expected a gash and blood, but there was only a small, red mark in the center of my palm.

I woke up suddenly, disoriented. Where was I? My heart was beating furiously. I realized I was home, in my bed, and not at my office. My first instinct was to retreat into sleep again. I wanted this dream to go away, but I knew better. I could no more keep the dream out of my conscious mind than I could keep the owl away while I was asleep. I *knew* the dream was prophetic. But what did it mean? And why had it come now?

I shook my head to clear it. It was still dark outside, the clock on my bedside table said it was the middle of the night. I lay quietly in the dark, replaying the dream. I had to capture it, write it down in the dream journal kept close by, in the table drawer. A touch to the base of the bedside lamp brought soft light into the dark. Without getting up, I wrote down every detail of the dream. The stark clarity of the images surprised me. Usually a dream begins to fade as soon as I awaken; this one did not. There was so much power in this one; I could still feel it.

From early childhood, I have remembered my dreams. Intuitively, I seemed to know they were important. Like most children and adults, I didn't know what to do with them. Even in college psychology, there wasn't much information about dream theory. It was a Jungian analyst in my psychiatric training who gave me the key to understanding the language of dreams. Our waking life experience, full of thoughts, impressions, and feelings, creates an overload for our conscious minds. This information must be stored for later processing and assimilation. Much like a computer, the conscious mind uses a code of symbols and images to convey information back and forth between itself and the unconscious. When we sleep, the dream code carries the valuable and important "data" to the conscious mind and we remember. Most people are intrigued by dreams but dismiss them like a foreign language they don't know. Learning to translate a dream is like mining for gold. Unless we value the gold of a dream, it is lost to us.

Now I was wide awake. I found my bookmarked place in *Atlas Shrugged* by Ayn Rand. Surely that would put me to sleep.

Chapter Six

My next session with Stephanie was six days later.

"We had a last minute cancellation," Sarah explained. "I left messages for several other patients, but Stephanie called back first."

As if summoned by our conversation, Stephanie came in the front door at that very moment. Her hair was down and uncovered, a beautiful shade of pale blond with streaks of gold from the sunlight. She wore a blue sundress that left her tanned shoulders bare. She had probably been walking the beach. She was the proverbial picture of health, and I wondered briefly if the diagnosis of leukemia had been a mistake. I knew better. Leukemia is an insidious and stealthy disease, often striking children and young adults in their prime and gradually sapping their health. Hadn't I learned that lesson repeatedly over the last twenty years, from both patients and friends? Wasn't it why I left pediatrics for a psychiatry residency? The initial chemotherapy was only the first battle of a long war. It was mild compared to what was coming.

I opened the waiting room door and brought Stephanie back into my office. Unerringly, she went to the painting that had so enthralled her on the first visit and again touched the image of the teacup. She then sat down on the loveseat.

It often intrigues me how patients make their decision where to place themselves in the office. I usually let them know where I sit. Psychiatrists stake a place to anchor themselves. It provides continuity for us. My chair is by the light with my reading glasses and water on the table beside it. Typically, I lead the patient into the room and make a sweeping gesture to the other wing chair, loveseat or leather desk chair. It is a revealing decision. Rarely will a patient say they don't care or ask me where I want them to sit. Once chosen, the place becomes "theirs." They will return to that place every succeeding session. If they bring a family member, friend or lover to a session, they will say, "This is where I sit, and Dr. Kai is there, so you can sit…." If they change places in their course of therapy, it is a big red flag signaling a psychological shift is taking place. They are ready to make a leap. Stephanie chose to change places in her second session. I was not sure what to make of it, so I asked her.

"I wanted to sit under the painting," she answered. "I feel safer here, and it's as close to the light as I can sit … since you have the only chair by the light," she added with a small smirk.

"It's where you tried to sit the first time you came. I may need to give you this seat," my voice assumed a questioning tone.

"No, I need to sit here." It was said with finality; the issue was settled.

"Stephanie, tell me about the leukemia."

She began speaking with a clear, resonant voice, looking me straight in the eye.

"I had just finished my second year of grad school in Chicago when I got the incredible opportunity to attend the Jung Institute in Zürich. I was thrilled to spend the summer studying and traveling in Europe again since I had spent my junior year abroad in Germany.

At first, I thought the persistent fatigue I felt was delayed jet lag and I ignored it. But it didn't get better. After a couple of weeks, I wondered if I was anemic. I also noticed I was bruising easily. I became worried when blisters from new hiking boots didn't heal. One seemed to be infected.

Finally, I decided to get help. The school referred me to a local doctor. I mainly went because of the bruises and the blisters. I almost didn't tell him about the fatigue and the feeling that I needed to sleep all the time."

Stephanie seemed to drift into her own reverie. "The doctor was so kind and gentle. He actually took time with me." She smiled to herself.

"We spoke in Swiss German, so I didn't know the words for some of the medical terms, but we got by. He ordered an antibiotic and blood work and asked me to see him again in three days."

She paused, remembering.

"It was Dr. Von Orelli who first used the word 'leukemia'. It's a similar word in German: *Leukämie*. He explained that my white cell count was extremely high. Normal was between five and ten thousand, mine was *150,000*. Equally troubling was the increase in red blood cells and platelets. He told me that many of these blood cells were abnormal, immature. He called them blast cells. They were young, undifferentiated cells that hadn't matured. All clinical data pointed to leukemia. The most basic cells in the bone marrow, the stem cells, capable of making any component of the blood, had given rise to malignant blast cells and were reproducing wildly. They were making too many cells."

Again, she was lost in her own thoughts. It was as if she was telling me a story about another person from long ago. Distancing the self from extreme threat is called denial. In early stages of life-threatening illness, it is often a "necessary denial," a psychological defense mechanism that helps a patient cope and function.

"I was in shock," she said. "How could this be? I'm athletic. I've always paid close attention to my diet, never smoked, hardly drank. I could *not* accept the possibility that I had leukemia. My classes were ending in two weeks, and I tried to bargain for time to finish the course work. But, Dr. Von Orelli was adamant that I see a blood specialist in Switzerland immediately, or return home to the U.S. for treatment right away."

She shook her head as if trying to dispel the thought. "I couldn't quit classes and lose six credits. I guess my denial and stubbornness prevailed. I rationalized that the fatigue came from too much hiking and partying. So, I decided to just continue taking the antibiotic and stop hiking for a few days."

"By the end of the week, the blisters were worse and I could hardly drag myself out of bed. I Googled leukemia. I stayed up half the night and printed everything I could find. I read medical journals, American Cancer Society protocols and treatment plans. I remember the exact moment that I admitted it. I said it out loud, '*I have leukemia. God in heaven, I have leukemia.*'"

I took notes on everything she said. She was succinct and quite clinical in her delivery, like Dr. Gellman had said. She was unemotional, distanced, almost disconnected from her own words.

"Did Sloan Kettering confirm the diagnosis?"

"They ran a battery of tests and their specialists studied every aspect of my blood and bone marrow. They even did a bone marrow extraction." She shivered involuntarily at the memory and skipped a beat in the rhythm of her story. "And it hurt. It hurt so badly. They're heartless when they do that. Have you ever seen the size of the needle they use?"

I nodded. In medical school, my pediatric leukemia patients hated bone marrow biopsies. *Hated* them. And I hated having to be party to causing them pain.

"They stuck it into my left pelvic bone, all the way into the middle of that large, flat part. And get this, no anesthesia. They really do need to put people to sleep when they stick that huge needle in. But, *no*, it doesn't hurt *them*."

I knew we would have to revisit her view of pain and the medical profession's enduring dismissal of the pain they cause in the attempt to treat the illness. It was a persistent, unresolved issue for all of us.

"Have they established the chemotherapy treatment regimen?"

"Yes, and it's real aggressive. I'm on daily Cytarabine injections until I go into the hospital next week. Then, for seven days, I get continuous IV infusions of two other long-named drugs. Hopefully, these will kill all the malignant cells in the blood. I will be in isolation for another two weeks until the stem cells reset and start putting out healthy new cells. They are trying to push the leukemia into total remission."

At this point, I remembered Rob Gellmans' other words to me on the telephone last week: "Won't stay in remission." I pondered the word *re*mission. It was used in the medical field to indicate a time during the life of the disease when there are no evident symptoms, when the disease is quiet and the patient appears well. Remission is not a cure. It simply indicates the dormant phase of an illness.

Remission, remit, forgive, pardon, relieve, abate. The remission of leukemia. The etiology of the word remission is interesting. In religion, we speak of the remission of sins; in medicine, the remission of disease. Did those of us in the medical field have any real understanding of the word that we had purloined from theology? In the hallowed halls of cancer treatment centers all over the world, "remission" is second only to "cure" in its power. Remission is the desired "way station". The longer a patient stays in remission, the better the hope for cure. Remission becomes cure when it lasts for at least five years. If a patient relapses, each succeeding remission is shorter and shorter until the disease will no longer remit. This is often the last stage that ends with death.

I heard Stephanie calling my name. This time, it was me who had drifted. She was talking about when she would start her hospital treatment and I realized I had not heard what she said.

"I'm sorry, Steph, could you repeat that?"

"I said I'll go into the hospital a week from today."

"Are you worried about this stage of treatment?"

Stephanie stared intently at me, through me. Now, she was drifting.

"Steph?"

"I was thinking about how the blister almost killed me. One little blister. By the time I landed in New York City, I had to be rushed to the E.R. at Sloan Kettering with a raging bacterial infection. All those extra white cells that usually fight off infection were defective. I had enough cells to defeat Napoleon's army and they were all blind to the enemy. They started IVs in the ER and flooded me with all kinds of antibiotics. I was really out of it; had visions of angels. My father and grandfather had flown to meet me. They thought I was going to die. Apparently, I almost did."

Stephanie stopped talking and dropped her head, her shiny blond hair forming a curtain of silk around her face, veiling her eyes. Her hands lay quietly in her lap. I held the silence with her. Finally, she lifted her head. With palpable sadness, she whispered, "Maybe it would have been best if I had…if I had just died then." Reality was leaking in around her wall of denial.

This was no longer a tigress speaking, no Joan of Arc; merely a tired young woman who had a long, hard struggle just to live ahead of her. In the recesses of my mind, a faint memory rose from its deep, hidden resting place: a little girl with leukemia who died with me beside her so many years ago. I banished it quickly, as I had many times before.

"I am thinking about the contract you brought to me last week, Stephanie," I said softly. "Number six said, 'help me try to live'. Do you still want to live?"

Stephanie was gazing out the glass doors. She slowly turned her misty emerald eyes to meet mine.

"In my best and highest moments, I think I'm not afraid to die. If what I've been taught all my life in the church is true, why should I be afraid of death? I mean, I have always believed in God. Surely, I will make it to an afterlife beyond pain and suffering. Still, sometimes I am afraid of the unknown, terrified of not 'being' anymore.

You know, by the time I flew back to the U.S., my whole body was aching as though I had the flu. Every time I moved my joints, they hurt like a toothache. I still don't know how I got to the airport and onto that plane from Switzerland. My hips and knees hurt while I was just sitting still in my seat. I wondered if people ever die on airplanes. I was eating Advil and Tylenol every hour; even took a sleeping pill. Right before I fell asleep, I remembered that little prayer I said at bedtime when I was a child. *Now I lay me down to sleep, I pray the Lord my soul to keep. If I should die before I wake....*" She paused, choked up.

"*If I should die before I wake, I pray the Lord my soul to take.*" Her childhood prayer...and mine...and countless others.

She started to weep, soundlessly. Tears spilled down her cheeks. My eyes filled with tears, too. Empathy is a matter of the heart, emotional resonance. It is not premeditated and can't be faked. It just is. I was *with* her. Stephanie cried for the pain and suffering that was to come, the incredible difficulty of it all. The unfairness, the threat of death - not just quiet, peaceful slipping out of this world into the next, but the agony between now and then. And the ever present fear.

Sometimes, tears say a lot more than words. So does touch. When a patient is facing death, it changes all the dynamics of a normal therapy. There is simply not enough time. Trust and alliance accelerate, instead of taking weeks or months to evolve. Boundaries soften and a unique intimacy can take place. I put down my pen and paper and crossed over to the loveseat. I sat down next to Stephanie. She turned into my arms and I held her, gently rocking her back and forth. Tears and touch melded us, creating a solid foundation for our future work together.

Sniffling followed. I reached for the tissue box. There were four or five boxes placed strategically around the room. We ordered the stuff by the case for the office.

Stephanie and I blew our noses together and then started smiling at the strange sounds we both were making.

"God, you sound like a horn on a tugboat," she sniggered.

We both laughed. When emotions become too heavy, the mind seems to call on the healing power of laughter for balance.

I looked at the seashell clock. We were ten minutes past the hour. We had done precisely what we needed to do. Our eyes were still red when Stephanie and I stood up and hugged one more time.

"God didn't take my soul when I lay down to sleep on that airplane or at Sloan Kettering," Stephanie said. She stood still in the middle of the room, a little apart from me. "I wonder if God has cast me aside...just forgotten me. Or maybe I'm being punished for something I've done. Maybe I pissed God off somewhere in my life. She paused. It's possible that God wants me to make a stand, to fight, to give it all I've got. God and me?"

I didn't try to answer her. Often, a patient waited until the last minute of a session to reveal the "gold," the deepest truth of the heart. I did know that every statement or question she spoke would be the seeds of future therapy sessions. Like following a trail of bread crumbs to mark the path, we would have to revisit them all in depth to make our way through this therapy together. Stephanie had just dropped a treasure trove.

"I need to see you again before I go into the hospital."

"Let's go check the schedule."

I knew before I looked at it that I would "tack her on" to my schedule at 6 p.m. on Tuesday unless something else opened up. The inpatient hospital phase of her treatment would be serious and grueling.

I was running late for my next appointment which always

bothered me. I hated making patients wait. It was a matter of respect. This had been a big issue with my father, too. Being on time meant respect to him. My patients usually came on time and I needed to stay on time. It was a constant juggling act. Today, Stephanie had needed the extra time. I would apologize to the next patient knowing one day they might need those precious extra minutes.

I quickly walked back through my office, opened the French doors, silently cursing once more that they opened only inward instead of outward, and stepped out onto the porch. The air was crisp; nature was dressed in multiple shades of green in stunning contrast to the backdrop of the clear, blue sky. I breathed deeply, trying to clear my mind. There was a rustling on a live oak tree where a bright red cardinal was perched, staring right at me. I stared back, looked quickly for the missing owl and remembered the dream again - now I began to realize that not only was my hand to be marked, but also my heart. I felt mildly anxious. Stephanie was *here*. I had signed on to be her guide. I honestly did not know if I was ready for this adventure or not. The cardinal was gone when I turned back into the office to see my next patient.

Chapter Seven

Owl dreams were haunting me. Even though Halloween was several months away, the commercial campaign was underway in every store. I had never noticed how many toys and inanimate owls were available in the retail world. Witches with owls were everywhere. Whatever happened to broom sticks and black cats? Halloween candy even included chocolate covered marshmallow owls. Inflatable owls festooned the candy aisles in the grocery store. Barnes & Noble had cardboard cutouts of Harry Potter and his white owl bracketing a special display table. Browsing through a collection of books "back in print," I found *I Heard the Owl Call My Name*. I had read that book years ago and been touched deeply by its theme about owls portending death.

Last night, I had another owl dream. This time, the small barn owl was under my bed covers, nestled over my heart. In the dream, I woke up with the weight of something on me. I gingerly raised the cover and was shocked to see the tiny owl with its head tucked under its wing, sleeping. Carefully, I lifted the creature only to find its talons gripping my nightgown and the underlying skin. The owl raised its head and looked me straight in the eye as if to say, "*I am here to stay, lady...right on your heart.*" I dropped the covers back down and felt its grip relax. Then I *really* woke up. I knew I couldn't wait; I needed help, *now*! The dream was upping the ante and I wasn't getting its message. My thoughts turned to my friend and colleague, Willa. I knew she would understand.

Willa had joined my psychiatric practice shortly after I had moved from Charleston to Mt. Pleasant, across the Cooper River. I had started my career with an established group of psychiatrists on the opposite side of the peninsula. When my husband and I moved to Mt. Pleasant, it was an expeditious time to strike out on my own and start my practice. The building I found had room for four other therapists and Willa was the first non-M.D. counselor to join me. She had come from the trenches of public mental health where burnout was legion. I was thrilled when she finally decamped to private practice which gave her more control over her scheduling, patient load and reimbursement. Over the years, our team of independent therapists evolved, each with unique specialty interests and training. This team approach not only allowed a broad spectrum of treatment choices for our patients, it became a strong support system for each of us as therapists. It was *critical* to my well-being. Psychiatry is a demanding emotional arena. It is not surprising that the suicide rate amongst all physicians is topped by psychiatrists. Dentists rank second. Both deal almost exclusively with pain and discomfort in their primary treatment.

As the only prescribing M.D. on the team, I often evaluated my colleagues' patients for medication. Weekly supervision with each therapist allowed me to review progress therapeutically and medically. Whenever possible, we did this during lunch hour. Getting out of the office was more than a change of location; it was a valuable change of venue.

As soon as I got to the office, I texted Willa asking if we could use part of today's supervision time to discuss my owl dreams. A note back from her reassured me there was plenty of time to review her cases *and* my dreams.

My morning with patients seemed to drag. I was distracted by my need to understand the dreams. They hovered at the edge of my conscious mind. I was downright anxious by lunch time.

Willa and I tucked into one of our favorite lunch spots that was quiet and secluded. After dispensing with patient medical issues, we turned to my owl dreams. Willa was our resident expert in animal symbolism. We had a monthly dream group composed of eight therapists from all over the area. We always titled our dreams: my first dream was labeled "Marked by An Owl". I read her the dream as she listened intently. I also gave her a quick account of the most recent dream, which I called "Owl on My Heart". Now it was my time to listen.

"Gal, gal, be cum full 'up de spirit wur'll, eh?" she spoke in Gullah, that almost extinct African-English language created by the early slaves of the sea islands of South Carolina. The cadence and rhythm of its sound was as unique as its words. Willa had spent most summers with her grandmother, Sophie, and her live-in housekeeper, Daufina. They lived on the sparsely-populated Yonges Island, south of Charleston. Daufina's ancestors were descendants of slaves from the old Toogoodoo Plantation who preserved and protected their Gullah heritage; Sophie's were the plantation's owners.

Daufina had taught Willa about the mysticism and rituals that still prevailed in some black communities on the barrier islands protecting the coast from the ravages of the wind-driven Atlantic Ocean. Willa was a curious mixture of her Caucasian and "borrowed" African heritage. She had been named by Daufina who had raised her own mother, Sophie's daughter. She and Daufina had a deep relationship rooted in love and respect. I read an article once by a genetic scientist that said spirituality was "wired" into human genes; that our spiritual strivings to know God and the universal realm of mysticism were genetically determined. If that is true, Willa and I both were born with a whole heapin' handful of those genes.

When Willa spoke Gullah, she was either being playful or dead serious. Dreams were a serious matter to us both.

"Tell 'um," I spoke back in my limited repertoire of Gullah.

"Dat owl bird ain't gwain dash away til e gits e meanin'."

"That's what I thought, too. Help me, Willa. Part of me

would just as soon forget these dreams. But I just can't. They'll only get louder and stronger. Are they warning me? Scares me. I once read that when the owl called your name, it can be a premonition of death."

"Okay, Kai," Willa was ready to get down to the work of interpretation, bringing her expertise and experience to bear.

"What are all your associations with owls?"

"Wisdom, mystery, predator, spirit animal for Athena (Greek goddess of wisdom and knowledge), 'night owl' which I happen to be, extraordinary vision and hearing. I think that's about it."

"Daufina would tell you that the owl is the messenger bird from the spirit world. You and I would translate that as a messenger from the unconscious or the unknown, shadow part of our psyche." This was pure Jungian theory in which we were both well versed.

"The barn owl's heart-shaped face and silent flight give it the name 'the ghost owl,' a 'plat eye' in Gullah. Think about a modern example. The owl is a messenger in the Harry Potter books which have so many archetypes of good and evil, light and dark, etc. Harry's white owl helps him and shows him the way."

"Me and Harry Potter," I mumbled. "What a dubious distinction."

"Don't knock Harry. You might be able to learn a lot from him as you get into your own adventure." Willa was serious.

"And the red bird that turns into the owl?" I questioned.

"The cardinal is the male of the species. That might connote animus or the masculine energy in a woman."

We both started laughing. Everyone in our dream group and our practice knew how "animus driven" we both are. Willa's father was a doctor who returned to England after her parents' divorce. She had almost gone to medical school before she came into our practice, but was saved by a late-in-life pregnancy and the birth of her son. The masculine traits of focus, discipline and perseverance are hallmarks of an animus woman, and are an absolute necessities to make it in the field of medicine. Most women who enter medical school or get graduate degrees are animus driven. The trick for us is balancing that masculine energy with the feminine qualities of feeling, expression, creativity, empathy and patience. It is an ongoing battle for Willa and me. Paradoxically, psychiatry and counseling demand a measure of both these energies.

Willa continued, "Red is the color of passion, life-giving blood, the vital energy of emotional fire."

Immediately, the image of Stephanie just before our first session reappeared: the tigress with its powerful, primitive energy. The association made sense to me. I told Willa about Stephanie and how the referral had come. The approximation of the first owl dream the night after her initial visit struck me with a different insight.

"So, this young patient fighting leukemia may have evoked the symbol of the red bird in *your* dream. The connection may be that both of you will need passion and vital energy to make your individual, yet parallel journeys."

"And what exactly is *my* journey?"

"The red bird morphs into a barn owl and gets through your window, screen, and hand. It's making a concerted effort to penetrate your mental defenses to get to a part of your body, your hand. What do you do with your right hand?" She asked.

"Touch, eat, wash, hold things, cook, write, create." It suddenly dawned on me; my creative life was virtually dormant. My painting and writing, even my creative romantic relationships with men were absent. I felt a stab of emotion. I knew intuitively that "creativity" was the correct symbol for why the owl impaled itself on my *right-write* hand. In my dream, I had thrown my hand up for protection after the owl broke through my outer defenses...a partially open window. Was I trying to keep this energy away? Was this the proverbial window of opportunity for a messenger to break through my defenses? I finally spoke all this out loud to Willa.

"What has happened to your creativity?" Willa asked.

"I don't know. It simply went away...was lost to me over the years. I was so creative as a young child, drawing and writing, even into early adolescence." I paused. I was confused...unsure what to say. All I could think of was Dumpling. Now, of all times. "After Dumpling died, ..." I made a strangulating sound that startled Willa. "Damn it to hell!!!!" I exploded. "Surely all this doesn't have to do with my grandmother. I thought she was dead, gone...."

"Gone where?" Willa's tone softened, "Where did you send her, Kai?"

We both knew that nothing ever died in the unconscious. It just waited, full of energy, creative or destructive, whatever we let it become. My own Jungian analyst, Dr. Ann Ulanov, had taught me to understand the language of dreams, to hear the guidance and healing they spoke. She was my mentor, my strong mother figure. I could hear her telling me of such energy being repressed for years until some experience evoked it, opened a door or window to bring it back into the light. She also taught me why we need a guide to help us. I needed Willa to guide me because I had been too afraid to "hear" the dream. I could not do this alone, no matter my skills with dream interpretation.

Now I began to weave the symbols of the dream together. "The old woman who came to see me in the dream was a messenger...a crone...a wise woman. It was she who made me step to the partially opened window...the portal? She stood with me when the owl came through; she made me deal with it. The owl went to her shoulder, creating an image of Athena, goddess of wisdom."

Willa interrupted, "On the deepest level of the dream, the old, wise woman is part of you. Perhaps the good grandmother, the 'mirror' of your own undeveloped images of the feminine. Maybe *she* is the key to retrieving your feminine creativity...if you want it back?"

I felt like crying. Something precious had been gone from me for a long time and I didn't even realize it. Want it back? Living without creative energy the rest of my life would be tantamount to a living death; like existing without imagination, inspiration or hope. Willa must have seen the anguish in my eyes. She reached over and put her hand over mine.

"The owl marked you, Kai. Even though it was painful, it was as if it was a reminder that terrible wounds heal and that your 'hand of creativity' can be restored."

"But, why now, Willa?"

"Therein lies the mystery, Kai. Why did this special patient come to you *now*? Does the dream-maker, spirit think it is time for healing and restoration in *your* life? Maybe you still have something to learn or to finish with your grandmother or your mother, especially if your creativity and well-being are bound to them. The owl knows the secrets of the night, those things hidden in the dark. Your job is to wake up, to choose to understand the message. See the possibilities and act on them."

I looked at my half-eaten grilled cheese. I really didn't want all this buried "wound stuff" to come out. I had a choice, didn't

I? I could ignore the dreams and go right on with my old ways.
I could, couldn't I? Didn't I tell patients this every day of the
week? Isn't this why some of them quit therapy?

"Lordy, lordy," Willa started standing up, "we bees late.
Time for we'uns to git on back ta work!"

Now she was being playful.

Chapter Eight

Stephanie was late for her appointment on Monday. She had to drive across the Cooper River Bridge from downtown. Before that, she had to navigate the labyrinth of huge buildings from the Hollings Cancer Center to the patient parking lot. She sat caught up in the heavy 5:00 p.m. traffic streaming over the bridge from the city to my office. She called and left a message with Sarah that her chemotherapy treatment had started late, but she was still coming.

It gave me time to catch my breath after a full day. I made a cup of Lemon Zinger herbal tea, hoping for a lift, and headed to my private porch. It had been overcast and misty all day, but seasonably warm. I sat at the wicker table and thought about the patient who had just left. Julia was one of many women I treated for depression. She was in her late forties, an empty-nester since her youngest had left for college. Julia had given her all to raising her three daughters and now they had each gone away into self-discovery. After twenty-five years, she was left in an empty marriage with a workaholic surgeon. Julia's symptoms began with frequent crying spells and low energy. Often she didn't get out of bed until noon. She lost her appetite and interest in life. She thought she was strong enough to ride out her problems, but her best friend convinced her she needed help.

"I'm so lost," Julia had said in our first session. Depression covered her like a thick layer of ashes. After three weeks in therapy and taking the antidepressant, Zoloft, she was beginning to feel better. She slowly became aware that something deep within had begun to "search for her". Julia's mother had died from a stroke at age forty-nine; her grandmother and an aunt had had strokes in their fifties. Julia was facing her mortality, wounds of separation from her children, and the disintegration of her marriage. Now that she had enough energy and willingness, she could tend to her "inner psychological and emotional" needs.

Women like Julia were the backbone of my practice. Eighty percent of a psychiatrist's patients are women. The other twenty percent are men who are recommended, sent, or dragged in by women.

The intercom buzzed. It was Sarah letting me know Stephanie had arrived. She and I dived in, making up for lost time.

"You know the craziest thing about chemotherapy is this: you lie quietly in a La-Z-Boy chair, sipping orange juice and reading trashy magazines while the doctor of your own choosing injects you with poison. I have just ended three hours of being poisoned, and I had to pay for it!"

She was exuberant. Her eyes danced like flames on a gas stove burner. "Irony of ironies," she declared.

"You seem to feel well," I said, wondering why she was in such a good mood.

"I do. I've been ravenous. You know the steroids they give me along with the chemotherapy make me hungry and manic at the same time. I knew I was going to be late, so I stopped in the hospital cafeteria and got a takeout cheeseburger loaded with onions, pickles, lettuce and tomato, and an order of French fries to boot. Ate the whole thing coming over the bridge. I'll apologize now if I have to throw up later. I guess we should have a signal if I have to make a run for it! The signal will be an abrupt leap for the door! Do you mind if I stretch my legs out on the loveseat?"

"Not at all." She was definitely edgy and had a "steroid flush" on her face.

"Did you deliberately get a couch that's too short for patients to lie down on?"

I laughed. "This one matched my décor. Plus, it goes so well with the red neon exit sign."

"But, seriously," Stephanie continued, "do patients ever lie down on couches anymore?"

"A few Freudian relics are still around for that kind of analysis. I'm afraid that modern psychotherapy requires sitting up. You could lie on the floor if you wish."

"On your lovely Chinese rug? I think I will." Stephanie angled down in a roll from the loveseat and settled on her back. Her long legs stretched almost to the desk.

"Remember, Dr. Kai, that poison is circulating throughout my body as we speak." She was definitely hyper, speaking rapidly and making small extraneous movements. It took her a while to settle down. Still, she surprised me with her next question. "Did you ever play that board game called *Risk*?"

It was one of my brother's favorites, I thought, as I answered, "I did, I did."

"My Dad and I played that game. I always chose the blue pieces, I think they were French. Dad was British red. Dad taught me about battle tactics in that game, including placement of the bombs, cavalry officers, and foot soldiers. I think chemotherapy is like that game. The doctors are placing the poison soldiers and cavalry strategically to battle the cancer cells in my blood."

"Tell me about your father, Stephanie."

She became still and quiet for so long, I thought she might not have heard me.

"He's tall, gray haired, handsome. Brilliant professor. He taught me to read when I was four. I loved Dr. Seuss's *Cat in the Hat*. I memorized almost every Seuss book, *Green Eggs and Ham, How the Grinch Stole Christmas*. I also loved *Tom Sawyer, Huckleberry Finn, Robinson Crusoe, The Last of the Mohicans*.

Some of my earliest memories are discussing those books with Dad. He made them come alive. He made me want to hear the next chapter. We used to even rewrite some of the chapters to add our own twists."

"Your parents are professors at the College of Charleston, right?"

"Dad is a tenured professor of American History. Mom teaches music part time. She also plays the organ at the Cathedral. It lets her get back to Mass without upsetting the 'Great Compromise'."

"I thought your parents went to Grace Episcopal?"

"That's it, the compromise. Dad grew up Presbyterian at First Scots downtown. Mom grew up Roman Catholic in Richmond, Virginia. I think her great-grandmother was the only Catholic member of the Daughters of the Confederacy. When Mom and Dad got married, he refused to agree to the Catholic rule that you had to raise your children in the Catholic Church. So, they eloped and later joined the Episcopal Church as a compromise. Mom's mother was mortified. They were Richmond blue bloods on the Mayflower Registry. Blue bloods do not elope.

My dad's people were French Huguenots who escaped persecution in Europe in the early 1700s. Straight-line ancestry through the males who were born and bred right here.

My great-great-great-grandfather, Etienne, was a successful indigo and rice planter who got mega rich. The original plantation was up near Middleton Place Plantation on the Ashley River. You didn't ask for my genealogy, did you?" She smiled innocently. "Am I boring you?"

"It's pretty fascinating stuff. I'm a transplant from Oklahoma, so I had to learn about this obsession locals have with ancestry."

"My mother's the one who is obsessed with it. She was a Jackson from Richmond, Virginia. Stonewall Jackson was somewhere in her family, the resident saint. Move over, St. Peter and St. Paul for St. Stonewall."

"He was accidentally killed by his own men in the Civil War, wasn't he?"

"It was a great Southern tragedy. To the Confederacy, that was like Jesus being betrayed by one of his own disciples. I always wondered what happened to the Confederate sentry who shot him. Did he hang himself like Judas...or did a Stonewall zealot 'accidentally' shoot him?"

"So, all this history is important to your mother?"

"Let me be clear, Doc, she breathes this like oxygen. It *is* her life. And she personally brought the Mayflower Registry together with the French Huguenot settlers of Charleston. She married into the St. Andrews Society and the St. Cecilia Society. She also got into the Carolina Yacht Club. She belongs to the Daughters of the American Revolution, United Daughters of the Confederacy, and lives S.O.B."

I had to laugh at the way she enunciated every letter. South of Broad Street is where the Charleston blue bloods live.

"I don't have a problem with any of it. I'm proud of my Southern heritage," she continued.

She laughed and turned on her side, facing me, pulling her knees up to her chest. I could see the top of her head, but her face was hidden from me.

"There's just one hitch to this story though. I don't belong in it. Actually, neither does my father."

"But, he's the historian who was born here. Why not?"

"He *teaches* history, but his lineage is not that important to him. He doesn't worship his ancestors. He loves history. You should sit in on one of his classes. They're packed. He's famous for his lectures about Abraham Lincoln and FDR. But he doesn't wear his personal genealogy as a badge of honor like my *lovely* mother. If you took all those societies and registries away from her, she wouldn't exist. Poof, a ghost. Well, maybe like the *Phantom of the Opera* with musical notes wafting out of the mist."

"And you don't belong, either," I parroted her words back to her.

Stephanie sat up abruptly. I thought maybe she was sick. But she pivoted around to face me with her knees pulled up to her chin, both arms hugging her legs.

"Sometimes I can't believe I'm her daughter. Granted, I look like her. We both have blond hair and green eyes. She has brown specks in one. Her hair is out of a bottle, though. I'm tall like my father and Mother's five feet two. I outgrew her by the time I was eleven. But I'm not musical *at all* like she is. Piano lessons were the bane of my life. She started teaching me when I was six years old. She finally gave up and got another piano teacher who used to rap my knuckles with a ruler when I made mistakes. I learned to play the piano, but I hated it. Still do. As soon as I finished high school, I never touched a piano again. Mom would drag me to St. John the Baptist when she played the organ at Sunday Mass. I had to sit under her watchful eye throughout the long service. I *finally* learned to sneak in a book and hide it inside a hymnal.

"And, let us not forget cotillion: gloves, manners, etiquette and ballroom dancing. I was 5'9" when I was thirteen. Skinny as a stick. In cotillion, you had to wear hose and low-heeled dress shoes. I hated it. My mother tried to mold me into her image. I went to Ashley Hall until eighth grade with all those girls. Cotillion was the only time I even saw boys."

I was struck by how different Stephanie's childhood had been from my own. I'd had nothing but boys in my life. The only gloves I wore were baseball mitts.

Stephanie continued, "Mother made me wear a hat to church. This is during the 90's! I'm a hippie at heart. I should have lived in Berkeley in the 60's. I was born out there when Dad was getting his doctorate at Stanford. He and Mom moved back to Charleston when I was a baby."

"Did all these struggles with your mother make your childhood unhappy?"

"I was happy away from her. I was happy with my friends and my Dad and my twin cousins. My Dad has one sister who lives here and she has twin girls, Janet and Linda. My Edinger grandparents are fun. They have a second house out on Wadmalaw Island. I spent most of my summers out there, with horses and dogs and rabbits. We'd go over to Rockville and swim all day. I learned to sail Sunfish there. Sometimes, I'd stay for weeks with Nana and Two-Pop and Dad would come on weekends. Do you know Two-Pop? He's president of the Medical University."

"Well, I know Dr. Stephen Edinger."

"That's Two-Pop," she smiled broadly. "I named him when I was little. He's quite renowned at MUSC for his research in genetic mutation."

"When did he leave the governor's office?"

"I was twelve when he started. He served two terms. It's hard to believe Two-Pop is so famous. He taught me to ride horses, go duck and dove hunting, and love the land. He was my special granddaddy. Nana taught me to cook and sew and paint. Those were happy days. They loved me and I loved them. That will never change."

"Did your mother go with you? Out to Wadmalaw, I mean."

"She doesn't like the country. She's a 'townie'. She thought it was dirty out there. Hated the animals. She's a control freak and she couldn't control nature, Nana or Two-Pop like she does Dad. He's too kind to stand up to her. Passive. I think he loves her and just plays the 'peace at any price' game."

"I was the one that rocked Mom's boat. I'm a rebel. I remember when I was three or four; I hated the smocked dresses she always made me wear. We had this big fight. I wanted to wear cowboy boots to Sunday school with one of those dresses. She was horrified. I pitched a fit, threw myself on the floor and screamed until I almost passed out. I lost. No cowboy boots. Just patent leather Mary Janes with lace socks. I would rip those dresses on purpose, especially if they had sashes on them! Once, I marked one up at school with a purple magic marker. It's the only time my Dad ever spanked me. She made him. She said I was bad and going straight to purgatory if somebody didn't stop me. Life was pretty good after I left home and went to Princeton with all those smart, sassy, sexy Yankees!"

"So, there you have it. Guess I'm pretty screwed up, huh? Control freak mother; passive, brilliant father? And I got leukemia. I wonder if rebels get leukemia more than other kinds of people. Nobody else in my family ever had it. Maybe this is divine justice. Maybe Mama prayed to St. Stonewall to teach me a lesson."

Stephanie yawned widely and lay back down on her side.

"Steph, you mentioned the board game *Risk* relative to your chemo, your war on cancer. I have a book I want to send home with you today, *Images of Healing*. It's about using guided imagery as a way to approach cancer. I'd like to do a short imagery exercise with you now if it's okay."

I heard her yawn again.

"I'm game. Never heard of guided imagery."

"Do you feel comfortable lying flat on your back again?"

She turned onto her back as an answer and closed her eyes.

"Take several deep, deep breaths and blow them out slowly."

Her chest expanded and I heard the slow whispers of her exhalations.

"Now, remember yourself lying on that recliner at the hospital. Can you see yourself?"

She nodded.

"This is an eidetic image: it has visual and auditory memory components, 'body imprints' as well as emotion attached to it. All of these together form an 'eidetic picture.' Imagine that the IV full of chemo is really full of thousands and thousands of little Pac-Man circles with mouths, like in the early video game."

"Pac-Man. This is getting far out, Doc."

"Stay with me. Can you see all the Pac-Men?"

"Yeah. They're all different colors."

"Now, climb on one of them and ride it like a horse."

"I don't know if I can do this, Doc." She was laughing.

"Get out of your judging self and let your imagination take charge. Put on your cowboy boots, Stephanie. Nothing is holding you back but you."

"Okay, I'm riding a big blue Pac-Man horse."

"You're charging alongside the Pac-Man cavalry through your blood vessels. Some of the Pac-Men horses are gobbling up the sick red blood cells, white ones, platelets. Others are veering off to your brain, spleen, liver. You're riding to the bones. You've just arrived at your left pelvic bone where you had the bone marrow needle biopsy."

"Oh, God. Oh, God, I'm here. There are hundreds of malignant cells."

"What color are they, Steph?"

"Black. Black. Black." She almost writhed on the floor.

"Time to eat them all. Kill them, Stephanie. Use your mind and do battle."

"There are so many, so many."

"Pac-Men are ferocious, they can eat them. Be aware of the cleansing going on all over your body."

I slid down to the floor and took Stephanie's hand and joined in the battle with her. I focused my mind on her Pac-Man horses, her cowboy boots, her immunity. I felt an arc of energy between our bodies through the closed circuit of our hands. Light, heat, quantum energy of motion. *Recreate this body. Make us whole and well,* my spirit spoke to its Source. Time slowed, seemed to stop. Then, abruptly, we were cast back into the "now."

Stephanie sat up and stared at me. I stared back. We were both shaken. I realized that Spirit had included me, too: "*make us well.*"

"What just happened, Kai?" Stephanie's voice quivered.

I shuddered. "I'm not sure."

"It was powerful," she replied. "It felt like being touched by God."

"Touched by God," my words echoed hers and hung palpably in the air between us, filling the silence that followed.

Stephanie leaned forward, closed her eyes, and gently touched my face with her fingertips. It was if she were tracing the very essence of me. It felt like the brush of owl's wings and I smiled.

She broke the spell by standing up, extending a hand to help me off the floor. My joints were stiff and I felt every one of my forty-six years. In all those years, I had never had an experience quite like what had just happened.

"Can you come visit me in the hospital? I have to be in sterile isolation for the next fourteen days with the IV infusions. I'm trying to figure out how to sterilize my laptop, or at least my iPhone, so I can text."

"Call and leave me the room number and I'll come after work," I told her, then gave her my cell phone number.

"Some people die from this treatment, you know." She said it casually. I heard it as another step in her dance with death.

"Stephanie, look at me. It is not time for you to die; not now," I said it slowly and with clarity.

"You think?"

"I know." I did know. I don't know how, but I knew.

"I hope you're right," she gave me a small smile.

After Stephanie left, I stood in front of "her picture" for a few minutes looking at the delicate tea set. Sometimes, life is fragile, too. I know that in human beings strength coexists with fragility. And Stephanie had a tigress inside, crouched and waiting, fueling her will to live.

Chapter Nine

I awoke early Wednesday as the ambient light of predawn was pushing away the silken dark of night. I had forgotten to close the plantation shutters last night and now became witness to the birth of a new day. I lay perfectly still in the bed, cocooned in the soft covers, facing the wall of windows. My eyes widened as the first rays of sun broke over the eastern horizon of fading marsh grass, as if each ray were a paintbrush on the palette of the sky, swirls of pink, rose and gold flowed from their tips to fill my view. In all my years, I had only seen a handful of sunrises. I was always too busy sleeping or getting ready to go somewhere or do something. But here, now, in the perfect stillness, I could see and know the miracle of morning.

My pager singaled. A call this early is never good. It was my answering service with an emergency call from Stephanie. I called her immediately.

"Kai, I'm so sorry to call at such an early hour, but I need to see you for a few minutes this morning. I have been up all night. I left messages on your voice mail at the office all during the night. I probably should have called your answering service or your cell phone, but...I couldn't. I just couldn't. It was like I had to get through the night...alone. Kai, I've never been through such darkness and fear...such despair. I'm supposed to check into the hospital at 11:00. I really need to talk to you. Please say you can see me, Kai." She hardly took a breath until she ended with my name.

"I can be at the office in fifteen minutes. Can you come right now?"

"I can be there by 7:15."

"Drive around to the back parking lot. My silver SUV will be back there. Follow the path through the trees to my back deck. The lights will be on and the door open. Are you alert enough to drive?"

"I've been driving around all night. Been to Folly Beach and Sullivan's Island. Parked at your office twice. Crossing one more bridge won't be a problem. See you."

I launched out of the bed, fortified with the power of sunrise, ran a brush through my hair, slipped into warm-ups and running shoes, left a note for the kids and poured a cup of coffee to smell. Seven minutes later, I was at my office. I turned off the alarm, flipped on the lights, punched on some air conditioning and listened to my voice mail. I could get a "read" on Stephanie's night from the messages she had left. The recording gave the times of the calls, as well.

12:13 a.m. "Kai, it's me, Stephanie. I just needed to hear your voice on the machine. I'm scared. So scared. I don't think I can go through with the chemo. I just...I just...I just feel like I'm going to die if I do. I can't breathe, Kai. Don't let me die. Call me as soon as you get this message in the morning. I know you come in early. I don't want to bother you tonight. Call me."

2:17 a.m. "Kai, it's me again. I've never been so scared in my life, even on the plane coming home from Zurich. I was too sick to be scared then. You know I could die from this chemo. They're going to blitz all my blood cells. Kill them all. What if they kill me, too, trying to cure me? I need to talk to you. I'm sitting in my car in your parking lot. It's as close as I can get to you. You said you knew that I wasn't going to die yet. You said that yesterday. But I think you're wrong. Call me, Kai."

When Stephanie spoke from the heart, she called me Kai. No Doctor Kai or Doc. All of this was straight from her heart. Why didn't she call my answering service instead of leaving messages on voice mail? Why couldn't she? She even had my cell number for emergencies...and finally used it this morning! What stopped her? My uneasiness was escalating.

4:30 a.m. "Kai, I'm sitting on the sand dunes at Sullivan's Island. It's high tide and the waves are crashing in. I'm dragging my feet through the phosphorescent foam. It would be very easy to walk out into the ocean, deeper and deeper. I could float away. I am so alone. So alone. I feel so lost, like nobody can find me. If I float very, very quietly, out beyond the breakers, maybe God could follow the beating of my heart and find me again. I don't want to die, but I would rather walk into the arms of death than keep feeling all this fear...terror. Would I be forgiven if I just let go and slipped under the water where I can find peace? I can't. I just cannot. I'm going to drive some more, maybe over to Folly Beach to watch the sunrise. Call me."

Folly Beach was on the opposite side of Charleston. She would have to have crossed three or four bridges to get from Sullivan's to Folly Beach. What powerful symbolism, I thought, this crossing of bridges.

I was shaking by the time I finished listening to the messages. Last night, while I slept so soundlessly and dreamlessly, Stephanie had faced death. This kind of experience had a name: the *dark night of the soul*. So many patients made that passage when they were facing deep loss or critical illness or some other cataclysm in their life. I had been there when my marriage died; when my brother Mark died. And my father. When death threatened, I felt utterly alone. It is a journey most of us make alone.

I walked through the back door and stood on the porch watching full morning light filter through the trees, my arms wrapped tightly around myself. I heard Stephanie's VW Jetta before I saw it. She pulled up next to my Pathfinder and I walked out to meet her. She had made it through the night and something had kept her out of the ocean...out of the arms of death.

I stepped down to the parking lot and stood outside Stephanie's car door. There was a look of serenity on her face as she looked up at me through the side window. She opened the door but remained seated, extending her left hand to my right one, the hand that had been marked by an owl. Our hands were clasped in such a way that I could feel her heart beating in her wrist.

Who found you last night, Stephanie? Who followed the beating of your heart? I wondered without words. I knew her crisis was over. Now we would walk back through it and in the telling, Stephanie would let me know what she had learned, and what she had decided to do.

The pomegranate green tea had steeped into a dark red color. I put a Splenda packet in mine; Stephanie added half and half to hers. We carried our tea into the inner sanctum where I bundled her into her corner of the loveseat with a cream and peach silk-wool throw that always lay close by, folded and ready, for such times. As the patient that knitted it once said, "Even in the middle of summer, emotions and air conditioning could freeze a body in here." The late autumn nights and early mornings were very cool. I asked Stephanie if I could sit on the other end of the loveseat and she nodded. I folded my legs under me and faced her; the steam rising from our tea cups created a mist between us.

"When is your first patient coming?" Stephanie started.

"I've cleared my schedule 'til ten." These kinds of shifts happened frequently in psychiatry. Patients in crisis did not always fit neatly into a schedule. In virtually every deep therapeutic piece of work, there would be one or two crises and they took precedence over scheduled hours. Always. Actually, most of them happened after hours.

"Did you listen to my voice mails?" Stephanie spoke tentatively as if it was hard to get started.

"I did."

"I'm embarrassed," she whispered around her tea cup. Tendrils of fine light hair curled around her hairline where they had escaped her ponytail.

"Don't be. They were like a journal of your night. They've given me a small glimpse of what you've been through. You know you could have called me at home or had the answering service page me. Surely you remembered that."

"I wanted to, Kai. The part of me that felt like a scared little kid wanted to. Another part of me felt like I was a twenty-six-year-old woman who should be able to take care of herself. But there was something else going on. Deep inside, a voice seemed to be calling me to be apart. Something deep, instinctual, primal seemed to be leading me. Gradually, it became clear that I needed to be alone. The phone calls to your voice mail were as close as I could get to you. When I heard your voice, I felt like you were there. I thought about driving to Two-Pop's on Wadmalaw, but that seemed blocked, too."

"There are some things we have to face alone, Steph."

"Like death?"

"At certain points in the journey of death and dying, we feel very alone," I answered. I had learned that from my brother.

"Well, we certainly, ultimately die alone. Let's face it, everybody who's ever lived on this earth has either already died or will die, and they do that final piece alone!"

She was talking about death of the body, not the family gathered around.

"Absolutely correct. What happened last night, Stephanie?"

She took another long swallow of tea and seemed to gather her thoughts.

"I was packing to go to the hospital. I looked at my clothes: underwear, t-shirts, pajamas. Suddenly, I knew I wouldn't need any of it. I would be wearing sterilized hospital gowns and socks. I picked up my iPod, iPhone and Fossil watch. This was my 'stuff,' I thought; if I die, I won't need it anymore. I wondered what Mom and Dad would do with it if I was gone. That stuff wasn't me, just outer things to make my life easier." She paused, looked down at her tea cup.

"My world collapsed. I think my denial just came crashing down and the reality that I might really die created a wave of pure terror that hit me like a tsunami. Maybe it was a panic attack. It was almost midnight. Mom and Dad were sleeping, but I couldn't go to them. I wanted to get the hell *out*. Run. Escape. I grabbed my stuff and ran to my car. Halfway to Wadmalaw and Two-Pop, I slowed down and pulled into a closed gas station. I couldn't breathe, like I was suffocating. I got out of the car and walked around gasping for breath. I had this horrible premonition that I was going to die, especially if I went to Hollings Cancer Center. That's when I called your office. After I hung up, all I could think of was first getting help for my panic attack. I turned around and headed back into Charleston, praying to every higher power I'd ever heard of. Kai, I swear God was completely mute. Silent. I felt utterly alone. I even wondered if God simply stepped into the shadows when it was time for one of us to die. I tell you, Kai, that was as frightening as the thought of death itself. Maybe this is what Samuel Beckett meant in *Waiting for Godot* - waiting for God who never came. Then I got mad. Hell no! I'm no atheist. I was angry at God because I believe there is a God, one capable of love and mercy! So, why the silent treatment?

When I pulled up to the emergency room at Roper Hospital, I totally settled down. It was like the feeling I get sitting in your parking lot after our sessions. Like a shot of virtual Valium. Then I decided to drive to the old playground on East Bay Street. I used to go there when I was little. I sat in one of the swings and let my body remember how to move. I pushed back to go up. Back and forth, higher and higher I went, recreating the safety of my childhood. Afterwards, I got in my car and drove to your office. I kept hearing you tell me that I wasn't going to die. Over and over I heard your voice. It was as clear as if you were sitting there with me. I heard another voice say 'keep moving'. So I went to the beach at Sullivan's Island."

"I need some more tea, Kai, and a pit stop." She extricated herself from the blanket and headed down the hall.

As I refilled the tea cups, memories of my brother, Mark, overwhelmed me. Mark's battle with pancreatic cancer had ended eight years ago. Stephanie's words were almost exactly those Mark had used in the year before his death. Mark's crisis had come after he had been in remission for five months and then developed brain metastases in the spring. At the beginning of his illness, he had had colossal faith that God would heal him. After the cancer spread, his beliefs were shaken to the foundations. He was furious, despairing. Yet, he had found peace before he died. My memory was interrupted when I heard Stephanie's footsteps.

She settled back into her blanket and resumed her story.

"On the dunes at Sullivan's, waves crashed in the dark, each wave dying on the beach while another took its place. This repetition had gone on for millennia, I guess, like cycles of life and death. Very clearly, I knew I had the choice to live or die. I had the total freedom to step into that ocean and get it over with. I *knew* that God would forgive me. I also knew that I could choose to fight for life."

Stephanie sighed and then continued.

"From the time I learned that I had leukemia, I've been denying that I could die. Dr. Gellman told me that some patients die during their initial chemo. If they survive, only twenty percent make it for five years! Still I was in denial. Until now."

I sat quietly and listened. I remembered Rob Gellmans' words when he had first talked to me about Stephanie and acute myelogenous leukemia. "Necessary denial" was critical to cancer patients. Without it, many patients would see suicide as a preferable alternative. Some end-stage patients did choose suicide. Was there any wonder why the ethical debate of euthanasia raged in every civilized society? Sooner or later, this *denial* of death had to give way so that truth could be faced, preparations made, peace found.

"Stephanie, what kept you out of the ocean?"

"The voice. God's voice. Over and over I heard, 'It is not time. Hope can balance your fear. See this journey through.'"

She continued, "I felt compelled to drive to Folly Beach to see the sunrise. You have to go all the way to Morris Island lighthouse to see the edge of the world and the sun. It was beautiful, Kai, my sunrise of hope. It seemed to fill me with peace. I know that I have to try this chemotherapy. It's the right thing to do."

Hope was the other thing Rob and I knew our patients needed. Hope of remission. Hope of cure. Quality of life and death with dignity. Hope that life after death was real.

"Stephanie, have you ever heard of *dark night of the soul?*"

"Something to do with mysticism?"

"The 16th-century Spanish poet and Catholic saint, John of the Cross, wrote about it. He describes it as a time in our lives when we must journey alone through profound spiritual darkness; when all we have known and been taught fails us in the face of some cataclysmic change, emotional loss, illness, or death. It is the deepest kind of psychological and spiritual quest, to find something deeper in the self to carry us. We are stripped of our illusions, our disguises. We begin to conceive that death is some kind of gateway. With the death of our old selves, the possibility of eternal life emerges. Life and death, and then life. It's what you did last night while I was sleeping. You faced the terror of death. You made it conscious and found the bridge of hope to life."

"That bridge for me, Kai, means that life does not end with death."

It is what Mark said in his last days, I thought to myself.

"Do you believe in miracles, Kai?"

"There are so many kinds," I replied.

"I mean miraculous physical healing. Do you believe it can happen?"

"I have had one case in all my medical career. A young mother with a malignant brain tumor. I had worked with her and her family as her disease progressed. She had been through surgery, radiation and chemo. Her doctors gave her no hope. She was at death's door, on a respirator, almost totally paralyzed. One night, she was miraculously healed. There was no medical explanation for it. Her oncologists and neurosurgeons called it a spontaneous remission. Several of her doctors, including me, called it a miracle."

"So you do believe it can happen."

"It is rare, but yes, I believe it can happen."

"In the sunrise this morning, I saw what a miracle looks like," Stephanie said.

I closed my eyes and saw my own sunrise. Miracles happen every morning if only we can see them.

"Thank you for being here for me, Kai. My real mother can't be here for me or maybe I don't want her to. All I know is I need a mother and you seem to be here for me. Is that okay, for you to be my psychiatrist and my mother? Is that what transference means?"

"It is perfectly okay for me to be a surrogate mother for a while. And, yeah, it's called positive transference."

"Just part of the job, huh?" she rejoined.

"You, my dear, will never just be part of the job."

We both smiled.

"I guess I'd better finish packing and go to the hospital. I'll call you and leave my room number. You have my cell number."

"Send word when you are ready for me to come. And you *will* call *me* this time? No voice mail?"

"Yes, ma'am," she said with a mock salute.

Chapter Ten

This whole business of mothering had me in its grip. Being a mother to my own children, to Stephanie; needing a mother for myself; having spent my life as a mother to my own mother; battling my mother's mother. I had done a lot of therapy on all this throughout the years, but the Stephanie energy in my life seemed to be stirring the proverbial pot of my feminine ancestry. This was part of my counter-transference to Stephanie. I needed to be very sure I didn't contaminate her with my own mother-grandmother wounds.

I had been reading in bed the night after I saw Stephanie. Memories of my mother kept breaking into the words on the page. Finally, I closed my eyes. Silver reflections shone from my mother's hair. It was silver gray when I was born. She was only thirty-three years old. Some people would have said she was "prematurely gray." But gray is not silver. Silver shines. You can see yourself in its reflection. Silver also tarnishes. It's an oxidation process that happens when silver interacts with air; when it "breathes". People get tarnished, too, when they breathe life. After years, they can no longer see themselves through all the layers of life's tarnish. Therapy is all about helping people remove the obstructive layers of wounds and fears so they can "see themselves more clearly" and remember who they were created to be.

Many people who need help never see a psychiatrist or any kind of counselor. They do the best they can by themselves. They become survivors, going inward to hide behind the tarnish. They thrive in simplicity and safety. Above all, they minimize risk, often running away when life gets too painful. One thing I've learned after years of working with tarnished survivors is that sooner or later, life calls them out. Love becomes greater than fear. Freedom challenges bondage. The template of true self, carried by the spirit within, yearns to develop into wholeness.

My mother gave birth to a therapist, but never had access to one herself. She was a survivor who ran away from her demons but ultimately came home to face them in the end. Life gave her a number of chances to heal.

Her name was Eva Angelica. Eva after her mother's sister. Angelica because as a newborn she looked like an angel to her mother. She was her mother's first child and only daughter. My mother's mother was Tiffany, named after the famous stained glass lamps that were popular when she was born. She was only fifteen when she gave birth to her angel. She then had three sons in quick succession, finishing her family at age twenty. Her husband, Jeremiah, was a decade older, part owner of a successful mill.

In my childhood, I was mesmerized by a picture of my grandparents sitting side by side on a horse-drawn buggy on their wedding day. In an ornate silver frame on my mother's bedroom dresser, the black and white photograph captured their youthful serenity and grace. Tiffany was a markedly beautiful young woman. Her long, black hair was swept up and pinned on top of her head in the fashion of the early 1900s. Her skin was flawless and pale, untouched by the sun. She had a beguiling expression on her face, a Victorian Mona Lisa. I spent long hours trying to reconcile this lovely, innocent young woman with the Dumpling she became. Her beauty was tarnished beyond recognition and she was heavily shrouded in mental illness. I could not see her as being both of these women with only age distinguishing them. I wish I had known her as she was in the photograph. Maybe I would have liked her.

By all accounts, life in the deep, rural South during the Great Depression was brutal. Just read Faulkner's *The Sound and the Fury* or Steinbeck's *Grapes of Wrath*. Poverty, hunger and helplessness. Little Eva Angelica was born into national collapse and chaos. Her father and his brothers held onto their business in Boykin, but they all lost their considerable stock market investments in the crash of 1929. Tiffany had married wealth, but it was lost within a year.

By the time her last son was born, Tiffany had run out of energy. This boy was never named. I didn't know that until after Tiffany and Eva had died. My nameless uncle told my brother, Jamey, about it at Mother's funeral. Seems everyone had just called him "B.B." all his life. When he joined the army at age eighteen, he had to go to the county courthouse to get a copy of his never-before-seen birth certificate. It read "Baby Boy Stoddard." B.B. No more angels, just more mouths to feed and diapers to scrub clean for the next changing. My uncle proceeded to name himself the most elegant thing that would also explain his initials: Baron Beaumont Stoddard.

My mother rarely talked about her childhood. After I got to know Dumpling, I had plenty of questions and no answers. I think my mother felt it was disrespectful to speak ill of her mother. It is even more probable that she needed to keep her memories safely buried under multiple layers of tarnish. Years after I became a psychiatrist, I was compelled to work on my own tarnish in therapy. My Jungian analyst was surprised by how little I had talked to my mother about her mother. She intimated that I was still protecting my mother by not confronting the issue. My father's death several months after this session set the stage for my mother and me to start rubbing together at our respective tarnish. I was thirty-eight years old.

My father was buried in Boykin on a Friday morning in late summer. He was seventy-two years old. I had sent the children home to Charleston with their father who was still legally my husband. We had separated the April before. It made my father's death even more momentous. I needed to spend time alone with my mother. Everything changed when Daddy died. My mother's primary protector was gone. Mark lived close by with his family and Jamey an hour away. It was me that had broken ranks and moved the farthest away. Gradually, over the twenty-three years since my grandmother's death, my mother and I had reached a détente...a kind of truce about Dumpling: we never spoke of the early years. Even so, unfinished business with her mother smoldered beneath the ostensibly calm surface of our family's lives. My father's death ruffled those calm waters as the dynamics shifted. It was time for my mother and me to talk.

After a quiet and restful morning, we were alone on the back "stoop" having lemonade and a light lunch. The green and white striped awning served as a rectangular umbrella to the light rain that had continued to fall since the graveside service. Its steady rhythm on the taut funeral tent stretched above Daddy's coffin the day before had sounded like the steady drone of an airplane, come to mark my father's last flight. Death had come and gone. Those of us left behind had to get on with the task of living and healing.

I knew that the best way to edge my mother into talking about her family was to get her to tell a story that had some humor in it, not unlike the stories I made up as a child to distract her.

"What was that story about you spending all day on Christmas Eve in a tree, hiding from your mother?" I craftily inquired. I never referred to her mother as Dumpling in direct dialogue with her. That was my secret name.

Mother smiled at the memory.

"It was a huge, old ginkgo tree in the front yard of our house up on the Camden Highway. That was the wood house with the gables." I knew exactly which house she had been born in and lived in until she was fourteen, when her family moved to a new brick house in town.

"Mama and I were busy cooking dinner for the Christmas Eve feast. There was a pot of green snap beans on the stove. I think she put them on the stove and left the handle protruding over the side of the stove. B.B. ran by and hit the handle. He knocked the pot off the stove and beans went everywhere. He was terrified and ran to hide under his bed, which was his favorite refuge from Mama's anger. So I took the rap for him. I was trying to clean it all up when she came in the kitchen."

Mother faltered ever so slightly here, then continued.

"Mama grabbed the pot and started after me, brandishing it like a sword. I ran through the house and out the front door like a scalded rabbit." (That was some kind of old phrase from her childhood that I'd never heard before, but I caught the meaning.)

"I shimmied up the trunk of that gingko tree in record time and hid. I wasn't dressed for the winter chill or tree climbing, but I was getting out of my Mama's reach. She stood on the ground and even tried to throw the pot up at me, but it almost hit her on the way down. She did smack the tree trunk a few times. Then, she stomped back into the house. I settled down to sit on a limb to wait for my Daddy who wasn't due home for hours. I was wearing a light sweater and cotton socks and began shivering."

Mother looked more serious as she continued to talk.

"It started getting dark. My shivering got so bad I was afraid I would fall out of the tree. There was no way I was coming down 'til my Daddy came home. I knew he had to come home to eat Christmas dinner. It was plumb dark when he drove up and parked beside the tree. Just as he opened the car door, I yelled, 'Jeremiah Stoddard, help me down out of this tree!' Don't ask me why I didn't just call out, 'Daddy.' I was half frozen and yelled out his biblical name. He told me later he thought the archangel Gabriel had wrought a visitation on him."

Mother said she laughed at the look on his face as he peered up into the dark arms of that old tree and saw his pale, shaking, angelic daughter instead of an archangel.

"I told him through chattering teeth, what had happened. 'You come on down and sit in the warm car 'til I can go see

95

what state your mother's in,' he said. So I started down that tree and skinned both my legs when my jumper rode up. I was in the car when Daddy came out and opened the door. His voice was always so calm and kind, no matter how loud and raging Mama was. He said, 'It's okay now, honey. Everything's all right. Come on in with me.'"

As I listened to Mother talk, I realized it was the only time her father had ever protected her. His normal brand of neglect and avoidance was often referred to as "benign." It wasn't, it was malignant. Deadly to his children.

"The table was set and the boys all dressed for dinner. Mama looked haggard but not mad anymore. She got the food done on time with no help from me." She trailed off and we sat in silence for a few minutes.

"Mother, I need to try to understand about Grandmother's mental illness and why no one did anything to help her."

"Kai, I don't know if you *can* understand," my mother pleaded for one last reprieve.

"Mother, I *need* to know. Now. Today."

"Mama couldn't help herself. She just couldn't handle life."

"She was *mean*, Mother. More importantly, she was mentally ill. With my training, I now see that she was bipolar, manic-depressive. Why didn't Grandfather get her help? Or you and Dad? Or Uncle B.B. or Uncle Jack? *Nobody* helped her!"

I was trying to stay calm and rational, but my anger was leaking around the edges. God in heaven, was I *defending* Dumpling?

"Kai, do you know what insane asylums were like back in the 30s and 40s? They were terrible places. You just didn't send somebody you loved to a place like that. That's how my Daddy felt. He told us we needed to help her. He said she was sick like somebody who had cancer, but her sickness was in her mind. The stigma of mental illness was terrible back then. Our whole family would have been scandalized."

"Mama, how old were you when the Christmas Eve incident happened?"

She had to stop and think.

"About nine or ten, I think."

"When did it start being so chaotic and crazy?" I kept on.

"I never thought she was crazy, Kai. Just angry. The least thing would set her off."

"What is your first memory?" I was unrelenting. We both needed to know.

"I don't remember her any other way. She was always like that."

"But what happened to you over all those years? And your brothers? Your childhood?"

"I was afraid all the time. She never expected the boys to

help her cook and clean. She expected me to help and I could never please her." Her voice sounded flat, helpless.

Her helplessness ignited my anger.

"Why didn't you fight back, Mother? You just caved in!" I accused. I would never have said that to a patient, but she was my mother. Problem was, I had been treating her like a patient most of my life.

"I was afraid Mama would lose control and hurt me or one of the boys. Especially B.B. She seemed to despise him. He was so cute, but she just rejected him."

"Why didn't you run away?"

"I did, one time. I walked all the way across town to Aunt Eva's house. She gave me Japanese fruit cake and sweet iced tea and had one of her sons drive me home. Mama really whipped me for that. She made me go out back to get a hickory stick and bring it to her. The first one wasn't big enough, so I had to go back out for another one. She switched my legs until blood ran down into my white socks. I had scared her when I ran away and all that fear turned to rage. I never ran away again until I ran away to college."

"Mama, you know you were abused. She physically and emotionally abused you." I teared up. I hated Dumpling all over again. Not just for traumatizing me, but for abusing my mother.

"Kai, I just thought it was normal. I survived and so did two of my brothers."

"Do you think Uncle Jere's early death was her fault?" I never knew my Uncle Jeremiah who died before I was born, the first son, his father's namesake.

"I don't know, Kai. Jere was kind of like Mama. He was not stable. He would fly off into rages as a child. He chased B.B. and even his friends with knives, axes and hoes when he got mad. He started drinking whiskey when he was a teenager and even physically fought with Mama and Daddy after I went to college. That's why they sent him off to a military boarding school in Georgia."

"Was he drunk when he had the car wreck?"

"Kai, do we have to keep talking about all this?" She had turned her body away from me on the couch. I couldn't tell if she was crying, but I could feel her discomfort.

"Mama, I know it's hard. It's just been buried for so long. There's so much tarnish on our lives from it all."

Mother turned back to me with a sorrowful smile on her face.

"I loved going to college. It saved me, Kai. Limestone was like a family full of sisters for me. I was no great student, but I loved home economics, sewing, cooking, and making a budget for a household. Granted, I couldn't do much math or science, but college was the great escape. I even spent holidays at the homes of my friends in Spartanburg or Charlotte. That's how I met your father. He was so smart and handsome. He went off to join the Marines and when he asked me to marry him and move to Oklahoma, I knew it was the right choice. Those were wonderful years," she spoke quietly, but resolutely.

"Why in God's name did you come back to Boykin, back to life two blocks away from a lunatic?"

I was filled with rage. I couldn't seem to stop myself. Was I punishing my mother for not protecting me all those years ago?

"Because I missed my family. My Daddy, Jack, and B.B. and their wives and kids. Jere was gone and I never got to tell him goodbye." Tears trickled down her cheeks. She pierced me with her next words.

"I *loved* her, Kai. Can't you understand that I loved her? I remember when she used to tell me I was her angel. I was just a little girl, three or four. She would take me up in her lap and rock me and call me her angel. *That* was my first memory. That's what I still remember now. I would do anything to be that little angel in my mother's arms one more time."

Her eyes were crying now and her voice was filled with anguish.

I just stared at her. I loved *her* the same way. Deeply. Devotedly. It didn't really matter if I witnessed the shotgun incident or countless other rampages. It didn't matter if my mother's survival cost me as much as it had her. I just loved her, too. But I couldn't *be* like her or Dumpling. Not passive and avoidant or aggressive and chaotic. I had been caught in that great, archetypal struggle between order and chaos, anger and passivity. Dumpling had been the queen of chaos. As it had fallen on my mother, her inability to contain it had allowed it to overflow onto me. We had both paid a huge emotional cost for it.

We hugged. I felt bad that I had made my mother cry.

"I'm sorry, Mama. I'm sorry," I said as I patted her back. We never spoke about her mother again.

Chapter Eleven

Charleston summers are miserable. It's hot, humid, muggy, stifling. There's a scene in Katherine Hepburn and Humphrey Bogart's classic film, *African Queen*, where the two of them are immersed in waist high, muddy, leech-infested water, dragging the boat (of the title) through the African jungle swamps. That's Charleston in late summer. Most of the natives head north into the Blue Ridge Mountains of North Carolina to places like Flat Rock, Tryon, and Asheville. You can breathe up there, float on an inner tube down cool mountain streams or cruise the Blue Ridge Parkway all the way to the Shenandoah Valley in Virginia. Those of us unable to escape stay on or in the water as much as humanly possible.

Tied to our short deep-water dock was an eighteen-foot Hurricane deck boat with a Yamaha outboard motor. It was white with red trim and a red, canvas Bimini to shade us from the hot sun. It was our personal conveyance onto the great tidewaters of the Lowcountry.

Gracen and Andrew had spent most of June with their father in Montreal where his family had rented a house for the summer. Trey returned to work several times, leaving the kids with their grandparents. I had two weeks with both children in July, interspersed with their camps.

I had this lone week with Andrew before he left for the Governor's School of Mathematics and Science in Hartsville. He was one of two rising juniors selected by the teachers in his high school, and had just celebrated his seventeenth birthday.

Andrew was a water rat. He had been taking the boat out since he was twelve. He seemed happiest trolling the tidal creeks, casting for shrimp bait, and fishing for spot-tail bass and trout with his friends. It was a great equalizer for him and me to be on the water together. There was no real angst or tension; we left that at our dock.

I had made a "date" with Andrew to spend the day on the boat, promising to take his favorite picnic lunch of a ham on wheat with mustard, deviled eggs, grapes, cheese, Fritos and brownies for dessert. Gallons of water and lemonade were staples. Andrew maneuvered the boat along Boone Hall Creek, watching for sandbars; the tide was ebbing. Herons and egrets were stalking around the pluff mud looking for lunch. Several white ibis and a wood stork joined them. We motored slowly by. I watched a great blue heron with its six feet of wingspan glide to a graceful landing on a small sandbar at a bend in the creek. She was my favorite of all wading birds in the marshes. The sun glinted on her feathers as she preened, reflecting blue, black and deep violet.

"I wish that I could fly with you," I whispered as we passed, careful not to disturb her.

Animal life along the marsh was in concert with the tides, that great movement of water controlled by the gravitational pull of the moon and the earth's rotation. Twice a day, ocean water rises and streams into the tidal basins and estuaries ringed by marsh grass. Its ingress continues along the paths of least resistance: the creeks and marsh itself. It takes some six hours for the tides to rise and flood the marsh, bringing food and succor. Our creek would rise almost six feet at the pinnacle of high tide. Interposed in the shift of tides was a lull when the salt water seemed to become placid like a lake, with only ripples from small fish to disturb its glassy surface. Inexorably, the moon's pull would wane as the earth turned on its axis and the water would reverse its course, making its way back to the ocean. Along the beaches, the same movement was dictated as the tide crept up to the dunes and back. I once heard that the tides were God's way to mark the passing of time. Surely, the tidal marshes were one face of Eden.

"This is my place in the world," I said softly, here on the creeks and estuaries of the sea. This is my lifeblood, as surely as that which flows through the vessels and capillaries of my body. It was a quiet declaration of interdependence. A paean of gratitude. It was also recognition of where I would lie after death. My will directed that I be cremated and my ashes spread over this great womb of the earth called marsh.

Andrew and I did not talk when we were moving through wide-open water at full throttle. That would hopefully come later. When he slowed the boat for a "no wake zone," I knew my boy-child's stomach would rumble along with the outboard engine's idle. Sometimes, it mimicked the gurgling sounds of the propeller churning water. I was sitting in the back of the boat under the shade of the Bimini when Andrew signaled his hunger.

"I'm starving, Mom. When can we eat?"

He had been snacking on grapes and watermelon since we left the dock. I truly believe that teenage boys have the metabolism of a hummingbird and appetite of a foraging elephant.

"Let's head back and find a place to anchor in Nick's creek." We had named this small inlet off the Wando for a friend whose house we could see in the distance. It was a quiet place cloistered by winding bands of tall green marsh grass.

The sun was at its zenith and a light breeze had picked up. Otherwise, it would have been too hot to stay there. I set up a small folding table and laid out our food. Andrew joined me in the back of the boat and dived into the deviled eggs. I hoped he left me one or two. I began to edge into conversation with this more introverted of my children.

"Are you looking forward to Governor's School?"

"Sort of." He popped another egg into his mouth.

"It's such an honor to be chosen."

"Guess so." Muenster cheese, down the hatch.

"Are you happy, Andy-san?" The old take-off on Andy-son.

He looked at me quizzically, "Why are you asking that again, Mom?"

"You seem happy, but we've had no real time to talk since you came back from Canada. Just wondering what was going on inside."

"I am happy, Mom. You don't need to worry about me."

Andrew was much harder for me to read than Gracen. Like most boys that reach puberty, they seem to withdraw from their mothers. Problem was, Andrew was not very close to his father, either. The two of them had just started playing golf together, which finally gave them a common interest.

Andrew was a gifted child. As a two-year-old, he was reciting children's books and knew more animals than I did. Hippopotamus was his favorite word. He bypassed baby talk. The teacher at his Montessori school didn't know what to do with him, so she taught him to read and do simple math at age three. His real gift was in spatial perception, a function of his right brain. He got that totally from his father. They played chess with two chess boards, one above the other. Pieces were moved traditionally and vertically between the two boards. I could never get it. I could hardly play a regular game. Video games were another disconnect for us. Pac Man was my limit. Andrew was obsessed with video games. It was almost scary.

We had to limit access to all electronics by the time he was seven, and to the Internet by nine. His saving grace is that he wanted to be a regular kid and not a nerd. His friends knew he was smart, but he downplayed it.

All in all, Andrew was a neat kid. He rarely got into trouble, but he was a teenager. When he was fifteen and had a daytime-only driver's license, he snuck out late one night to go to a forbidden party. I wouldn't have found out if his car hadn't stalled on the bridge at six in the morning on his way home. I grounded him for a month and forbade him to drive at night for six months, even after he was legal! After the divorce from Trey, I put Gracen in a group therapy with other kids going through similar life changes. She worked out a lot of her anger, confusion and grief in the group. Andrew refused to go. He said he was fine and he acted like he was. In all honesty, I probably relied on him too much as the only male left in the family.

"Andy-san, you know how much I love you? You will always be my firstborn, my only son."

He smiled.

The wind was picking up and the sun beginning to lower when we pulled anchor and started home. Andrew stood with one knee on the seat behind the steering wheel console. He was tall and lean, dark hair blowing in the wind. I was suddenly struck by what a gift he was to me. What did I ever do to deserve this incredible child? We had been through a lot these last few years. Divorce, the death of two family members, a move. I had not been able to shield him from some harsh realities. Yet, we had survived…together. Somehow, we were stronger, wiser.

Andrew turned around just at that moment, lifted his sunglasses and winked. I wanted to hold that image of him forever.

Chapter Twelve

The days of Stephanie's hospitalization seemed to fly by, as I had an incredibly busy week. I was usually off on Fridays, unless patients had to be seen and there was no other time available. This Friday was one of those. I saw three patients and finished by noon. While running errands, my answering service texted me. "Dr. Stephen Edinger, Please call ASAP." Stephanie had left me a message the day before that she was doing fine in chemo. Now her grandfather, the head of the hospital where she was being treated, was trying to reach me. The page troubled me. I called him right back.

A deep male voice answered, "Dr. Edinger here."

"Dr. Edinger, this is Dr. Kai Ingersohn returning your call."

"Yes, thank you, doctor. I was just calling about my granddaughter, Stephanie."

"Is everything all right?" I couldn't mask the anxiety in my voice.

"Yes, yes. She's holding up. I was just with her and she told me about the work she has been doing with you. She's a pretty tough nut, but she seems to need to touch base with you. I was wondering if you could come down here today."

"What time would be best?" I asked, remembering that I had a three p.m. dental appointment.

"The sooner the better. Frankly, under all her bravado, she seems tired, fragile. She didn't want me to leave her this morning. Her dad was on the way up when I was going out. I don't think she was hallucinating, but she was talking about Pac-Men riding horses and outrunning death. You know, she almost died up at Sloan Kettering. Scared Stevie and me to death. Can't let anything happen to my baby girl." He cleared his throat and paused.

I spoke reassuringly, "She was simply recalling some work that we did on Tuesday. She's *not* hallucinating. I'll come on over as soon as I can."

"You know she's in an isolation unit. We all have to wear gowns and masks, even gloves. I always like to kiss her, but can't risk it now. Dr. Ingersohn, we really need your help. You know I'm an academic, research most of my career. I'm having to update on this leukemia thing. Our oncologist, Rob Gellman, doesn't pull punches."

"Yes, I spoke to him earlier about Stephanie. I'll read his notes and look at the chart when I come over. I'm not really on the staff at MUSC. Can you or Dr. Gellman get me special consulting privileges?"

"I'll see to it right now. Speak to Kitty Drummand when you come to Hollings Cancer Center, 8 East. She's the head nurse up here and an old friend of my wife's."

"I'll do it," I replied. "And please call me Kai. Stephanie says she calls you Two-Pop."

His laugh seemed to choke up.

"Yes, Stephanie called her father 'Pop' when she was little, so I became Two-Pop. Makes me feel helpless to see her in isolation. She looks so small in that big room all by herself. Even the food has to be sterilized. She has her iPhone in plastic wrap, so she can still send text messages and make phone calls. I wish I could take it on myself, just take the leukemia from her. I may need a psychiatrist myself before all this is over."

He cleared his throat again.

"She knows how much you love her, Dr. Edinger. She loves you the same way. I am very grateful that she has such loving and supportive grandparents. Many of us do not. I'll be there in an hour. I'm happy to talk to you any time about Stephanie."

I ended the conversation. My mind cut to my maternal grandfather who turned his hearing aid off when family crises occurred. He worked all the time and was a pillar of the Baptist church. But, in essence, he was gone, emotionally and physically, to his family. Why hadn't he helped Dumpling or my mother or me? I said a little blessing for all the loving grandfathers and grandmothers in the world. How many of my patients had told me stories about how a grandparent had been there for them at a critical time in their lives.

Some had lived with this extended family when their own parents couldn't or didn't want to keep them. Others simply helped carry the parenting load. It was the unwavering love and support of their grandparents that saw many of them through life.

Chapter Thirteen

I still had a list of errands before I could visit Stephanie. I found myself battling heavy traffic all over Mt. Pleasant. Fridays here took on overtures of NYC's Fifth Avenue during rush hour!

It's remarkable how much of my work with patients is processed in my car, especially if I get caught in traffic. When my mind switches to neutral, my unconscious repository of patient information is transferred back into the conscious. I call this backfilling; it is a very valuable part of therapy, particularly if a patient's mind is doing the same thing on some parallel track. As I was finishing errands, thoughts of Stephanie jostled with other patients. I remembered her asking me how I got my nickname. It had been years since anyone had asked me about it. It was one of those things that slipped into life and stayed. It happened in the first grade. Now, I was backfilling about myself.

My parents had always called me Katie. My first grade teacher was so strict she was like a rubber band pulled too tight. No one could please her. Suffice it to say that the alphabet I printed did not measure up to her standards. After endless drills of printing our ABCs, I got more proficient with my name: Katherine Ann Ingersohn. Once, at the blackboard, in front of my class, I proudly wrote my name in chalk in tall letters that only slanted downward a little. Later, at recess, my friend, Anne Marie, who had seen the letters K, A and I as bigger than all the others, started calling me Kai with the "i" as the main sound, not the "a." Nicknames in the South when I was growing up were like getting the chicken pox. Once a special name made an appearance, everybody "got" it. So, Kai stuck. My big brother, Mark, picked it up from the other kids at school and took it home. Katie gave way to Kai. It seemed to fit better anyway with my being such a tomboy.

I had always idolized Mark. He was almost four years older than me and a natural born "leader of the pack."

Our neighborhood in Boykin had ten boys of all ages and me, the only girl. When I wasn't guarding my mother from Dumpling, I was playing with the pack. They did not play girly games, ever. When I played with my dolls and tea sets, I did it alone or invited a girlfriend home after school. Anne Marie would come when she could get away from taking care of her little sister with Down syndrome. She was probably the closest thing to a sister that I had growing up. The boys played hiding, army and touch football. We raced bicycles, built forts and tree houses, and dug foxholes.

Once, Mark brought a huge, dead vine out of some nearby woods and nailed it to a tree so we could play Tarzan. I got the role of Jane by default. It turned out to be a poison ivy vine, its leaves missing in late winter. That vine nearly killed me. A number of the pack got poison ivy, but I was violently allergic to it. It spread like wildfire all over me, causing my face to puff up like a toad and my eyes to swell shut. I was hospitalized for five days and was left at night in a large metal hospital crib with such high sides that I could climb out only with great difficulty. Eight years old and imprisoned in a hospital, itching to death. That kind of itching all over your body really is a unique kind of agony. Alone and afraid. Trapped. My mother couldn't drive then, so she came with Daddy after work. They stayed for about two hours. The nurses checked on me often, but their faces changed a lot. There were many hours between visits. Hospitals have progressed over the years. When Gracen had her appendix out last year, I did not leave her side. I slept on a pull-out chair beside her. Sometimes thoughts of my mother coming to be with Gracen and me would come. It was a physical-like longing.

There were hazards to belonging to that group of boys, but amazing rewards. I was a really good athlete and could play any sport. In middle school and high school, I excelled at swimming, basketball, and tennis. Competition was born and nurtured for years in the pack.

I began first grade at five the September after our move to Boykin. This was important because it took me out of the house and out of Dumpling's emotional line of fire during the week. It also diminished my ability to protect my mother. Our house was only three blocks away from my grandparents and Dumpling could walk the distance in two or three minutes flat. School was a twenty-minute bike ride. There was always a sense of pressure to get home and check on my mother. I tried a lot of bike routes to see if I could shave time off the twenty minutes, but until I got older and stronger, that was my best time. Mark had to ride his bike with me for the first few months until my parents thought it was safe for me to ride alone. It was during some of this time that I shared "Dumpling's" secret name with Mark. For the rest of our lives together, he kept the secret with me. Inclement weather meant Dad took us in his 1970 blue and white Chevrolet Impala. If the rain stopped, Mark and I walked home. That took nearly an hour. On those days, I would dash into the kitchen loudly calling for my mother so I could "get a read". This was like taking her emotional temperature. I didn't know to call it "body language" back then. If her reading was normal, all would be well. She would be starting supper, perhaps country fried cube steak smothered in gravy with rice and baby sweet peas. She might be in the middle of kneading dough for biscuits or an apple pie. She would be humming and smiling and cheerful. This would be a "Dumpling-free day". A "Dumpling-encounter-but-okay day" meant homemade spaghetti and meatballs with garlic bread and banana pudding for dessert. When I smelled nothing cooking, I knew Mother's body temperature would be on cold, immobilizing her. It meant Dumpling had hit before I could get home. Mother would be sitting at the kitchen table, red eyed from crying or in her bed. That's when she would need me to comfort her and make her laugh. I would pull out my art work and write, "Love Kai." It was all I could write at that age. Most of the time I just drew a heart for the word, Love. Usually, I could get a tiny uplift to the corners of Mama's mouth, but her eyes would still be dull and lifeless. Then, I would tell her funny stories.

"Mama, you should have seen what happened to Mrs. Goforth today. It was so hot that she opened all the windows in our room. When she slanted that last bottom window pane open, a yellow jacket wasp flew right in and made a dive for her 'blue hair'. She freaked out and started running around the room, batting at that wasp. It was a real dive bomber. We were laughing to beat the band and pulling for the wasp."

"Oh, Kai," Mama said, "you telling me the truth?"

"Yes ma'am. That wasp could have been in the Marine Corps alongside Daddy's jet Hornets. It was making rolls and split S turns around Mrs. Goforth. Finally, she opened the door and ran down the hall screaming. The kids finally tallied up the results: wasp 10, teacher 0."

"Kai, you can sure tell some whoppers," Mama said with a smile; I knew everything would be all right.

Another thing I did after school was stand guard in case Dumpling came over for a late afternoon visit. I would usually do my homework on the front porch. That gave me a block's notice of the storm clouds rolling along with Dumpling. In later years, I called that stretch Tornado Alley. If I could head Dumpling off, I could save my mother for a day. So, I started lying to my grandmother. If I spotted her coming, I would run down to meet her and tell her my mother wasn't home. I'd make up some story about a circle meeting at the Baptist church or a trip to the grocery store. She usually believed me and went back home. I felt guilty about the lies, but felt they were for a good cause.

That changed when it was time for bed and the dark came, bringing Mr. Death to visit. In my later years studying child psychology in residency, I was particularly interested in a child's view of death and my own embodiment of death as a person: Mr. Death. Jean Piaget, the famous developmental child psychologist in the 1960s, wrote that children could not conceptualize the reality of death as irrevocable loss until the age of eight or nine years old. Until then, death was subject to magical thinking wherein a child could "will" a dead pet or person to reappear. Reality was always subject to the power of the child's "magic" to control its world on all fronts. If Spot, the dog, died and was buried, a child would resurrect Spot and ask endlessly where he was when it was time for Spot to eat. Eventually, the child forgot Spot, but never fathomed Spot's true fate.

I seemed to be an exception to Piaget's rule. By the age of six, I had created Mr. Death. He took you away forever and you never came back. I understood that Spot would have been history in his dark grave of earth. What I wasn't sure of was how long you stayed buried until you got to heaven to live with God. The prayer I prayed every night with my mother was perplexing:

Now, I lay me down to sleep,
I pray the Lord my soul to keep,
If I should die before I wake,
I pray the Lord my soul to take.

So how long did the Lord wait to come and get you? I thought Mr. Death's job was to take you to that place in the ground. Then, hopefully, God would take your soul to heaven from there. I had no idea what my soul was, but I figured God did.

To make matters worse, the house built for us by my grandfather had only two bedrooms, one for my parents and one for my brothers. My grandfather knew full well that girls did not sleep with their brothers, at least not in the Deep South. I never asked him why he didn't build a bedroom for me, but it spoke volumes about the man. So, I had a daybed in one corner of the dining room. I kept my clothes and toys in my brothers' room where there were bunk beds, a crib for Jamey, two dressers and a closet.

At night, after prayers, Mother would tuck me into the made-up daybed and close the door to the hall. My parents' room was directly across that hall. The door was beside the head of my bed. There was always the dilemma of whether to open the door to feel closer to my parents, thus creating a wall of shadow by the head of my bed. Or close it, remove the shadow, and possibly stifle my own cries for help if Mr. Death came to visit and decided to take me away with him. If I got really scared, I would sneak into Mark and Jamey's room and climb up to the top bunk to sleep. I had to train myself to wake up before my parents did and creep back to my daybed. I didn't go in my parents' room and wake them up because that was considered foolishness by my father. You might get a swat on the behind as you were sent back to bed. No, I went to my brothers' room in case of emergencies. There was something very comforting about being close to Mark on those dark nights, hearing the soft rhythm of his breath as he slept on the bunk below me. He was my big brother, second only to my father as a talisman of safety. When Jamey moved from crib to lower bunk, I would make a pallet on the floor beside both my brothers.

As an adult and a psychiatrist, I see now that the combination of the fear of my grandmother, my mother's emotional helplessness, my father's emotional distance, a precocious understanding of death, and the guilt from telling lies all fed into the conjuring of death as a realistic nocturnal threat. The great ephemeral concept of death became a man dressed in a black monk-like habit, his head covered in its cowl, his face in shadow. To show respect, I called him Mr. Death.

I became rather adroit at dealing with Mr. Death's visits. It was hard for me to believe that he really wanted a skinny little girl that could barely read and write. I would tell him all the reasons he shouldn't take me yet. But I told lies. And he knew it. My mother was a staunch Baptist. Our church was almost puritanical and taught that telling lies was a sin and you went to hell for that. Hell was not where the Lord was; it was dark, hot and you burned up there. So, add Christian fundamentalism to the aforementioned mix and Piaget would say I was a neurotic in training.

In psychiatric language, a neurosis means a conflicted state of mind and emotion. The conflict generates enough anxiety or depression to interfere with normal life. Somehow, I sidestepped neurosis and became a child that had an abnormal relationship with death. As I grew and developed, I never lost sight of the reality of death as a powerful force in shaping all of life. In my work, death had been a prominent theme that forced me to face it on a regular basis. What I could not abide was the death of a child.

Death altered the landscape of my life permanently when I was sixteen and the Dumpling years officially came to an end.

When she was sixty-three years old, Dumpling had a debilitating stroke. My grandfather reluctantly agreed to put her in a nursing home in Camden, fifteen miles away. I would often accompany my mother on weekend visits because my father and my brothers refused to go. The last time I saw Dumpling alive was one lovely spring Sunday after church. Mother had carefully packed leftover fried chicken and made-from-scratch biscuits along with a large slice of chocolate cake in a small picnic hamper. She put sweet iced tea in a thermos bottle and the two of us set off to have a picnic with my mother's mother.

There was something haunting about the tender care with which she packed all this food; we both knew Grandmother was slowly dying. She was hardly able to sit or eat, and had not walked since the stroke. But this I learned from my mother: no matter how badly an *adult* child is treated by their mother, they never give up trying to gain the love that they never really had. There was a time when I thought my mother was masochistic by continuing to subject herself to her mother's irrational emotional abuse. When all was said and done, she loved her mother as only an adult child of abuse can love the abuser. She craved to be affirmed by this woman who gave birth to her.

We arrived with the picnic basket and were directed to the sunroom, a closed-in porch with a wall of windows that faced west and let in the afternoon sun. As we entered, I saw my grandmother sitting in a wheelchair twenty feet away on the opposite end of the sun porch. The nurses had tied her in the wheelchair with long swaths of white sheets, but she still leaned forward with her head hanging down. Her long gray-white hair had partially escaped the confines of its bun, gathered at the neck and draped over one shoulder. She wore a flowered day-dress that she had always favored.

As we approached, she lifted her head and stared desperately at my mother, screaming at the top of her lungs, "Angel, my angel! Save me, save me from this place!"

My mother stopped in mid-step. She dropped the picnic basket, chicken and biscuits scattering across the dingy tile floor, followed by the crash of the thermos. Mother turned and fled. She ran out of the porch, out of the nursing home, stopping only when she got to the car.

If I could have killed my grandmother with my thoughts, she would have died on that beautiful spring day. I was furious as I turned away and followed my mother to the car. She was leaning over the hood, sobbing and beating her fists on the hot metal. My timid, quiet, ever-restrained mother finally released her anguish to the universe.

When she calmed down, I drove us home. As we turned into our driveway, I parked and turned to Mother.

"I will never again go to see your mother with you. I understand that you need to go, but I can't go with you." It was my first step toward emancipation from the most convoluted triangle of my life. It was something my father had done years before. I stifled the immediate guilt that always kept me from stepping away from their dysfunctional relationship. Bravado, fueled by anger, helped me break away this time.

There were to be no more visits for either one of us. Tiffany Eliza Blackwell Stoddard died at dawn the next Sunday, alone in her room at the nursing home. It was in the early morning of my sixteenth birthday. Honestly, it was the best birthday present I ever received. That sounds terrible...disrespectful, even to me. It embarrasses me now to admit I felt this way. I am simply trying to tell the truth now.

The rituals around death in a small, rural town had not changed much from the turn of the century, at least for my grandmother's generation. My memories crystallized on the invisible screen behind my eyes as I watched the crisp, sharp images that time had stored in my personal archives. Images from thirty years ago.

They laid my grandmother out in the sunroom parlor of their West Church Street house. I had always loved that room. It was full of beautiful white wicker furniture bathed by the sunlight rising on the east side of the house. I visited on the first evening of her "laying-out". After Daddy came home from work, he and I walked together to my grandparents' house. He was still my emotional talisman. I have no memory of my mother going there before me. Normally, my mother never went without me. Maybe she was safer now. Mark hadn't gotten home from The Citadel, and twelve-year-old Jamey hid in his closet until the whole fiasco was over. Back then, the older folk always thought young people should view the body, but the very idea of looking at a dead body freaked Jamey out. I felt that I had to go. I wanted physical evidence that she had *really* died.

The minister from our church was holding court in the living room. Dressed in black, his matching demeanor cast a somber pall over the whole assembly. Grandfather was speaking in hushed tones to the mostly aged visitors. My great aunt, Eva, kept ushering me toward the sunroom.

"Katherine Ann, you need to go in and pay your final respects to your grandmother," her voice, sounding like velvet and steel, called me by my given name. She didn't like nicknames.

It was dark in the parlor except for the glow of a small lamp in a distant corner. The only other light in the room was a tall, white candle standing on a high brass stand. Its flickering flame cast ghostly shadows on the shiny dark wood of the coffin, its hinged half top open and lined with white satin. I wondered if Mr. Death was dancing in those shadows. No, he would have taken her soul by now. Anyway, I hadn't used that name in many years.

When no one else was in there, I crept into the eerie sunroom and stood by her coffin. Dumpling's wax shell body was there and had every appearance of being dead.

I was horrified that the little jingle from the Wizard of Oz started playing over and over in my head, "*Ding, Dong! The witch is dead!*" To me, it didn't signify anger or revenge, it was a song of relief. Like the Munchkins who celebrated that their nemesis was dead and gone, I couldn't help feeling as though a burden had been lifted for me as well.

Irrepressibly, the scene of the Mayor requesting the legitimacy of the witch's death played in my mind:

We've got to verify it legally, to see if she
is morally, ethically, spiritually, physically,
positively, absolutely, undeniably and reliably dead!

And then the Munchkins' glad proclamation:

This is a day of independence!
Let the joyous news be spread...
the wicked old witch at last is dead!

I pictured myself skipping and singing out of this death room, but I knew it would have been too profane for the occasion. I did smile as I turned away and went to find my mother who was now gracefully offering food to the visitors who had come to bring solace, at last, to this family of survivors.

How naïve I was. Dumpling was dead, but not gone. At sixteen, I had no concept of how deeply entrenched she was in my psyche.

Chapter Fourteen

Driving over the new bridge connecting Mt. Pleasant to downtown Charleston always gives me a thrill. From a distance, the supporting white cables of the eight-lane suspension bridge looked like the sails of an old ship that made the colonial port of Charleston so successful. As I approached the zenith of the highest span, my sight was captured by glints of sunlight reflecting on the wave caps in the harbor. The light seemed to be dancing with the water. I was mesmerized. I was aware of all of the motions of driving, but my sight extended beyond...I was finally on my way to see Stephanie. I wanted to share this with her, take these images to her sterile room full of artificial light. I wanted her to know that even though her body had to be there, chained by necessity, that the essence of her, her soul and spirit, could soar and dance with the light.

I was unfamiliar with the University parking lot and with the layout of the cancer center. The parking place closest to the Hollings Cancer Center was in the "E" lot. After walking a half mile, I found the right entrance. I checked in at the information desk and was told to go to the "E" bank of elevators which I would find down the hall to the right, through the atrium, turning left by the cafeteria. What was it with "E's" today? How about E-nough? E-ternal hassle? I started chuckling to myself. The atrium was beautiful and seemed to rise at least three or four floors. Was it possible that some visionary architect had wrapped a cancer center around an atrium? I smiled at the thought. I slowed at the cafeteria. I decided to get a burger for Stephanie, with fries.

Armed with food and memories of dancing light, I ascended the elevators to the eighth floor. Although I had never met her, I spotted Kitty Drummond from the classic cap and crisp white uniform instead of the more casual brightly colored scrubs favored by younger nurses. In teaching hospitals, the head floor nurses were the backbone of the medical system. Students, interns and residents came and went. Attending senior doctors flitted in and out. I knew from experience that the charge nurses ran the show and provided continuity and invaluable experience to the transient medical students, interns and residents. Some of them could have been drill instructors in the Marine Corps for a second job. Kitty was a tiny woman that exuded a commanding presence. I approached her to introduce myself.

"Hello, Dr. Ingersohn," she said, before I could speak.

"You must be Kitty Drummond."

"Welcome to 8 East," she said with twinkling blue eyes as she pumped my hand.

She had known immediately who I was. Dr. Two-Pop had obviously communicated with her. Well, he was the president of the whole medical university. I wondered how many of the staff and professors knew what a tender heart he had.

Kitty led me down to the isolation units. Unfortunately, the atrium did not come up this far. There were six units ringed around a nursing station. She handed me Stephanie's chart. I read all of Rob Gellmans' notes and the nursing notes. The charting of her blood counts showed a steady drop. Transfusions might be necessary at some point, Gellman noted. Her blood type was AB negative, the rarest type of all.

I followed Kitty into a prep room where I stored my purse. As in my med school days rotating through surgery, I was helped into a paper gown, hat, mask, and foot covers. Then Kitty held the latex gloves so I could slip my hands in. She had put the burger and fries into a heavy duty plastic bag that would seal itself when heated. Finally, she put it all in a special sterilizing microwave.

"Stephanie's father just went out for lunch. I'll keep visitors out while you're here," Kitty spoke to me as she would to any medical consultant. She led the way to Room E.

I knocked on the door to Stephanie's room and entered, bearing her gifts. She was in bed in a white hospital gown with a white scarf wrapped around her head. The bed linens were also white. A plastic tube snugly fit under her nostrils feeding an oxygen mixture into her lungs. With the chemo, the malignant white cells being killed compromised her immunity and required the sterile surroundings. The red cells that carry oxygen throughout the body had also been seriously depleted. With only a small percent of healthy red blood cells left to carry the load, the percent of oxygen she breathed had to be higher. Purplish blotches on her face and arms showed where she had bled under the skin from diminished platelets. The same dark tint painted half-moons under her eyes.

"Are those French fries, Dr. Kai?" Her dull eyes emitted a tiny sparkle.

"Fries with cholesterol, salt and carbs," I answered as I turned over the booty to her.

She tore the protective plastic covering off while asking, "Any sterilized ketchup packets?"

"Arrrrgh. I knew there was something else. There's some on your burger."

"Manna from heaven."

I pulled up a white plastic folding chair close by her bed and sat down, watching her eat.

"Did Two-Pop call you?"

"Sure did. He was worried about you."

"He's not doing so well with all this. Neither is Dad. Nana brought cookies that she blitzed in the microwave. It melted all the chocolate chips." She was talking between bites.

"Has your mother come yet?"

"Not since the first day. She's not very good at 'sick stuff'. She can't handle it. She didn't come see me at Sloan Kettering either. Plus, I think she is afraid that I will die. She just cries."

"How are you handling all of this?"

"Better than I thought I would. I think you were right when you told me it's not my time to die yet. Dr. Gellman said I've got a good chance at remission. He said about seventy percent of us go into remission at least once, especially someone my age. If I go into remission, he wants me to go back to Sloan Kettering to prepare for a probable stem cell transplant. They do them here but a doctor up there actually specializes in AML. My family needs to be tested to see if anyone's a genetic match. If none of them are, they will try to match me to a donor list."

My thoughts were bouncing between her words and my memories from prior patients who had had leukemia or lymphoma. How many of them were still alive? I really didn't know. A number had died. A small flicker of the first leukemia patient to die in my training passed quickly through my mind…a little girl. I banished the thought, as I always did.

"Well, isn't this the latest in sterile décor," I said, looking around the room, "lacking in taste, but also microorganisms." Another unbidden image crept into my head, this one of my thirteen-year-old daughter's bedroom. I was torn between labeling it a pig sty or a disaster area. Piles of both clean and dirty clothes were wrinkled, balled up, and partially buried on every available surface. Magazines, papers, books and food wrappers overlaid what was barely distinguishable as a bed. She studied in that bed. I think she slept there, too. There were probably enough bacteria, viruses and other living beasties to keep a microbiology lab supplied for years. Just this moment, I was so grateful that she was healthy that I made a mental note to get off her case about her room! At least for now.

Stephanie was halfway through her food, licking mustard from the edge of her lip.

"They say white walls are soothing. It feels futuristic in here to me, like a condo where angels would live," she said flippantly.

"Actually, most angels I've seen seem to favor stained glass; robes of white surrounded by bright jewel toned glass fragments," I answered.

"Ummm," she mumbled with her mouth full. "Like in Notre Dame or St. Peter's Basilica. I hadn't thought of that."

"Have you been nauseated at all?" I asked.

"Taking meds for that. Doesn't seem to be a problem yet. The hair came out in chunks last night. One of the nurses helped me shave it off. Want to see?" she asked as she pulled the scarf off, revealing her bald head.

"Amazing symmetry, girl. Way to go," I spoke admiringly. "You have one of those beautifully shaped heads."

"Yeah, me, Bruce Willis, Michael Jordan, and Sinead O'Connor," she shot back.

"Sinead O'Connor?"

"You know, the Irish singer that shaved her head in protest one time. She also ripped up a picture of the Pope on *Saturday Night Live*. She did ultimately apologize. I've never had the courage to be that overtly rebellious."

"I do remember her now. I'm surprised you do. Wasn't that before you were born?"

"I read, Kai. Plus, I identify with her passion. I wish I had cut my hair and donated it to Locks of Love before I began losing it. I really didn't believe it would all come out. I feel a little neutered without my hair. Like I'm unisex, especially in this hospital get up. But, hopefully, only eleven more days."

"So, you have more than a week to rest, relax and recover."

"You make it sound like a vacation."

"No, just an opportunity for you to spend some quiet time reflecting, sorting out some of the questions you've raised, deciding what you want to take away from this experience."

"I hadn't thought of having leukemia as an opportunity," she scoffed. "I'll think about that."

She then did something that would be a hallmark of her therapy. She rapidly switched gears.

"I want you to tell me a story about your childhood. Only caveat is it has to be a happy story. I'm too tired to talk anymore. I just want to be still and listen. Just *be* with you."

She rolled onto her side facing me and tucked her right hand under her cheek. There was still a dot of mustard at the corner of her mouth. I reached over and blotted it with my latex glove. There was a pause as I thought about her opening the door to me. It harkened back to her set of rules from our first session. *Number three: agree to share some of my life with her as she shares hers with me.*

In psychotherapy, this was usually considered a ploy to avoid. Today, it was appropriate to let her go there. I had really made that decision in the early days of our therapy. Meet her, no therapeutic dodges, encourage transference and be acutely aware of my own counter-transference. Walk the path with her, help her not to fall off or stop or walk in circles.

Almost immediately, as if I heard the opening of some closed gates, my mind recalled the childhood game I played only as day was giving way to night. Images flashed in muted shadows of dusk and it was then that I felt the freedom to continue.

"I'll tell you a story about a game I played outside, just as night was falling, called Kick the Can. I played it with my brothers and the neighborhood. Lost Boys, á la Peter Pan," I told Stephanie.

"Someone would kick the can – usually a Campbell's tomato soup can with the label peeled off to expose the dull-shiny silver tin. The can would arc into the twilight, landing with a rolling sound, and the kid who was 'it' ran after it, captured it, and returned with the tin talisman to home base defined by a circle of pebbles. The rest of us dispersed into the graying evening light, running and hiding at the same time. We flitted from tree to tree, hugging the bark. We ran to the corner of a house or behind a trash can, always moving, always keeping an eye on home base crowned with the tin can. The whole idea was to make it to that tin can without getting caught by 'it'. I remembered slinking and sliding from one place to another, edging closer to safety. When 'it' saw you, you had to freeze in the shadows. That was when the crickets seemed to play the loudest on their leg fiddles, as bullfrogs picked up the bass of the cadence. These were the sounds of my childhood. 'It' always caught someone and the game would end only to begin again, the 'it' of late kicking the can and peeling out to join the other hiders. In the interim, during those minutes between kicks, a rush of pure freedom overtook us."

Stephanie broke into a big smile at this. She had been transported along with me back to my childhood.

"Dusk was turning to dark when the fireflies came from their secret hideaways," I continued. "We fell into step with them, chasing and swooping, mesmerized by the fiery little chemical beacons on their abdomens. Joy was to catch one, to feel its buzzing wing sound on the palms of our hands. We cupped our hands and opened a sliver of a peep hole at the top to see the firefly at rest. The light turned on and off with some kind of rhythm. We could count it...'one, two, three, on; one, two, three, off'. The firefly caught us every time with the wonder of itself. Then we threw up our hands to the sky and the little firefly sailed off into the night becoming one with the stars of heaven."

Stephanie lay very still with her eyes closed. I wondered if she was asleep. She spoke without opening her eyes. "You're a poet, Doc, masquerading as a shrink." There was no malice or sarcasm in her voice.

The poet sacrificed on the altar of science, I thought. Tinkerbell chained to responsibility. The tin-silver of the can tarnished with rust and unfettered shouts of childhood silenced by age. This was part of what had been lost to me – this kind of creative play.

"Fireflies," Stephanie mumbled.

I shared with her the images of the sunlight dancing on the water under the bridge...the something beyond. As I trailed off, a voice seemed to say: "Are *you* listening? There was a time *you* danced. You could again."

"Fireflies of the night and morning," Stephanie yawned.

After that, we gave over words to silence, me remembering my childhood freedom. Stephanie lost in her own thoughts. I noticed her eyes filled with tears.

"Just before I was admitted on Wednesday, I went with Dad to Boulevard Diner in Mt. Pleasant. You been there?"

I nodded. It was a hole-in-the-wall kind of place only a mile from my office.

"Well, I asked to go there for my last lunch before hospital food. They have turkey and dressing with cranberry sauce on the menu every day. Kind of like Thanksgiving on demand."

That and the coconut cake were two of my favorites.

"Anyway, as we were going in, two little girls were playing hopscotch right outside the entrance."

As she was talking, I had a clear image of the permanent hopscotch pattern painted on the concrete walkway.

Stephanie continued, "I wanted to play with them, throw the pebble in one of the boxes and hop on one foot. I tried, but I was too weak. When I bent to pick up the pebble, I lost my balance and fell. And I couldn't breathe. Even the simplest exercise leaves me breathless. I can't even scotch one hop, Kai. What if I never play again?"

I reached out for her hand, and through the latex barrier could feel the heat of her body. I wondered if she was running a fever. A vein was pulsing in her forehead. A single tear had made a track from the inside corner of her eye across the bridge of her nose.

Softly, silently, I sat beside her, holding her hand. I looked at our hands and realized they made a solid bridge.

Underneath it was our oh-so-human vulnerability floating in a little lifeboat across dangerous currents.

We stayed like that until Stephanie's hand relaxed in mine and I heard the regular breath of sleep. I left quietly, retracing my steps through the narrow hallway.

Chapter Fifteen

I stripped off the latex gloves and shed the paper coverings and walked out to the nursing station. There was no sign of Kitty or any other nurses. I went through the exit door, emerging into the eighth floor. I must have made a wrong turn, as I found myself in a corridor I didn't recognize. It dead-ended in an ICU unit: intensive care for cancer patients. I had been in a place like this before. Memories assailed me. I was back in medical school again.

A hush descended over the room like a gossamer shroud gently falling, falling to cover her. Septicemia, a massive blood infection, had finally claimed her. She had been brought to the emergency room some hours before in a deep coma with a black, swollen right leg. She was five years old, and six weeks into outpatient chemotherapy treatment for leukemia. She, unknowingly, reflexively, had scratched a mosquito bite on her leg. Had the staph infection been on her fingernails? No matter, it had made its way into her bloodstream meeting no resistance. Her immunity had been suppressed by powerful drugs intended to be a cure. How utterly ironic that the cure had killed her. I was a senior medical student, taking an elective course in pediatric hematology and oncology, preparing for a pediatric residency. I was part of the team that gathered helplessly to bear witness to her death.

I stood at the head of her bed as if held by some glamour, some unforeseen force of spirit. Over and over, I stroked her long dark hair that had only just begun to loosen and fall out. Surely she slept, but then there had been a whisper of something touching my face as the hush fell. Was it simply a draft of air, or the touch of her spirit, its cool spectral wings slipping from her body on its upward journey? I backed away from the bed and bumped into the metal bedside table, rattling its contents as I spun around, clawing my way through the divider curtains surrounding the bed. I passed the nursing station, fled down the hall and ran, away from the loss of a child, away from death.

Panic welled up in me again as I stood outside the double doors to the ICU in the present. I wanted to run again like I had done twenty years ago. I stumbled into a small waiting room right beside the intensive care unit.

"Breathe deep," I told myself. "You're not back there, you're here, now." The memories of that five-year old girl were not to be dispelled so easily this time. They were just so real. I could almost feel her long black hair under my fingertips; see her pale lips move silently; watch the rapid eye movements of her comatose dream sleep; feel that same brush of air as her spirit slipped away, stilling her heart and her eyes forever.

And, God, her name. Her name had lain dormant in the deep vaults of my subconscious for twenty years. It could not be, but it was. Her name had been Stephanie.

When I had run out of the ER so many years ago, I vowed never to work with children who had cancer ever again. With that decision, I capped the well of raw emotional pain that threatened to overwhelm me. I had loved children and wanted to take care of them. Kai, who had placated Mr. Death, had not been able to save little Stephanie. Losing that battle with death years ago had only made my fear of death worse. With the remembering, the tears came. Now, I could cry. My tears were for all of us: Stephanie the child and Kai the child, Stephanie the young woman and Kai, the young doctor, and the two of us here in this hospital who were being healed.

Chapter Sixteen

I replayed that moment of emotional release repeatedly in the days that followed. I have shared these kinds of cathartic moments with so many patients over the years, when some deeply buried memory is safely brought back up through the layers of covering to be cleansed with understanding; energy lost to the repression retrieved and freed to be used creatively in life.

I have been asked by so many people why it is necessary to deal with these locked away traumatic memories. The answer is always the same: not only are they thieves of our energy, they also fester and eventually leak through as anxieties, phobias and obsessions. They chain us to wounds as surely as Atlas, the Greek hero, was bound to shoulder the world forever as his penance.

I had done psychotherapy as part of my psychiatric training and had even flown to New York City years later to do Jungian analysis over a four-year period. Yet, I had never experienced catharsis like I did in the hospital that day. Something else had happened as well. It was a moment the old Irish Celts called the "thinning of the veil" when human spirit transcends the barrier between the human, physical world and the hidden spiritual realm becomes transparent allowing us to "see" clearly what human eyes cannot. It is a glimpse unhindered by time, that renders perspective that heals. To look through the veil reminds us that our time is finite, yielding to the eternal.

I needed sanctuary, a place of peace away from everything. There is a kind of saturation effect that happens to most psychiatrists when our mental and emotional sponge is full. Being cloistered to rest, relax and recharge is the only thing that helps. There are many places in my life that I claim for their tranquil beauty and stillness. But there are few sanctuaries. The one I longed for that day was Melrose Plantation on Daufuskie Island. It was an easy two-hour drive south to Hilton Head to catch the ferry across Calibogue Sound to the Island. I decided to go.

My former husband, Trey, introduced me to Daufuskie Island. That and my treasured son and daughter are all I have left of our twelve-year marriage. It was one of my greatest failures. My ex-husband's given name was Henry Andrew Renault Legare, III, a harbor pilot with a long Charleston pedigree, whom I had met at my cousin's wedding halfway through med school. Charismatic, smart and sexy, we'd shared a love of sports, sailing, and travel. But there were so many other things that created discord. I had unerringly chosen to marry Peter Pan. In retrospect, I think I wanted to be Tinkerbell and fly with Peter. In reality, I became entrenched as the responsible Wendy.

Reclaiming places once known in the context of a former marriage can be a healing process. Was that another reason I chose to come back to Daufuskie? Or, was it simply her ageless island beauty that beckoned? The old plantation house had been destroyed by a terrible hurricane in 1896, and the Atlantic Ocean had long since pounded the northern beaches. The beauty remained breathtaking. Huge live oaks covered the grounds with branches bending gracefully, draped in long Spanish moss. Palmettos, cabbage palms, cedar trees and wild dogwoods were plentiful among stands of regal pines. Bogs of cattails and miles of marshland dominated the island's western point. It felt like hallowed ground to me. It wasn't much different from the days of early settlers, or the even earlier inhabitants. Cusabo Indians had left huge oyster mounds and arrowheads to mark their passage through the place.

After an hour-long crossing from Hilton Head, I disembarked from the ferry, checked out a golf cart which was the only allowable transportation around the resort, and headed to the beach. My luggage would be delivered to my room. The wide, white beach was littered with sun-bleached bones of live oaks felled by the same tides that had taken the old plantation house. The trees lay as dormant sentinels, reminders to those of us who came to disturb their haunting memory that life full of beauty and grandeur had once prevailed in this place. Inexorably, it had given way to the spirals of time as surely as all life does. I sat under the shade cast by one of the trees, leaning my back against its sturdy trunk. The rough bark had been sanded smooth by the fine white grains of sand, endlessly blown by the winds of time. The sun was descending from its peak and glints reflected on the waves like crystal fire. I took handfuls of the tiny quartz sand and let it run through my fingers. I am Kai and I am here. Alive. Alive. And the sand, marking time, fell through the hourglass of my hands.

I don't know how long I stayed in the pure "being" of that place. The sun was lowering in the sky as it dipped towards the horizon. Ocean breezes had picked up and storm clouds scudded overhead as the temperature dropped. I felt a chill. It was time to head back to the inn.

I walked up through undulating sand dunes, brushing my outstretched palms along the tops of sea oats clustered on their leeward sides, watching for resident sand spurs lurking in the interspersed vegetation. My little white golf cart awaited to carry me back to the inn. I emerged from the shadows of the remaining live oak stand into a small clearing. Suddenly, a great horned owl in full wing spread, swooped through the darkening sky across my pathway. It was so focused with its keen sight on some small animal on the ground that it did not see my converging cart. I thought owls only came out to hunt at night. Had the darkened sky lured one out prematurely? Were they following me now, even into my sanctuary? Stalking me in real life? An involuntary shiver ran through me.

The owl was many colors of brown, the feathers of its outspread wings outlined by a single shaft of sunlight streaking between the dark clouds. She descended with outstretched talons, leaning in to capture her prey. When she landed, her head dipped in vicious repetitive pecking motions as she "hooded" her kill by covering it with her wings.

I brought the cart to an abrupt stop and stared, stupefied at this primal drama unfolding before me. Predator and prey.

I was riveted as the owl, finishing her kill, began to rise. A small gray squirrel was hanging below her. I was so close that I could see the fine scales of the yellowish-gray talons that gripped the neck of the squirrel, which had no signs of life. The squirrel's body was eclipsed by the mighty wings of the owl as it struggled to be airborne, wobbling in its ascent. There was a lone tall pine, ten feet to my left. The owl, in its wobble-flight, fought to hold on to its prey and flew toward the tree. It landed on a sturdy horizontal branch of the pine, whose long needles spread in multiple clusters at its tip. I craned my neck from under the top of the cart to see the owl perched on the branch some fifteen feet above the ground, precariously balancing herself as she held onto the squirrel. The squirrel was mercifully dead, with no hope of escape or recovery. A gentle breeze pushed it into a graceful sway below the tree limb; its destiny of feeding a huge owl fulfilled.

"What?!" I wanted to yell at the owl. "What?" I had come here to rest, for God's sake, not attend a passion play staged by nature. Regardless, I could *not* tear myself away.

This is our strength.

This is our surrender.

We are all predators.

We are all prey.

See them all together. The great prize is Balance.

I clearly identified with the squirrel hanging lifeless. I was well acquainted with the role of prey...victim. I had learned it at my mother's knee. I had even played a variation of that role in my marriage to Trey. I was half of the dysfunctional relationship that we choreographed together. I had chosen to play the role of responsible Wendy, the parent of the unfettered Pan. The underlying wound to my feminine was part of the reason I chose Trey and stayed with him. Learning that in therapy had been a hard pill for me to swallow. I had been so confident in the role of doctor and later mother; perilously, I had looked to Trey to make me a real woman. He had done the male version of the same thing. Neither one of us could. Fracturing the emotional and physical stranglehold we had on each other turned out to be our only hope.

I felt like a fool and questioned everything about myself in that dark time during my divorce. In all honesty, my self-righteousness probably turned me into a predator. An image of me digging my talons into Trey formed in my mind's eye. I used talons of blame, punishment, abandonment. I had not been ready for the owl's deep wisdom. It had taken me years of therapy to come home to my own sense of self and value as a woman. Coming to Melrose, immersing myself in her beauty and serenity, was part of how I had learned to nurture myself. I hungered for the great prize of balance in my life. Being able to hold such extreme opposites in the self – predator/prey, masculine/feminine, love/hate – was very hard to do. It was one aspect of wholeness. The owl-god could see and be them all.

Today, I could thank Trey for giving me a love for this place, for co-creating our children, and for teaching me to fly. Memory no longer had to be tainted by our failures together. Melrose, or Ms. Rose as I now dubbed her, could hold me, nurture me, show me my own beauty and essence. It could help restore my true feminine nature.

Raindrops began falling as I left the owl and the squirrel to make my way to my room. I wanted to burrow under the soft down comforter and take a long nap. Pamper myself with room service. Revel in the joy of being a woman in sanctuary.

Chapter Seventeen

As I was healing, so was Stephanie. My initial visit to her in the hospital had been her lowest point since the onslaught of her chemotherapy. She had required two transfusions in the days after I had seen her, to boost her red cell and platelet counts. What a difference a week makes to the wondrous physical creations we call "bodies." I had a cancellation on Tuesday before lunch and called Stephanie to see if I could swing by for a visit.

"You may come and share my lunch. Two-Pop brought Nana's fried shrimp and hushpuppies with coleslaw which will transform to hot slaw in the sterilizer."

"What can I bring?"

"Chocolate, which becomes a kind of sludge. It has a low melting point. Same flavor, though. I like to eat it with my fingers."

"Ah, the taste of chocolate laced with latex. Sounds divine." Stephanie was concentrating on her laptop so intensely, she didn't hear me come to the door. Nurse Kitty had zapped Nana's food in the sterilizer while I was putting on the protective garb. She waited on the Godiva chocolate and Chessmen cookies to dip in our fondue. I must have looked like an astronaut with vittles. I stood at the door and watched her fingers flying over the keyboard. She had on a hospital gown, festooned with Disney characters. Goofy was showing above the laptop. A matching scrub cap featured Daisy Duck. The colorful materials lessened her skin pallor making her look almost festive. I knocked on the door, startling her.

"You scared me to death!"

"I've been standing here for a while. Didn't want the food to get cold. Except the hot slaw."

We arranged the food on the portable tray top that had been doubling for a desktop moments before. I sat on the edge of her bed as she tore open the plastic covering to reveal succulent shrimp and steaming hushpuppies.

"Your appetite is still good," I said as I watched her eat with gusto.

"Need to gain some weight back. I lost almost six pounds the first week. Food tasted like cardboard. Chemo really affects the taste buds."

"I truly hope you can taste these hushpuppies as I am delirious with hushpuppy joy," I mumbled with my mouth full.

Stephanie chuckled. "Hushpuppy joy, huh? I'll have to pass that on to Nana."

"What were you working on so intently when I came in?"

"A letter to my thesis advisor at U. Chicago. I want to change the topic of my doctoral thesis and *that* is no small feat.

It will take the approval of an entire committee."

"What do you have in mind for the new topic?" I inquired.

"*Fear of Death in Life-Threatening Illnesses: Impact on Spiritual Awareness.*"

"That's a mouthful," I said with my mouth still full of shrimp.

"When my brain began functioning again yesterday, I was struck by the unique opportunity I have to write about extreme illness and the fear of death. Let's face it, twenty-six-year-olds don't worry about it until a parent or grandparent becomes ill. The last time I really dealt with death was when I was seven. Samantha, my favorite dog…a gorgeous white Lab who lived on Two-Pop's farm. She got bitten by a snake and barely made it back to the house from the horse pasture. She died in Nana's arms. I was off riding with Two-Pop. It took me forever to get over her loss. I almost drove Two-Pop crazy asking him questions. Where had Sam *gone*? Did dogs keep living after their bodies died, like people did? Would I see her in heaven? I helped Two-Pop bury her in the apple orchard. I didn't want to leave her there, alone in the ground."

Stephanie sounded emotional, even after all these years. Memories intruded of Mr. Death coming to me in the dark. Sooner or later, most children are confronted with death in real life. Some of us do it alone. Stephanie had Two-Pop and Nana to help her.

"You remember Sam's death clearly," I commented.

"Very clearly. Last week when I was so sick, I dreamed about her. We were together again on Two-Pop's farm. I woke up wondering if that meant I would die and see her again. Anyway, losing Sam was the last time I was touched personally by death. Reading Küng and Becker's books about death and dying were just academic exercises. Now it's *real* to me. I can do more than create some intellectual treatise on the subject; I can add my personal experience to existing literature and research. It's right up my alley." Stephanie was excited. Her green eyes always lightened when she spoke passionately and now sparkles looked like little green fireworks. "It's the perfect topic to integrate biology, metaphysics and religious studies," she continued. "What do you think, Kai?"

"Stephanie, can you tell me exactly what metaphysics really means? I have an idea, but find the whole concept confusing." This was clearly a hole in my education.

Stephanie just looked at me…the kind of look a parent gives their child when asked where babies come from. I could hear her brain shifting down to basics.

"I think I can use a simple analogy to explain this better. Visualize a lamp plugged into an electrical socket. Concentrate on the bulb with its tungsten filament enclosed by the glass. This is like our physical bodies. Next, consider the electricity available in the socket. It is similar to a pure, unseen source of energy. For the sake of our human analogy, let us call this electrical energy "spirit". Now, in your mind, turn on the lamp, allowing electricity into the bulb. A third emergent is created: *light*. Light is not the lamp and it is not electricity. This light is analogous to the human's living soul: our unique personality capable of thought and reasoning, feeling and expression, belief, and relationship. If we flick the lamp off, the light goes out...or the human being dies. The study of this light or human being is metaphysics. The sub-disciplines of metaphysics are philosophy, psychology, theology and religion, cosmos-ology (the outer universe) and physics/quantum theory (the invisible universe within all matter). Have you ever heard of the God particle?"

"Yes, I have, but don't ask me exactly what it is," I sputtered.

"Its real name is the Higgs boson. Years ago, Higgs theorized that on the subatomic, quantum level, there existed a particle that constantly shifted from matter to energy and back. It has recently been scientifically substantiated to exist. Higgs conceptualized this shifting point as the interface between God/Spirit/Creator and time/space/matter. He postulated that this particle/place is where God energy and our physical cells (that make up our bodies) intersect. It's like science is proving how God uses natural law, gravity, time and space to create and sustain life."

"Is this the new controversy over creationism versus natural selection?" I asked nervously.

"Spare me," she groaned. "Scientists, especially physicists, are pulling theology and science back together! Religion and science split several times in history. By the time Copernicus used astronomy to prove the sun was the center of the universe, the church threatened to burn him at the stake. Same thing later with Newton. Darwin waited twenty years to publish *Origin of Species* because he was afraid of the church."

Stephanie stopped and looked at me. We both took a deep breath. I was getting a crash course on her life's work and I wanted to understand it. For her and for me, but I was lost with the quantum level God particle, and my face showed it. She wasn't finished yet.

"Another aspect of metaphysics is thanatology...the study of death. After I got sick, this became a strong area of study for me. Adding the idea of the God particle expanded everything I was trying to integrate about physics, metaphysics and religious studies. It's all here, now, in my life, Kai. Add some mystery and…." She trailed off. "No wonder so many physicists believe in God. It doesn't collide for them. It all fits together, if you don't get mired in religious dogma. God is the great unifier."

She was breathless, enervated. She was trail-blazing something deeply personal and creative. What she was saying made sense and wasn't inconsistent with anything I believed. I told her so.

"This can be my thesis! I am so psyched, Kai!"

"I think life threw you a curveball and you have the potential to hit a homerun! It could be good therapy, as well, to document your own responses to this illness, fear of death, healing, etc." I could see it now.

"It will help with the boredom, too. The hours drag on and on in here. All you can do is watch TV or check Facebook. Too much reading makes my eyes watery and tired. Writing is easier; I can type with my eyes closed. At least now I have some energy to do it."

"Any idea how much longer you will be in isolation?"

"Probably seven to ten days. Healthy blast cells forming right on schedule. They can turn into the white cells I need for immunity. Can't afford an infection with nothing to fight it."

"Stephanie, I want to tell you what happened to me the last time I visited you up here."

I hadn't planned to tell her about the other Stephanie and my healing cathartic experience. It just seemed like the right thing to do, especially in light of our previous discussion.

"You look so serious."

"Somebody I knew died a long time ago. I was so afraid at the moment of her death that I fled, both physically and psychologically."

I told her what happened outside the cancer ICU. I told her about that first death in the emergency room at MUSC my senior year in med school. The recovered memories. I told her the first Stephanie's name.

She was rapt, listening to my every word. When I was finished, she leaned back and let out the breath she had been holding.

"That is an amazing story, Kai. I come along, how many years later?"

"Twenty."

"I come to you with leukemia and the same name; twenty years later, you start dealing with it. That Stephanie died. I hope for your sake, I don't die, too. Will you be okay if I die, Kai?"

"I would be very, very sad if you were to die, Steph, but I've come a long way towards understanding death in the last twenty years."

"Then again," she brightened, "I could beat the odds and outlive you!"

God, she was beautiful when she smiled. Even skinny, pale, and bald, her smile made me think of hope.

"Kai, there's something special about us being in each other's lives, isn't there? I mean, I *know* why you're in my life. I just haven't thought before why I'm in yours."

"When I saw you the first time and you brought that contract for me to sign, I knew our work together would have to be 'out of the box.' I had no idea how far out."

"You won't quit me, will you?" She teased.

"Not a chance."

Chapter Eighteen

At work the next week, thoughts of Stephanie regularly intruded. Most of the time, I could banish them with a breath prayer for her. Every time I started worrying about her, my brother Mark's voice would override my fear. When Sarah told me my five o'clock patient had cancelled, I was so grateful I wanted to pay her for not coming. I needed to drive to the beach. Like Stephanie, I was often drawn to the beach as a place to clear my head. I don't think I was aware at the time that it was a place to be close to Stephanie, as well. It was on the way home, anyway. The kids wouldn't expect me until 6:30. As I turned onto the four-lane connector to the beach, late afternoon traffic was still heavy. I was oblivious.

As I approached the crest of the bridge over the marsh, the ocean rose into my line of vision. The breadth of it filled me. Daylight savings had given me that precious extra hour of light even as the sun was well into its downward arc. I crossed the Isle of Palms and Breach Inlet, pulling into a public walkway on Sullivan's Island. I kicked off my shoes and trudged along the sandy path. I climbed one of the sand dunes and looked across the ocean trying to spy a tall ship or maybe Bermuda. Stephanie had been here weeks ago in the wee hours of the still-dark morn. I ran down from the dune and stepped into the rising tide which still held the warmth of the sun. I began turning in fast, tight circles, whirling back through time, through years. I lay down on the sand, mindless of hair or clothes and remembered what Mark had taught me.

It was Thanksgiving at Mother's house eight years before. Remnants of turkey and oyster dressing with giblet gravy, green beans almandine, macaroni and cheese, and sweet potato casserole lay strewn upon the good china plates that Mother had inherited from Dumpling. Chairs scraped the floor as each of us carried plates to the kitchen sink and made our way to the buffet table for a slice of pecan, pumpkin or German chocolate pie. Whipped cream was optional. The aroma of freshly brewed Jamaican blue mountain coffee wafted throughout the kitchen and dining room. I smelled my fill as other coffee lovers loaded up on sugar and cream. No Splenda today. When we were all seated at the long, gleaming cherry wood table again, Mark clinked his water glass with a spoon. Our voices quieted and he began to speak.

"I know all of you are missing Dad as much as I am," he gestured towards the empty place at the head of the table, to the untouched place setting of china, silver and crystal. We had buried Dad in August. He had died suddenly walking the back nine of his beloved golf course. How incredibly fitting that he had died doing something he loved so much.

Mark continued, "You are never the same after a parent dies," he glanced at Mother, "I feel Dad's mantel has fallen on me to carry on the Ingersohn family traditions." He stopped and took a steadying breath, seeming to fortify himself to continue. I had no clue as to what he would say next.

"But, it seems I, alone, cannot be the leader. I am going to have to ask all of you to join together and carry this family forward."

He took another steadying breath and gazed directly at our mother.

"I have recently been diagnosed with pancreatic cancer and they have given me less than twelve months to live."

We were stunned. Only his wife, Angie, looked away, the burden of her secret now relieved. Mother and Mark held each other's hazel eyes. He stepped around the table and knelt by her. She cradled his head against her breast and crooned softly so that only he could hear. It did not seem possible that my mother would lose her firstborn. I was thunderstruck. Unbelieving. Trey and I had separated in February; Dad died in August and now Mark had pancreatic cancer. No way! I struggled furiously with the reality that threatened to capsize me in its stormy waters. Rather than lose my composure completely, I left the table and fled to the back yard, leaving my chocolate pie untouched.

I went to the old water oak tree in my parents' back yard where Mark had nailed the Tarzan vine. I climbed up to that branch like I had done so many times as a child. I slammed my mind shut to the outer world as I began my angry tirade with God, speaking out loud, "You will not take another man that I love," I spoke menacingly, "I forbid it. This one you cannot have!"

I put my hands over my ears and started to hum as if the sound were a talisman to ward off Mark's words. I hummed and hummed. Finally, I heard Gracen calling me.

"Mom, Mom! M-a-h-m-a!" She must have been screaming by then.

"Go away." I tried to answer in between the hums.

"Are you okay?" She was shouting.

"I will be, but I don't want to talk right now." Hum....

"Mom, I think they need you inside. Everybody's upset. Grandma Eva's crying. Uncle Jamey and Aunt Courtney are crying. Mom, you always fix everything. We need you."

I didn't care who needed me. I had to finish threatening God.

"Gracen, I am not coming down. Now, go tell Andrew y'all can play some video games. Tell Uncle Jamey I'll be in later. Now, go away." I left no room for argument. She went away.

I was ready to do battle with God. Our relationship was nothing if not passionate. And it was personal. I had never seen God as some distant, remote deity. Whatever power I had, I mustered in the face of my personal Almighty. I was afraid I would be struck down with a single omnipotent thought directed my way. But God had created me with that great glitch, free will, and I was going to use it to do battle.

"*God,*" I called to the sky and clouds from my tree limb. "*Come down here. I want to talk to you.*"

Okay, no burning bushes, but I decided the Almighty could hear me.

"You took Trey and maybe I deserved that. I know I was part of that dance. It still hurt, though. It hurt! You took Daddy. I didn't even get to tell him goodbye. He was only seventy-two years old. I needed him to help me with losing Trey. He was the only Daddy I had." I was yelling the words in God's general direction, wherever that might be.

"And now, you're going to take Mark? My Mark? My big brother? What is the deal here? We're all down here trying to be good people - good God-fearing, live-right kind of people. Especially Mark! He's a deacon in the Baptist church of Boykin! He's the superintendent of the Sunday school program. He goes to church every Sunday, and Training Union at night, and Wednesday night prayer meeting. He is a prayer warrior for so many others! And this is his reward? Pancreatic cancer?

He's only forty-two years old." I began to falter. God was being too quiet.

As if in silent answer, memories of Mark and me began falling like dominoes. We were playing in that hot Oklahoma sun. Mark was barefoot and shirtless with a cowboy hat, bandana tied around his neck and double holsters with six-guns riding his slim hips; me with my bow and arrows slung over a shoulder, cheap Indian moccasins, and black braids wound with pop beads. Mark riding his red bike and me running alongside begging him to let me ride on the back.

There was Mark driving Dad's 1977 Pontiac Grand Prix. Me standing in the driveway watching my big brother drive off to pick up his date.

Mark marching in full dress uniform with Company D at The Citadel's Friday afternoon parades.

Mark in the Marine Corps in battle fatigues.

At his wedding to Angie in the Summerall Chapel at The Citadel.

Mark with his two little girls. I saw the joy and triumph of all those years flash before my eyes. And I felt God's sorrow along with mine.

"Well, I'm asking. Please heal Mark! It will take a miracle. You know how to do miracles. I'm asking, now, for a miracle."

Mark calling me intruded. The real Mark.

"Kai! Kai, where are you?"

Was the miracle just Mark? My thirty-eight years of life with Mark?

"I'm up here, Mark," I yelled back at him.

He walked over and looked up at me.

"Come down, sister of mine, from thy lofty perch!"

"Ha, ha," I retorted. "You come up!"

Mark climbed up the old tree that had held us in its arms countless times before. I thought of Shel Silverstein's book, *The Giving Tree*, a bittersweet story of a tree that gives its all to a little boy as he grows to manhood. Mark settled down beside me fifteen feet in the air on that gnarled old limb.

"Who were you talking to?" he asked.

"God."

"Want to share?"

"I asked God for a miracle to heal you."

"Thank you," he grinned. "I've asked for the same thing. God works in mysterious ways. Remember when that Huey helicopter crashed at Camp Lejeune when I was in the Marine Corps? I was supposed to be on it that morning. I was sick as a dog from food poisoning from mess hall food the night before. Me and about twenty other guys. I was the only one doing maneuvers with the group on the Huey. Twelve other Marine pilots died that day. I was twenty-two. Almost half my life ago. I met Angie and had the girls. I've had a good life, Kai. And I'm going to do chemo. I'm going to fight. Help me.

I'm going to need you to deal with the medical profession. I've got so many questions and I need a translator, a mediator. The whole family's going to need you, Kai. You understand all this medical language." His face shone with hope. After all these years, Mark needed *me*. What a twist. Did he even understand yet that he was going to die? At that moment, I hated being a doctor. I didn't want to *know*. I just wanted to hold on to him and keep him safe. Protect him from death. I put on my brave face. I hid my fear as a gift to my big brother. "I'll walk with you, Markham," I used his given name. "Every step." Inside, I just felt sick. What if I couldn't do what Mark needed me to do? What if I broke and ran? I didn't think that was possible. For the love of Mark, I would stay and intercede. I would use denial to cope, which is kind of a cardinal sin for a psychiatrist. Maybe *we* need necessary denial, too. I would pray that Mark would be one of the two percent that survive. Could I hold love and fear together at the same time like I did as a child? Could love triumph this time? Deep inside, I knew that love is stronger than fear. But I swear I didn't think I had the faith to believe that Mark would survive.

He reached out for my hand and squeezed it. Mark jogged through his first round of chemotherapy. He was a marathoner and in peak condition when he was diagnosed. But he started losing weight even with a healthy appetite. He believed that if he could eat, he could live.

"Kai, the day I leave a plate of Mama's homemade chicken and dumplings is the day I'll be boarding the bus to glory." He used to say things like that all the time. And he ate all the time.

His chemo was palliative, to shrink the tumor and relieve the pain. It was not intended to be a cure. The doctors wanted to give him as much quality time as possible. When the pain became too much to bear, they could induce a coma until he died.

I went to Boykin to attend Easter Sunday services with Mother, Mark, and his family. Jamey and Courtney brought their two boys; Gracen and Andrew filled out the second pew at the church.

I did love the music in the Baptist church. I had taken those songs with me to the great sanctuaries of marsh and salt water in my beloved Lowcountry. My spiritual journey had led me out of the confines of four walls. I had opened my belief system to the many faces and names of God. Somehow, it was all of us…people…who had carefully dissected God into so many different religious groups: Jews, Muslims, Hindus, Catholics and all manner of Protestants. Subset after subset. Yet, somewhere underneath it all, lay the essence, the archetype of God, undivided. Today, in Mark's church, I would make yet another petition for my brother's life. I would do it in the place and language with which Mark and I had first come to know God.

I would make it again and again as the marsh grass marked the turning of the year: from the silver gray of winter to the nascent shoots of spring. I would pray that Mark would see the brilliant greens of summer; watch as the grass faded to yellowish green; see it turn to gold like the wheat fields of Kansas. By then, Mark would have come full circle to Thanksgiving and beyond.

He barely made it through Easter. He had a terrible reaction to one of the chemotherapy medicines and it almost killed him. His liver began to shut down. Mama called Jamey and me to come. The doctors decided to rest Mark's body by inducing a coma. They chilled his body to slow the metabolic functions of his vital organs and fed him intravenously with strong sedatives and life-sustaining nutrients. Over the next few days, he stabilized. With the doctors' assurances, I went home to be with my children. I returned on Friday to spend the weekend by Mark's side in the hospital.

Trey agreed to keep the kids again. He was being very kind during this most terrible of times for me.

"We are going to wean Mark from the coma and bring him back to consciousness," his oncologist, Dr. Bennington, said to Angie and me. "His liver enzymes are almost back to normal and the pancreatic enzymes are better in spite of the tumor. We are going to stop all chemo from here on out. Too risky."

"Does that mean the tumor will start growing again?" Angie asked timidly.

"Yes, in all probability, it will," Bennington spoke in his normally loud voice that matched his oversized body. He gave me a knowing look that doctors often telegraphed to one another. It meant, the good part is over and everything is downhill from here. I closed the interaction by turning Angie away and said goodbye to the good doctor over my shoulder. I walked her to the elevators.

"Go home and rest," I told her. "I'll be here with Mark. You and Mama rest. I'll call if there's any change."

Mark woke up about ten o'clock that night when his liver finally cleansed the sleep meds out of his system.

"Kai," his voice creaked from disuse. It sounded rusted, like an old gate hinge.

"Hi, Markham. Where you been?"

He smiled.

"You won't believe me, little sister."

"Tell 'um," I said in Daufina's Gullah language he had heard during his years at The Citadel.

"Kai, I've just been on the other side."

"Where is that?" I wasn't sure if he had been hallucinating because of all the drugs.

"No, no, no. It's not a place. My spirit was there with God. Daddy was there."

"Did you see God?"

"It's not like that," he explained. "You don't see with your eyes. I was just *with* God. *In* God. It's true what they say about traveling down a tunnel and hearing loud noises, bells and clicking sounds toward a grid of bright light. But I didn't pass through it. It's not time yet. If you pass through the light, you can't come back."

Mark was speaking fast and his eyes were burning with some kind of ethereal light of their own.

"There's nothing to be afraid of," he continued. "It's so peaceful there."

"But, I thought you didn't pass through the light. Where were you?" I couldn't follow him.

"A peaceful, quiet place. With God."

Mark went on, "It was like I was bathed in soothing waters of peace. But my body wasn't there. I was present in spirit. My spirit was with other spirits. I couldn't stay. They asked me if I was ready to stay and *BE* with them and I said no. I needed to come back to the physical realm and finish with my family. Say goodbye. Kai, say you believe me," he was speaking through shining shards of crystal-like tears.

This was Mark. While his body had been asleep, his soul/spirit had skipped its bounds and had journeyed to the other side, but not to stay. To glimpse some mystical, otherworldly place that could hardly be fathomed by the rational mind.

Because it was Mark speaking, I knew that he believed what he had experienced was real. If he had hallucinated, so be it. What was psychosis anyway but a mind breaking out of its rational ego bounds to fly into realms not known by the rest of us. Mark had been somewhere outside his body and he was trying to share it with me.

"Don't you see, Kai? We don't have to be afraid. Death isn't the enemy. Death just frees us from the body. Death can be our friend. Oh, Kai, I have my miracle. I will be healed through death; I will live forever."

He pulled me into a bear hug with some kind of strength that he shouldn't have had and said he was famished.

I raced down the hall and told the nurses he was awake and he needed something to eat. I felt kind of crazy while I waited for the food to arrive. I had read about near death experiences, called NDEs. I had even had one patient who had died during surgery and come back to speak of the same thing Mark did. His surgeon was shocked when the man told him he had on socks that didn't match! I had heard enough and read enough to believe in these kinds of experiences. Now, my own brother had been to the other side and come back to tell me.

What did it all mean? I felt overloaded. I needed a run on the beach. I needed to call Angie and Mother. I needed to get food to Mark before he starved to death.

I began to see the greater vision of Mark's journey, beyond the confines of my own selfish ego needs. My prayers opened up as I acknowledged that Mark and God were in this illness together, even to the end; I, for the first time, accepted that Mark might die. But could I give my blessing? Not yet. I had a few more things to learn.

Mark never made it home from the hospital. He said his goodbyes, began to turn inward. Away from all of us. I was with him that last night. Angie had gone home for an hour to see the girls.

He was in so much pain. I knew he was ready to go.

There was a young oncology resident on call that weekend. He was not a member of Mark's team. My last gift to Mark would be to save him from the youthful brashness of a doctor in training. It was clear to Mark's team that he would ask to go into an induced coma in his final days. But the orders Dr. Kid-dare wrote were aggressive and designed to give Mark more conscious palliative relief. Mark was refusing to take the medicine. He was ready to go into end stage coma. He had long ago learned to ask about medicine he didn't recognize. Once I fully understood what was going on, I went in search of the young resident, who turned out to be a handful. He was feeling his authoritative oats and was only talking to a psychiatrist, after all.

Rather than slug the little bastard, I suggested we go talk to Mark.

Mark was eloquent, "I understand perfectly. Clearly. I cannot tolerate any more pain. I am ready to go to sleep...and let my body go."

He was looking directly into the young doctor's eyes. I saw the fear that was underneath the medical bravado; I felt empathy for him. I remembered my own fear during my early years of training. It was only now, with Mark, that I realized how often we doctors were called upon to stop treatment. Paradoxically, we had to protect dying patients from our own technology and our own fear of death.

The doctor nodded and went out to change the orders. I'm sure he had just learned something, too.

"Thank you, Kai." Mark's voice was full of affection. "He would never have listened to me."

I smiled and took his hand.

"You going now?"

"I am. It's time." He was so serene. He would also wait for Angie to return.

"Kai, don't be afraid of death anymore. You will need to walk this journey of death and dying with others. Walk with them, without fear."

With those words, he bestowed his final gift to me as a healer.

He was healed through death. I was left to live life without him. Even though I understood in my head, my heart was broken.

The rising tide finally called me back from my memories of Mark. Foamy salt bubbles outlined my body as the waves inched higher and higher around me. As they receded, the power of the water sucked at my clothes and skin, tumbling the sand around me back out to sea.

Mark and Stephanie. It was Mark who had taught me to be present to Stephanie. Mark, who, by inviting me along on his journey, had helped me confront my own fear of death. Instead of running, he had called me through love to stay and see death through...to find peace along the way. This is what I brought to Stephanie as ballast in her storms.

Chapter Nineteen

When the marsh grass had turned to a burnished gold and the Lowcountry trees wore leaves of red and amber, Stephanie went into remission. It was official. Rob Gellman called me to exult and we reveled in one of those rare moments that oncologists allow in between their perpetual vigils of preparing for the worst and hoping for the best.

"Kai, darlin', how in the world are you?" Rob crowed over the phone.

"I'm hearing a smile on your face, Hunk," I replied.

"She's in remission, Kai. Blessed, beautiful remission."

"Thanking you and God for that, Rob."

"Have you seen her since she left the hospital Friday?" he asked.

"She's coming in on Thursday."

"I probably should have let her tell you, but I really wanted to share my relief with you. Can you act surprised when she tells you?"

"She reads me pretty well. It won't stop our celebration. It's really a miracle, Rob. Something as vicious as AML can just retreat, become invisible. Are you pretty sure it's not a cure?"

"Almost never is. Most come out of remission within a

year. We used to try to push it into remission a second time, but now find better long term statistical survival with earlier stem cell transplant. As soon as she's feeling up to it, I'm sending her to the transplant center at Sloan Kettering to Dr. Peter Halverson for a work-up."

"Even *before* evidence of relapse?" I asked.

"We have to be ready to move at the first sign of recurrence. Can't let a patient get too sick before the bone marrow is irradiated and killed."

"More sterile isolation after the new stem cells are implanted?"

"Thirty days."

Thirty days in the wilderness. I winced.

"So, what can she do in remission? Go back to school?"

"She can do just about anything. Obviously, we don't want her going to Africa and getting malaria. Otherwise, she can live pretty normally."

"You've helped her a lot, Kai," he continued. "The psychological impact of leukemia can be devastating and critical to recovery. Stephanie told me about Pac-Men riding horses. We need to have lunch so you can tell me about that."

I was becoming infamous for Pac-Man imagery.

"I'll hold you to that, Rob."

"What a spitfire spirit. I can't say that I've ever had a patient quite like her before. Dr. Edinger's a pretty happy man, too.

He's talking about starting funds for an academic 'chair' in my honor. He needs to wait a while before he does that."

"So you're hopeful for her?"

"Cautiously. Realistically hopeful that she stays in remission for five years."

"Why couldn't she be one of the ones that doesn't need stem cell transplant?"

"That's the thing we can't predict, why those select few respond so well and the others don't. Research is showing us a genetic link in some cases of leukemia and lymphoma. Some of the aberrant cases, with no genetics, may have a better chance of survival."

"Well, apparently, there's no history in Stephanie's family on either side," I said confidently.

"You know, Dr. Edinger said something to me in the hospital last week when we were talking about the genetic piece. Possible glitch. He kind of mumbled it and I couldn't get any more out of him," Rob added.

"I don't have a clue about that. I'll nose around it with Stephanie on Thursday."

"Okay. Gotta run. It's a fine day today, Kai, a fine day. Remind me of that some rainy day in the future, when it feels like everybody is dying, will you?"

"Let's remind each other. I appreciate you, Rob. I'm glad you're in my life."

"Kai, there was a time when you prayed. If you still do, remember Stephanie. Gotta go now," he said before I could respond. That surprised me. Rob and I had never mentioned anything spiritual to each other before.

I closed the conversation, reminding myself to include Rob in the prayers that felt like breathing to me now.

Chapter Twenty

My patient, Julia, was continuing to get better. I had seen her weekly like clockwork. The antidepressant was working well. She was ravenous now, emotionally and physically.

"I'm always drinking water," she marveled during our appointment. "I am also craving tangerine frappes and chocolate, chocolate, chocolate. It's as though I ignored my body for years, just stayed in survival mode."

This was a typical reaction for a patient who is awakening from years of depression. She fit the psychiatric motto to a T: "Impression without expression becomes depression". It was time to give her repressed anger some expression. She was questioning everything and currently mad as hell at her husband. She was stamping back and forth in my office, shouting loudly.

"Dammit to hell!" Julia railed. "My husband, the workaholic, has probably fallen in love with a nurse – my three children have left home – how dare they?" Julia had found her voice and was feeling betrayed, shamed, devalued, discarded and abandoned. Oh, I knew how she felt. She was letting it all out!

I let her vent for a while, then began to ask her gentle questions. As she calmed down, she would have to look at who had really betrayed her; who had abandoned her first?

Amid the swirling emotions, my job today was healthy containment – to help Julia manage her rage without incinerating herself, or those she loved. She had unleashed a fire from her deepest self that could devour them all. Julia needed safeguards. She needed to harness this new energy in constructive ways. She agreed to call me if she felt the anger taking over. I felt depleted after she left, like I had been holding a corral door closed with a raging bull on the other side.

Stephanie was due in at four o'clock. Transitioning between patients was a critical time for me. It was imperative to store information and emotion from the patient just seen into a safe, retrievable place, and clear the way for the next person. That's one reason we jot notes during sessions-that and the legal demands that we document our work in the rare case that a patient gets entangled in the judicial system. Putting notes in a file is easy. Storing memories and emotions is a more complicated process. As I stepped out onto my back porch, I could feel the clearing and storing, like theater workers changing the stage between scenes of a play.

Stephanie bounced victoriously into my office. No longer the tigress of her first visit, this time she reminded me of Tigger from *Winnie the Pooh*. She wore a wig of long, red hair and carried a small gift box. She had just had a facial at a local day spa and, considering what she had been through the past month, her skin was glowing. Oh, the resilient human body. It stands at death's door and within days can restore itself. It never ceases to amaze me.

Stephanie launched into the session, seated Indian-style, on the loveseat that had become her throne.

"You know that swan I chose from your collection? You told me that when one of your patients really began her work of feminine transformation in therapy, she could choose a swan to take home and keep as a reminder. I took the ivory enamel swan. You asked that one day they bring a new swan to leave on the table for someone who would come later."

Her green eyes were translucent, her inner light seeming to shine through. I smiled in acknowledgment of all she had said. She had just completed one amazing spiral in her battle for life.

She handed me a white box with thin, pink grosgrain ribbon tied around it. From the layers of tissue, I lifted an exquisite enameled black swan with delicate gold trim. A "Schwarz-schwan," as it was called in German, was a rare black swan found only in a few places in the world. I had last seen real ones swimming in the lakes of the Keukenhof tulip gardens outside

Amsterdam where Gracen and I had made a mother-daughter trip to celebrate her twelfth birthday. It seemed important that she and I create some special ritual to welcome her onto the emotional pathway of the adult feminine, the one that had been blocked to me. In addition, we both loved tulips, so we chose a trip to the Netherlands. I remember her astonishment when she saw several black swans swimming together. It was her first sighting. To me, the black swan symbolized the dark side of life's journey, a counterpart to the grace and goodness of the white swan. As a healer, I had come to understand the necessity of suffering as a teacher to us. And its paradoxical beauty. I loved black swans. Stephanie would have seen them in Switzerland, too.

I was deeply touched by Stephanie's gift. No one had ever brought me a black swan. I cradled it in the palm of my hand and held it up for us both to see.

"I christen thee Stephanie, the Black Swan of Healing," I intoned solemnly, honoring her hard-won remission.

Stephanie joined in the spontaneous ritual and responded, "And I give thee this black swan in memory of our work together and the life I have left to live. And I pledge that I will live every day to the fullest of my ability, not with fear, but with hope."

I stood up and gave it a place of honor on one of my bookshelves, at eye level, amongst some of the other treasures from patients. The Stephanie swan looked regal there. She was a queen amongst swans. She would never go to the communal table for swans.

"There is one more small surprise down in the bottom of the box," Stephanie was struggling to keep a straight face.

I caught my breath in surprise. It was a perfect replica of a firefly, carved out of amethyst with an amber stone inset in its abdomen to simulate its light. It was to be worn as a pendant for a necklace.

"The firefly is a reminder of the freedom of your childhood." She seemed to speak with her eyes as well as her voice. They both shone.

Stephanie was delighted that she had surprised me and her delight made me smile. It was a time for unbridled joy and it filled the room. Here, again, was one of the moments that carried me through the counterpart valleys of shadows and darkness that were always part of a meaningful therapy.

Stephanie was heading back to Chicago. Her papers turned in at the end of her six weeks at the Jung Institute had been received with flying colors. Even so very ill, she was a gifted essayist and had added six hours to her graduate work. She needed one more year to complete her doctorate and she was going for it. Her doctoral committee had accepted the new topic for her thesis. She was going to have to work much harder to finish it by the end of the next year.

In the interim, Stephanie would need to travel to New York to be worked up for a potential transplant at Sloan Kettering. Her family would be included in the process and receive more in-depth testing of their blood and bone marrow. If any matches were found, they would both meet with a social worker, as well.

Stephanie and I planned to meet again when she came home at fall break, the end of October. We planned some phone sessions to keep in touch in the interim.

"Kai, thank you for walking so softly beside me. We both know this isn't over yet. Stay with me 'til the end." She was tentative, but serious.

"The question is, will you get too busy to remember our phone appointments?"

"Ain't gonna happen, missy," she sassed back.

I had learned from other cancer patients that when they felt really well it was difficult for them to stay with their inner work. Often, they just needed to forget for a while. I did, too. It was always a balancing act for me to be available emotionally and yet protect my own energy. Steph and I would take a rest while another patient would ramp up their work. Usually, there was a natural ebb and flow of need/demand in my practice. If not, a serious energy drain could sap me.

"Okay, then. God speed, Stephanie," I said.

We hugged and she bounced out the same way she had come in. We had finished early for a change.

I walked out onto the porch and stretched luxuriously. I loved autumn. The hot, humid, stifling dog days of summer were over for a while, and no hurricanes had hit the Southeastern coast yet. It was getting dark and wasn't even seven o'clock. I would miss the summer light. I heard a soft cooing sound and looked for a dove on the ground, but a fluttering in the branches of a dogwood riveted my attention. Nestled in the red and brown camouflage of the changing leaves was a small brown owl. It had been a "hoo-hoo" that I heard. Was it a benediction or was the messenger to speak again?

Chapter Twenty-one

Stephanie did not come to Charleston over fall break. She went to Sloan Kettering instead. We had scheduled a phone session for five o'clock that day.

She had driven to New York City and was ensconced in her hotel room near the medical center. She had seen the transplant doctor who would be the head of her team. Blood studies and bone marrow extraction would start the following day. Bone marrow extraction. Steph and I had visited that issue only briefly in our imagery work, and here it was again.

"So, how will you deal with the extraction differently this time?" I asked.

"I'm not sure what my options are," she said.

"How about we make a pain management plan?" I suggested.

"Okay. How does this sound? Morphine, valium, marijuana?" We both laughed.

"You know, the drug Versed is a real possibility. I've had it twice for shoulder dislocations and it's magical. It puts you to sleep in seconds, is short acting and creates a cloaking amnesia, to boot. Ask your doctor about it," I suggested.

I didn't need to worry about Stephanie being assertive now, but many times patients are afraid to be their own advocates. They abdicate their most basic rights in the face of medical issues they don't understand to doctors they have elevated to the status of minor gods, instead of partners in the pursuit of their own health. Some of that distance is closing as we make headway in holistic, preventative medicine.

"Tell me about your doctor," I continued.

"He is hot!"

I sighed and tried to remember that Stephanie was a normal twenty-six year old, although her love life was almost as bleak as mine. Marriage had scalded me; Stephanie's illness had consumed her.

"How old is he?"

"Old. Late 40s. But hot. He's not married, either."

Late 40s is old? I took silent umbrage.

"Is he divorced or gay?" I teased her.

"Neither. He told me his wife died in a car accident several years ago. He has a daughter who looks about sixteen in her picture on his desk."

No one escapes death, I thought. Not even transplant surgeons.

"What's his name?"

"Dr. Halvorsen, Peter Halvorsen."

Ingersohn is son of Inger. Halvorsen is son of Halvor, I thought.

"Scandinavian?" I asked out loud.

"Swedish ancestry. He's been to Charleston and even knows Dr. Gellman. They consult each other on stem cell transplants. I told him about you."

"You did? What did you say?" I perked up a little. I had been doodling on my yellow pad and stopped.

"I told him you were an outstanding shrink and a beautiful brunette and tall. I told him you were as smart as he was."

"How about doing my bio for match.com," I jibed.

"I would love to do that for you!"

"I'm kidding, Stephanie. Really, that was a joke! I would never do that."

"Why not?"

God, please save her from the trolls of the world, I silently prayed. She was somewhat naïve for twenty-six. Very smart, ambitious young women like Stephanie were often girl-nerds. Late-bloomers. Rejection between men and women comes in so many different packages. Getting back out in the dating scene always gave me pause.

"Anyway, I told Dr. Halvorsen I'd send him a picture of you on the Internet. Are you on Facebook?" she asked.

I wondered if she was kidding me now. "I told you I would never use a matchmaker service. That includes you, Miss Edinger."

"It comes free with the Stephanie package, Doc. Don't get in a snit. He's a good guy. Tall, too. Probably six-three or so. Sandy hair, blue eyes. You're not dating anybody seriously, are you?"

I could tell she wasn't letting go of this. Stephanie had always been curious about my personal romantic life and left few stones unturned. She didn't understand why I had never remarried.

"Stephanie, you are seriously pushing the boundaries of our relationship. Understand?" I was telling her to back off.

"My, my, you are sensitive."

"No, I am not dating anyone seriously," I capitulated.

"Well, I've met someone myself." She had obviously been waiting to spring this on me. Now I understood why she was matchmaking.

"And?" I prodded.

"He's working on a doctorate in genetics, like Two-Pop's field. But Two-Pop is an M.D. He is some kind of smart and sensitive. We spend a lot of time outdoors. Drove to Wisconsin last weekend and hiked all around some of the lakes and forests."

"How long have you known him?"

"Since the semester started. We met at a poetry reading at this little coffee shop near school - it was Rilke night."

"Rilke?! He's a biologist and likes Rilke?"

"A geneticist who is a romantic. He says poetry and music are universal languages. I think this also means I need to talk to someone about birth control. After getting leukemia, I thought I'd never have sex again."

"*When* are you coming home?"

"Thanksgiving, but I can stay over 'til Monday and see you. I've got a lot to talk about."

"Call Sarah and get it on my books as soon as possible." Days around holidays were always jammed.

"Okey dokey. Now, one last thing. I need a picture of you. Email one to me."

"Later, Steph. Later," I said as a goodbye.

So, Stephanie was ready to risk love, even with her future so uncertain. So, why was I so reactive about her sending my picture to her transplant surgeon? I had dated very little since my divorce. Every time I got lonely, I seemed to harken back to the emotional trauma of a bad marriage and painful divorce. Was it really worth trying again? Besides, my two children were all I needed. Maybe Stephanie was simply more courageous than I in *affaires de coeur*? This was not a competition, but our lives had so much parallelism.

Chapter Twenty-two

Thanksgiving had come and gone, taking November with it. My mother's love of Thanksgiving flowed to me and I hope it has passed on to Andrew and Gracen, as well. The coolness of the air in November, the grand feasting, and the gathering of family made it one of my favorite times of the year. It had also been marred with Mark's cancer and my Mother's death on Thanksgiving Day two years ago.

My brother, Jamey, and his family had just left after brunch. The kids had gone with their father for the rest of the weekend. I was settling down into some blissful reading on the deck off my bedroom when my cell phone rang. I almost didn't answer it, but remembered my family on the road. It was Stephanie and she was hysterical.

Stephanie was crying so hard, I could hardly understand her. I was alarmed. I exhorted her to calm down and take some deep breaths. She was wailing in between garbled words, like a wounded animal. I was afraid someone had died, maybe Two-Pop. The roller coaster ride with her had slowly made its way to the top of another arc (almost like a simulated *real* physical spiral) and hung precariously at the descent.

Finally, it became clear that I needed to meet her at the office for an emergency session. There was no question of her coming here. Patients did not know where their therapist lived. Violence is part of psychiatry. Keeping physical boundaries is part of our safety and rarely violated. Thank God I wasn't out of town. I was concerned about her driving in this condition, but she said that her father would bring her and join the session.

I had a sense of foreboding in my gut as I drove to the office. I felt the owl's eyes piercing through the veil. It had clearly not finished speaking. Stephanie and her father were waiting in his blue Jeep in the parking lot when I arrived. I drove past them to park at the back of my office. I prayed to all the feminine faces of God that I could think of: the marsh, mother nature, all the Marys, including the black Madonna. An image of Michelangelo's Pieta in St. Peter's Basilica in Rome flashed through my mind. That lone, alabaster marble statue of a mother holding the body of her lifeless child on her lap. Holding, having been unable to protect.

I unlocked the door from the waiting room to the front porch and stepped back to allow Stephanie and her father to enter. Before anyone spoke, Stephanie launched herself into my arms wailing. I held her, gently crooning, slightly rocking. I patted her back and glanced questioningly over her shoulder to her bewildered father. I was wondering where her mother, Victoria, was.

Finally, Stephanie's cries quieted into whimpers and some hiccups. "Do you want time alone with me before your father joins us? Is your mother coming?"

She shook her head and said no to both. I motioned for her father to follow us down the hall.

Stephanie went straight to her place on the loveseat by the windows. I leaned over to turn on the lamp on the end table by her, but she motioned me away. She huddled in the corner of the small couch, drawing herself into a ball. I turned to her father who was still standing in the doorway and offered my hand.

"I'm Kai," I said.

"Steve Edinger," he replied, then turned to sit on the opposite end of the loveseat next to his daughter.

"No! Not there!" Stephanie yelled at him. He froze.

"I don't want him to sit here," she explained, waving at the other end of her loveseat as she looked at me. "He can sit over there." She pointed at the green wing chair by my desk. So, this has to do with him, I thought.

I offered bottled water, but social amenities were clearly not in order. I sat down in my chair and waited for one of them to speak.

Steve was still bewildered. He kept shaking his head as if to dispel some kind of fog in his mind.

"You tell her," Stephanie said. "You did it. You're the great liar of the world. You and that, that," she sputtered, "that woman who's *not* my mother." Her words hung in the air tinged with the fire of her acrimonious indictment. She meant Victoria and it implied her absence was important.

Silence. I turned towards her father who was hanging his head and wringing his hands. He looked up, catching my eyes with his same-green-as-Stephanie eyes.

"It's true," he started. "We have all lied to Stephanie her whole life. Victoria, my wife, is not Stephanie's birth mother."

"God, I should have known. I should have *known*," Stephanie interjected from her huddle.

Steve told me the story he had finally told Stephanie some hours before.

"When I was a graduate student at Stanford, I had an affair with an undergraduate student who was in one of my history classes. She was eighteen and I was twenty-five." He faltered as his memory retrieved the details.

"Twenty-five or twenty-six. Anyway, it just happened. We were infatuated and there was an amazing chemistry between us, physically and intellectually. Stephanie looks a great deal like her mother did back then. Her name was Alexandra, but everyone called her Lexy. I'm afraid we weren't as careful with birth control as we should have been."

Stephanie was staring hatefully at her father. She shifted her body somewhat and sat up straighter.

He went on, "So, after about six months, Lexy told me she was pregnant. We were both shocked."

Stephanie's voice dripped with sarcasm. "And you screwed a student!"

Steve flinched but went on. In that pause, I realized what the "glitch" was that Two-Pop had mentioned to Rob Gellman all those months ago; Stephanie had a hidden genetic ancestor.

"We were faced with what to do. Lexy didn't want an abortion. We told her family together. They were totally supportive of her decision to carry the baby to term and then give it up for adoption. I felt the final decision was hers."

"Did you ever consider marrying her?" Stephanie lobbed comments from her corner. Now she had her legs straightened along the length of the loveseat.

"It might have been the noble thing to do, but she was clearly not ready to be married. I cared about her, but I didn't love her enough to make a lifetime commitment."

"So, I wasn't a love child from the free love California set, huh?" she spoke bitterly.

Steve shot her a look, but went on with his story.

"She went home to Sacramento to have the baby and arrange adoption. Lexy's father was disabled and her mother supported them on a librarian's salary. It was a hard time in her life."

"I have grandparents in California. And a mother, and maybe brothers and sisters." Stephanie's voice was rising to a crescendo. "All these years I thought I was an only child. All these years, Mother's…," she corrected herself, "*Victoria's* parents were icebergs who lived in Virginia. No wonder they didn't like me. I wasn't their *blood*."

Stephanie startled her father and me when she stood up abruptly and started pacing like her old tigress days when I first met her.

"I could have *known* my mother." She threw the comment at her father. "Have you ever talked to her? Have you ever told *her* about me? Have you ever sent her pictures of me? I've wasted twenty-six years not knowing my mother or her family, maybe some half siblings. God in heaven, is there *no justice* in this world? Now I might die and all that time has been lost, lost, lost!"

Stephanie turned her back on her father and shivered uncontrollably with anger and sorrow. I stood up and put my arms around her from the back. I visualized another kind of Pieta with God holding the two of us.

"I'm okay, I'm okay. I want to hear the rest of this." She shook me off and we both sat down.

Her father was sitting on the edge of his seat, watching us, helpless in the face of the pain he had created with his deception, unsure how to continue.

"There's more," he said. "Your mother wanted to sever all ties with me...and with you. She said she couldn't bear to give you up and be reminded of that pain the rest of her life. We both decided to never tell you the truth. And so did Nana and Two-Pop."

Stephanie shot him a glance that could have killed.

Steve went on, "When Lexy decided to put you up for adoption, Two-Pop and Nana wanted me to bring you home so they could help raise you. And I wanted to bring you home to Charleston. I *wanted* you, Stephanie." He stared straight at his daughter, holding her with his eyes.

"With their help, I saw that I could do it. I could keep you. I would be finished with my doctorate about the time you were born. I could make up some story about you being born to a friend of mine. I never had to do that. I met Victoria before I brought you back to Charleston and started teaching at the College of Charleston. It was love at first sight with Vicky, and she loved *you*. Both of us. So, we married when you were three months old and told almost everybody that you were our child." He was pleading with her to understand. He clearly was casting Victoria in another light. She was no wicked stepmother. Had this been underneath Stephanie's blame of her "different mother" over the years?

She answered, "There must have been people at the college who knew."

"There were a few. They drifted off and our closest friends kept the secret with us. So did my sister and Vicky's sister and parents."

"The *secret!*" Stephanie exploded again. "I am the *secret*. Damn you all. Just damn you, secret mongers. You liars. And if I hadn't gotten leukemia, I would have never known?" she accused. She turned to me and continued.

"Dr. Kai, do you know why the secret finally came out? Because of the DNA matching I needed for my stem cell transplant! Mother wouldn't do the blood work. Just kept dragging her feet. Tried to blow it off saying she couldn't do a bone marrow extraction. Well, that didn't come off too well! My *mother* wouldn't give me stem cells if I needed them? It forced them to tell me. What have I done to deserve this? What?" she spewed as she jumped up. Stephanie had so much rage and she was pinning it all on Victoria. We would have to get to the bottom of this eventually.

"Stephanie, sit down. I need to tell you the rest of it," her father said.

"There's *more?*" she sneered.

"Yes, there's more."

We all paused. I was wrong about no hurricanes visiting the Lowcountry. There was one unleashed in my office. Time to batten the hatches and hope I could anchor Stephanie during this terrible storm in her life.

"I stayed in touch with Lexy's mother, your grandmother. Her name is Rebecca Sanderson. She is loving and kind. Her only request was that I write her occasionally and send pictures. Rebecca was willing to honor Lexy's wish to sever all ties and that you not know about her or her family. Rebecca was very sad that she wouldn't know you. I sent pictures three or four times a year and told her about you." He stopped and took a deep breath.

"When you were ten years old, she wrote me that Lexy had died. She had been sick for several years. By this time, she had married and did have another child."

He stopped and looked straight at Stephanie again.

"You have a sister, Stephanie. She's nineteen. Her name is Alexis."

"After Lexy's death, your grandmother asked if the ban could be lifted, so she could see you. I'm afraid Vicky and I were too afraid to tell you at that point. I'm sorry, Stephanie. So very sorry."

Stephanie was in shock. Stunned. So was I.

"My mother is dead? She's dead?" Now she was shaking her head in disbelief. I felt helpless at that moment. No one should have to endure such pain. My witnessing it was agony. There was nothing I could do to protect Stephanie from this brutal truth.

"She died of leukemia, Stephanie."

"No! Oh, God, No!" She burst into tears and covered both ears with her hands in some futile attempt to block out the excruciating pain. Before I could react, she pulled open one of the French doors and fled through the back porch and down towards the wooded area beside the building.

Steve and I both started after her. I motioned for him to stay on the porch and I followed her on the small path that led into the trees. Now I was afraid for Stephanie. This kind of hit could shatter her ego defenses. Crush her. Years before, a patient kept running to six-lane Highway 17 South and over the Cooper River Bridge. Thank God she got home safely.

I didn't have far to go. Stephanie was crumpled in a heap in a small clearing ringed by towering pines. An outdoor chapel of tears, grief and sorrow. She was on her side drawn up into a fetal position, nestled on the pine straw. I sat down beside her, but didn't try to talk. There is some sorrow too deep for words. I simply held vigil, watching over her as she lay with her profound human grief, weeping it out. Garbed in nature to cloister us, the divine waited. Softly, I heard the notes of a lullaby.

"Hush, little baby, don't you cry, mama's gonna sing you a lullaby...." I can't sing. Have never been able to carry a tune, but it was my voice singing this most beautiful melody. It was spirit music come to soothe us.

Time elapsed. Sunlight filtering through pine needles changed angles as the sun moved across the sky forming a radiant arc of light over us, a halo of protection. Whispers of the poet Mary Oliver's words from *White Owl Flies Into and Out of the Field* seemed to fall around Stephanie and me:

...so I thought:

maybe death

isn't darkness, after all,

but so much light

wrapping itself around us....

As the words faded, I started thinking again and realized I had not planned anything that had just happened. Where was Steve? I was sure he was alarmed. Perhaps he had crept to a place where he could see us, but not be seen. My admonishment for him to stay back was at least being honored.

Finally, Stephanie rolled over onto her back and held out her hand to me. Only my hand moved to join hers, my right hand. There, in the sanctity of that small woodland that buffered us from a bank and a post office, she began to process the great wound of the mother that was lost to her again.

"My mother died of leukemia." She spoke so softly it could have been gentle sounds of a breeze. "I wonder if it was the same kind that I have? So there is a genetic link, after all. My sister, surely she couldn't have inherited it, too?" she asked me, but posed the question outward, heavenward. "Surely not," she repeated.

She turned her head toward me and opened her eyes. The smudges underneath somehow made them look darker green. She looked so very small.

"Does God have no mercy on His children?"

Words continued to fail me. Over the years I've seen a lot of suffering. Sometimes, words could bring comfort. But in times like this, all I could do was be present. Hold the suffering in a cauldron of *two* hearts. My perspective of God's mercy was ever changing. I had no answer for Stephanie. As if in answer, the wind picked up. The painted leaves of the hardwoods were rustling in between the sentinel pines. A sense of peace began to settle upon us much as the music and poetry had. I had never had a psychiatric session out here. Years ago, I met with a woman for a few sessions on the banks of a small retention pond beside my office. Once, I held court in my car because we lost the office air conditioning in the middle of July. But this place was not chosen by me.

Stephanie stirred again.

"I wonder how heavy it is to carry a secret like my Dad did all those years?"

Empathy for her father. Someone else's pain. A beginning of compassion. Did she realize that Victoria was controlled by the secret too?

"It's so like Nana and Two-Pop to have brought me home to the Lowcountry, to the marsh and to the tidelands. To bring me home to their hearts," she spoke calmly.

We sat in silence some more and I remembered lessons learned from another patient, a bereaved mother who had lost her only two sons to death. She had come to my office so many years ago to teach me the power of silence to heal. Truly half of our therapy had transpired without words.

Finally, I broke the spell. "Are you ready to go back and deal with your father again?"

"I have so many questions...about my mother, my grandmother, my sister. You know, Rebecca or Alexis could be a match for me. I need to let Dr. Halvorsen know about this. Maybe you can call him for me."

I agreed with Stephanie that one of them could be a possible match.

We stood up and brushed the pine needles off our clothes and walked side by side back to the office. The secret had been brought out into the light. It had ravaged Stephanie with its harsh truth, but there was emancipation in its telling. And perhaps a cure as well.

Chapter Twenty-three

Secrets. The word reverberated in my mind as I drove back to my office the next morning to see Stephanie one last time before she flew back to Chicago. So little time left to process and contain the potent power of her parents' secret that had hit Stephanie like torrential floodwaters from a ruptured dam. Was it only yesterday that the secret had been unleashed? Days and days ago yesterday?

I remembered when Gracen had told me her first secret when she was five. Eight-year-old Andrew had figured out how to override the parental monitoring block on the television set. He had sworn her to secrecy as they watched some forbidden program while the babysitter was downstairs studying. Children can't keep secrets. They are fascinated by them and it is a great milestone in a child's life to recognize their value, and the power of telling. It's another milestone altogether to keep a secret: teenagers are masters of the art form. Adults progress to the major leagues. Their secrets incubate in the deep underground caverns of their minds and hearts, protected from the conscious mind by multiple layers of rationalization. They seal the secret with good intent like, "it is better for everyone if we don't tell". This was the exact reasoning used by Stephanie's parents. One fine day, the secret slips out accidentally; or is forced out by necessity; is pieced together by sharp minds; or the dream betrays the truth. With Stephanie's family, revealing the secret of her birth was an attempt to save her life.

Stephanie was sitting in one of the dark green rocking chairs on the front porch of my office building when I drove past on the way to the rear parking lot. She was hugging herself as she rocked back and forth in a steady rhythm that didn't change as I approached her. I sat down in the rocker to her left without speaking. I began rocking alongside her. Soon we were in synchrony. The only noise was the gentle creaking of the carved wooden rockers on the oak slatted flooring beneath them.

"I dreamed about a snake last night," Stephanie began, never breaking the rhythm of her rocking.

"It was a small black snake with red and yellow bands, and slanted black eyes. Definitely poisonous. Maybe a young snake, it was only nine or ten inches long. I was in my room in our old house on Legare Street."

"How old were you in the dream?" I asked.

"Nine or ten. I was playing on the floor by my bed. I decided to have a tea party with my Barbie dolls. I always used my soft, white Blankie as the table cloth because it's just the right size for the play table. I kept it under one of the pillows on my canopy bed. I jumped up off the floor and was reaching behind a pillow sham when I saw the snake coiled up between the two pillows I sleep on. I almost touched it." She shivered involuntarily. She also picked up the pace of her rocking and we momentarily dropped out of sync.

I was very aware that she had started the session while we were still on the front porch. Inappropriate to move inside now. We would have our Sunday go-to-meeting service right here like in the old timey camp meetings made famous in the South. "Right out in front of God and everybody," as the old folks used to say.

Stephanie started again, oblivious to my thoughts. "I froze. Its head was raised and I could see slashes across its black eyes. Neither one of us moved. All I could think of was that a sudden motion would cause it to strike me and I didn't know how fast or far out it could reach. I wanted my Daddy but was afraid to startle the snake by calling out for him. Finally, the snake seemed to slither under the right-sided pillow and disappear. I was terrified. I *hate* snakes —*hate* them!" She spit out the final words.

"What does it mean? It freaks me out." She stopped rocking abruptly and turned to face me.

"Is this dream some kind of omen? Does this mean I'm going to die? Don't lie to me, Kai. If the snake had bitten me, I would have died in the dream."

I kept rocking. She dared me to tell her the truth.

"Do you know what a caduceus is, Stephanie?"

"The doctor symbol thing? With snakes wrapped around it?"

"That's right. Do you know where it came from?"

"No idea." She looked puzzled.

"The caduceus evolved from one of the earliest healing rites of the ancient Greeks. A man named Asclepius built a temple dedicated to healing. People with physical or mental illnesses would come seeking to be healed. Asclepius, who is considered the father of modern medicine, was a physician who studied with the great Egyptian physicians of his day, as well as many eastern mystics and healers. When seekers arrived at his temple, they were cleansed in pools of water and dressed in robes of pure white. Then they were led to small, dim chambers to rest and sleep and *dream*. If they dreamed of snakes, it portended of healing energy. If they were bitten by snakes, they would *always* be healed. That is how snakes around a staff became the symbol of healing that has lasted hundreds of years to the present.

"Snakes are healing? What kind of idiocy is that? Poisonous snakes kill people every day!" she said.

"We extract healing agents like streptokinase to dissolve clots from snake poison." I kept on rocking. "And think about how that symbolizes the chemotherapy 'poison' pumped into your veins that put you into remission."

She gaped at me with her mouth open as if she would countermand what I had said and couldn't. She started rocking again.

"Stephanie, dreams are symbolic. They don't always translate like you think: they are our deepest 'archetypal' language. All people in every culture in the world dream. Most of the symbols are the same, but there are regional differences. Mothers, fathers, gods, death, healing, good and evil are all universal symbols in a universal language, but with individual interpretations."

I continued. "Let's put your dream in context. What has recently happened to you, at home, that concerns you and your childhood?" I wanted her to learn to work with her dream instead of shutting it down in fear.

"The *secret* came out. What has that got to do with snakes?" She seemed exasperated and was rocking angrily, thumping the back rear curves of the rocker against the floor.

"The secret of your birth, it's out in the light now. As long as it was hidden, it couldn't be healed."

"Well, it *was* like a snake bite, jumped out of nowhere and struck me."

"What else happened around the time of that snake?"

"My birth mother died. She died when I was ten years old, but I didn't know it."

"Not consciously, but in what we call our 'collective unconscious', you did know. This may be where spirit resides, interfaces. Spirit knew. It sent you a message to put on hold, like a saved text message on a cell phone that we're not ready to open."

"The snake carries the message?" she asked.

"Perhaps. In the myth of creation, what did the snake do in the Garden of Eden?"

"Talked Eve into seducing Adam to bite the forbidden fruit."

"Which symbolized?" I prodded.

"The knowledge of good and evil."

"Consciousness."

"So, my birth mother's death..." she faltered.

I continued for her, "is no longer a secret and knowing it opens up the possibilities of so many levels of healing. Before, you had only glimpses, like the intuitive response to the painting in my office about the wounded mother who couldn't choose to love her daughter."

"Oh...my...God," Stephanie enunciated slowly.

"Another glimpse was your reaction to your adoptive mother, Vicky, and the feeling of 'not belonging'. You've been so angry with her, but the die was cast before she ever came along with your father's decision to take you to Charleston. Vicky chose to marry your father and take on a three-month-old baby. In the end, you were all she had. Granted, she tried to channel all her history into you to carry on her name and culture. She was as bound by the secret as you were. Was that some of her anger with your father and grandparents?"

"Hold it right there, Kai! Are you on her side now?" She asked sharply.

"There are no sides, Steph. There is only your truth to sort out; it's your work!" It was a pronouncement. Her childhood was over, innocence lost. Time to grow up.

She stood up and walked to the porch railing, her back to me. She hugged herself again. I wondered if she would walk away. Quit me. Refuse this wonderful, horrible journey to consciousness. So many in therapy did walk away at just such junctures as this one.

"My birth mother gave me away. She didn't want me." It was a toneless statement, but she was still with me.

I replied, "She was very young. Much younger than you are now. Away from home, a freshman in college. Your grandmother, Rebecca, can tell you a lot more about it all. We don't know enough about your mother yet, Steph. Try not to judge her too harshly."

"I would probably have had an abortion." She dropped the statement like a ten-pound weight. And there it was. Her mother had chosen to give her life and then had given her away. Abandonment or salvation?

"I just wish I had met her, just once. Just heard her voice. Do you think she saw me after I was born? Held me in her arms?" I could hear the tears in her voice. Good tears. Healing tears.

"I don't know, Steph. We can find out from *her* mother. Are you willing to ask her?"

"I'm going out to meet her if she'll let me come. Dad said we could call her tonight. And my sister Alexis. I have a sister! She's nineteen, a freshman at U.C. Davis."

"And if their blood and bone marrow match...'? I trailed off.

"I could be healed. Maybe the snake who brings consciousness is a symbol of healing," she breathed.

I heard a piece fall into place in the great puzzle of her life. I had a surge of pride in her. She was doing her work. Was it psychological or spiritual, or both? Metaphysical? Sometimes I couldn't tell. Would it benefit her body, her physical self? I was sure of it. They were all intertwined; the medicine of the whole person here in living color.

Remission of leukemia. Remission of sin. Pardon, forgiveness. Could Stephanie learn to forgive them all? The secret was lanced. The *knowing* a healing balm. Stephanie's conscious journey had begun. I silently prayed that she would have enough time in her life to walk it to the end.

We stood quietly, side by side, watching the breeze play in the treetops. A slight chill was in the air.

"Are we done for today?" I asked.

"I'm fried, Doc."

"Then, let's go home."

Stephanie headed down the steps and then turned back again, "Did you call Dr. Halvorsen?"

"Will do, pronto." I had promised to call him after the last traumatic session.

As I drove away, I marveled once again at the healing power of dreams. I was thankful that the dream maker continued to speak to all of us, guide us, teach us. The only problem was that many did not recognize the value of the dream or know its language. Even if our dreams escalate to virtual shouts, they are often ignored. Today, Stephanie heard and understood the power of her dream. My dreams continued to disturb me. For all my expertise with dream analysis, I was still struggling with my own owl dreams. Owls had even broken into my waking life and I still wasn't sure what it all meant.

Chapter Twenty-four

The office number Stephanie gave me for Dr. Halvorsen turned out to be the central one for the Hematology and Oncology Division of Sloan Kettering. I left a message and phone number for Halvorsen to return my call. Then, I forgot about it the rest of the day.

Gracen was bouncing off the walls when I got home at 6:30.

"Ma-ma, ma-ma, ma-a-a-ma," she was sing-songing.

"Hello to you, too, sweet pea." Something was afoot. Gracen was born charming and even remained positive, statistically compared to other young teens. I was dreading the fourteen-year-old-from-hell time to come. I hated my mother when I was fourteen. I was an arrogant little bitch and cringe when I remember all my back-talking and complaining. It was somewhat controlled by my father who handled teenagers like he did Dumpling: zero tolerance for hysterical or crazy behavior! I deserved anything I got from Gracen as I had gotten a "bye" from Andrew. At fifteen, I grew out of the age-related obnoxiousness. My mother loved me through it. That was my plan when Gracen morphed. I did love "Little Miss Sunshine" just now.

"Party at Susie Gellmans' house Friday night!" Big smile.

"With parents?" Rob and Lucy Gellman could ride herd on the little darlings.

"Of course, Mom. I know the rules." She gave me a mock pout.

"Will you need a ride?"

"Andrew can probably drop me." Andrew would make sure she got to the Gellmans" and back home. He was a protective big brother even if she drove him nuts sometimes.

"Where is he?"

"Grabbing a burger with the basketball guys. He sent me a text and said to tell you."

"I'm hungry...how about you?"

"Grandma Eva's famous spaghetti sauce was defrosted when I came in," she said. "It's simmering on the stove. Water is ready to boil for the pasta."

After forty years, spaghetti was still a comfort food for me, nurture from my mother. I had clearly passed that down to my kids.

My cell phone chirped from the den. I was on call and needed to check it. I answered it without paying attention to the caller ID.

"This is Dr. Peter Halvorsen returning Dr. Ingersohn's call." Nice voice and very formal tone.

"Thank you for returning my call, Dr. Halvorsen. Stephanie

Edinger asked me to call you after we found out about her adoption. All the biological/genetic implications of her having a birth mother with leukemia are unsettling to her and to me."

"She apparently had no idea about that," he replied. "She sent me a long email about it all."

"It was a shock to us both. I absolutely did not see it coming."

"I thought psychiatrists saw everything coming," he said with a slightly snarky edge that offended me.

"Is that like stem cell transplants always working?" I retorted.

"My apologies, Dr. Ingersohn. I was trying to get this call made before rounds. It's been a long day."

I glanced at my watch. It was 7:45 and he hadn't even started rounds? An unfortunate norm for his field. I thought Stephanie said he had a daughter? Where was she at this time of night?

"I appreciate that. I won't take much of your time. The question from both Stephanie and me concerns this new genetic inheritance issue. Her mother died of AML when she was twenty-nine. Stephanie is twenty-six. Scary." I felt apprehensive.

"Bottom line is not good. Randomly emerging AML has a better prognosis. It's the aggressiveness that is most alarming. Her mother's AML was aggressive enough to kill her in a year.

Stem cell transplants have improved greatly in recent years. That gives me the most hope for Stephanie."

"She has the utmost respect for you. You have earned her trust."

"Thanks for that. She tries to commandeer her treatment on a regular basis," he laughed.

"Pushy broad for sure," I laughed, too. "Entrusting herself to both of us is a big step for her. She's begun acupuncture and yoga, too."

"Did you recommend that?" the edge was there again.

"No, but I support both. Alternative therapy can't hurt her."

"I've never seen it create remission, either. Psychological pie in the sky."

"I thought hematology-oncology was more open to including alternative modalities," my own edge was apparent.

"Like Dr. Oz, the wunderkind of modern medicine, or should I call him The Wizard Oz?"

I refused to answer that. I was so over the surgeon-psychiatrist split and tension in medicine. "I would really appreciate being kept in the loop with your treatment notes and updates."

"Will do. Good night." He hung up.

"Spare me!" I said loudly to myself.

"What did you say?" Gracen yelled from the kitchen.

"Nothing!" I needed a big plate of spaghetti.

Chapter Twenty-five

Thanksgiving gave way to the Christmas season with all its frenetic energy. The child in me loves it. This year, I insisted on the tallest Frazier fir that would fit in our two-story great room. The tree was so tall that I had visions of the headlines in the local *Post and Courier*: "Local Psychiatrist Maimed By Falling Christmas Tree".

I finally made Andrew climb up on a ladder and anchor it to the wall with fishing line to secure it. He, Gracen and I spent several days hanging favorite ornaments, icicles, and arranging cascades of richly-brocaded ribbons which spilled from the flossy Victorian angel shining on top. Our trees were works of art and bound us together as much as the Christmas carols, cookies and exchange of presents. My inner Tinkerbell did all she could to banish the dark side of Christmas because I had learned long ago that not everyone was happy at Christmas.

Dumpling taught me that lesson. Her emotional instability took on a different quality under the pressures of Christmas. She seemed to internalize the high expectations, resulting in an almost audible hum of anxiety like a plucked guitar string that keeps resonating. She was stressed out over the idea of all she had to do. And do it right. Like the two days she set aside a week before Christmas to do her layers for her cakes. They would be mixed, baked, wrapped, in damp layers of gauze and sealed in decorative tin cans. Then put away to be frosted just before Christmas. One year, when I was part of the baking day, she threw away almost half her layers because they weren't just right. One of her sour cream pound cakes hit the trash because one side was lower than the other. I sneaked a hunk of the cake out of the trash when she wasn't looking. It was delectable.

As the days of December were marked off the calendar, Dumpling's anxiety rose exponentially. It leaked through her pores like the juice of raspberries through a sieve. It was the same vermillion color, too. I could hear it, see it, almost taste her anxiety as it emanated outward to cover us like a fine net. The irony is there were no explosions. By Christmas Eve, she seemed to fall into despair. Everyone began to tiptoe around her and whisper as if the denouement to a great tragedy was eminent. Christmas Eve dinner would be a somber affair. All the trappings were perfectly laid out. The silver candelabra fairly shone and reflected the light from red candles dripping wax just so, down the long tapering stems. Masses of ruffled red camellias, white roses and sprigs of evergreens held court at the center of the table. Grandfather carved the turkey solemnly and Dumpling set the tone of quiet desperation.

By the day after Christmas, Dumpling had taken to her bed which meant she was exhausted and in a deep depression.

It had been a gradual descent down the slippery slope of her own elevated expectations until she hit bottom.

I've seen that same scenario so many times as a psychiatrist. I finally dubbed it the Great Christmas Dichotomy, meaning the coexistence of despair and sorrow alongside joy and exuberance. It's easiest to understand this syndrome if you visualize the high jump event at a high school track and field competition. If the bar of happiness is normally set at four feet, it rises to six feet at Christmas. Depressed people can barely make it over three feet on a good day. Trying for six leads to despair. Anxious people false start and balk at the brink of the jump so many times, they burn out or erupt into emotional flames. Manics soar over the seven-foot-high school record bar and crash on the other side. It all means unhappiness wrapped in beautiful paper and ribbons. Being present to this great emotional divide without falling prey to it is one of the hardest things that a therapist has to do at Christmas, as the bar of happiness moves up for our patients and *ourselves*. There is no escape for any of us. Church, school, and work are permeated with the season of joy. Music, decorations and parties fill every space of our lives. If you are not happy, there is something wrong with you. Extra sessions and phone calls are standard Christmas fare for shrinks. This year, two of my patients had to be hospitalized. Ironically, I knew there would be reminders of Christmas there, too.

So, Tinkerbell and the Spirit of Christmas Present were doing all they could within me to balance this dark side of the Christmas season. To make their job even harder, I was on call for my consortium of eight psychiatrists until noon on Christmas Day. Andrew and Gracen were rotating with their father the week before Christmas and would come home late morning after "Santa Claus" with their Dad and his parents. Then the three of us would fly to Denver, pick up a rental four-wheel-drive SUV, and drive to Breckenridge for a week-long ski trip with my old college roommate, ZZ, and her family. I could then recharge and renourish my own emotional batteries on the beautiful, snow-covered mountains of Colorado and have some adventure with Andrew and Gracen on the way.

I had last seen Stephanie right after she finished her exams and arrived in Charleston for Christmas holidays. Her personal bar of happiness was raised near the seven foot mark as she anticipated meeting her lost mother's biological family at Lake Tahoe over the holidays. I had misgivings about her level of expectation. I had experienced the emotional fall-out of many disappointing adoption reunions with long lost parents and families. Expectation and reality often did not align. They were occasionally daunting, if not disastrous. I tried to warn Stephanie without dampening her enthusiasm.

"Just be aware that people who have been lost to us often become ideals rather than real people."

"You mean Rebecca and Alexis will be real people, and not like on the TV soaps?" Stephanie's sarcasm could be an automatic response.

Stephanie had already talked to Rebecca by phone for hours. She and Alexis were texting, emailing, and face-timing on their new iPhones. The quality of the phone pictures was better than my camera. Stephanie had been astonished how much she and Alexis seemed to be alike. The pictures showed similar heart-shaped faces with high cheekbones, freckles on their noses, and blond hair. Even so, I still carried a small frisson of anxiety about the reunion. It was my job to stay on high ground and anticipate potential negatives in the patterns of my patients' lives. It was clear from the Thanksgiving storm that even psychiatrists get blindsided.

Stephanie was grinning when she came into my office. I didn't think she was taking me very seriously.

"Seriously, Steph, you've got a lot riding on this trip out to see them. How do your father, Victoria, Two-Pop and Nana feel about you spending Christmas somewhere else?"

"They seem to be okay with it. I think they still feel guilty about all the years they kept the secret. You know, I hated my father when he first told me. I was even mad at Two-Pop and Nana. Now it feels different. I can understand more of it, especially after hearing Rebecca talk about my mother. Is this the beginning of forgiveness?"

The power of the question took me by surprise. The beginning of forgiveness. The middle of forgiveness. Finishing forgiveness. Healing the wound — not forgetting, but being released from the wound. It was deep stuff for such a young woman and for a forty-six plus woman like me.

"Yeah," I said. "I think it is. It's a process like anything else. It seems to me that forgiveness as an ultimate response to emotional wounds is much better than burying them. So, just be yourself and give it time. Call me a day or two after Christmas and check in, okay? I'll be skiing in Colorado and using my cell phone."

"You asking this for me or you?" she asked straight-faced.

"Both," I said as we bear hugged and then started out the door.

She stopped halfway down the hall and turned to face me.

"Merry Christmas, Kai."

"Merry Christmas, Stephanie."

Stephanie met her grandmother, Rebecca Sanderson, and her half-sister, Alexis, on Christmas Eve at Lake Tahoe. Her Sanderson forbearers had built a small, rustic log cabin on the lake's western shoreline in Tahoma, California. Multiple generations of Sandersons had been convocating there for decades to hold vigil on Christmas Eve. Even though her husband had been dead for many years, Rebecca had stayed close to his family. It seemed somehow fitting to me that Stephanie came to this new Quaker family during this expectant finale of Advent as they waited for hope to unite heaven and earth.

Stephanie called me late on the second day after her Christmas reunion. My fears were allayed as soon as I heard her voice. It sounded like a song, some combination of *Joy to the World* and *Silent Night*. Definitely an anthem of peace and not despair.

"I have found the rest of me, Kai. It's some kind of beautiful." She sang the words. "Just touching Rebecca and Alexis, I can feel my mother in them."

It was palpable over the phone. A trinity of love, reconnected, out of the dark. Maybe there was hope for my own disconnected trinity: myself, my mother, my grandmother.

"I have so much to say, but I'll save it for the new year," she said, referring to our next appointment in January.

"I'll be waiting to hear every single detail. Can't wait."

"One more thing before we hang up," she added. Somehow, I knew a "Stephanie thing" was coming.

"You know I'm big on presents for people. I usually go hog wild on Christmas. But this year is different. I brought a lot of presents and stuff for Rebecca and Alexis. They're still in my suitcase. I just don't need them here. This family is not into material things. They wrap up wishes for each other. They write poems. They promise visits and smiles and love. It's just heart gifts this Christmas."

"Doesn't surprise me, Steph." It wasn't hard to understand that, especially from the little I knew about Quakers.

"So, I want to 'tell' you your gift, Kai. It's something I've learned since I've been out here. I think you know it already, but I'm not sure."

I was very quiet on my end of the phone.

"Do you remember when I ran out of your office that day that Dad told me Lexy, my mother, had died of leukemia?"

A powerful, visual image immediately came to me of Stephanie lying in a fetal position in a nest of straw in a woodland chapel. The sounds, smells, visual imprints and feelings all flooded me again.

"Vividly," I replied.

"I asked you a question that you didn't answer while I was lying out there and you were holding my hand. Do you remember what I asked?"

I wasn't clear about what she was referencing. Most of my memories of that experience weren't words.

"I'm sorry, Steph. I don't remember."

"That's okay. Today, I got the answer for myself. I wasn't sure if you didn't answer me that day because you didn't know or you just wanted me to find out for myself."

The buildup to this present was starting to tingle up the length of my spine.

"So, here's what I know and I give it to you with love." She picked up the cadence of her voice song again.

"Hold out your hands like a chalice, Kai, so I can put it right into them."

I cradled the phone between my ear and shoulder and cupped my hands.

"Ready." I quivered with anticipation.

Stephanie's next words sounded almost like an annunciation, "God *is* merciful to His children." She paused. "God is merciful to *me*."

I stood transfixed.

In benediction, she ended, "I wish you to know that mercy today, through me."

I didn't say a word, I just received it. Stephanie was teaching me about mercy. One more time in my experience with patients, one of them had become the rabbi. I had understood the concept of mercy for many years but had stayed safely on the sidelines as an observing therapist. It had just become very personal.

"Goodbye. I love you, Kai."

"I love you, Stephanie. And thank you."

Joy vanquished the darkness for me that Christmas Day. The sorrow, the despair, the hurt of a wounded world. For one, brief, shining moment, Stephanie gave me the greatest gift she had and the only thing I needed.

Chapter Twenty-six

The bunny slope at Breckenridge was full of kids. Little kids. It was embarrassing when three and four-year-olds swooped past me with their short skis and no poles. I had just finished the second lesson with my very young ski instructor from Tasmania. I hadn't known its location in the world and would have guessed it was off the coast of Africa. Actually, it's at the southern-most tip of Australia, west of New Zealand. It was news to me that there were mountains and snow in Tasmania. After all, it's in the world's southern hemisphere with Antarctica below it. I wondered if Jeffrey had a Tasmanian devil in his lineage? He could ski with their famed ferocity. I admonished myself to concentrate on walking in skis. Andrew and Gracen had been skiing for years, thanks to their father; they were on the black diamond runs at the top of the mountain with ZZ and her teenagers. Jeffrey returned me to the bunny slope at the end of our lesson. I walked in my stiff ski-boot shuffle to the lift for the intermediate slope.

As the ski lift jerked to a start, the chair swung back and forth like one on a Ferris wheel when it stops at the top of its arc. My breath caught when I gazed out over the landscape. The view was so unimpeded; it looked as if pristine snow covered the world. The higher I rose, the farther I could see. The sun felt hot on my face.

"Is this a picture of mercy?" The question crystallized as my gaze swept the great, white expanse. I had not shared the conversation with Stephanie or her gift of mercy with anyone else. I had savored it like a rare confection that I wanted to keep all to myself. Besides, I had caused a disaster in the kitchen last night. No one told me that marshmallows swell to four times their size at high altitudes when they get hot. When I opened the oven to check for doneness, they looked like a huddle of Pillsbury Doughboys, all stuck to the broiler! When I yelled for help, Andrew and Gracen raced to the kitchen.

"Gosh, Mom, did you commit homicide in Frosty the Snowman's hometown?" Andrew quipped.

Soon everyone stood around the open stove marveling at the white sticky mess. It took hours to clean after dinner.

Throughout the ski vacation, Stephanie had come unbidden to mind. She was so *young*. It was not natural for such a young person to understand the "wide expanse" of a concept like mercy. She had given me the gift of mercy, but I wasn't sure what to do with it.

As usual, I quasi-fell off the chair lift when it stopped. I could never ski off the damn thing gracefully. Righting myself, I hesitated as I looked down at the steep slope below me. This would be my first solo run from up here, I thought as I pushed off. Mindlessly, I flew down the slope, executing textbook turns to control my speed. Not bad, I congratulated myself. I was doing this alone and I loved it. Me, the snow and the mountain. I made three more runs and decided to reward myself with hot chocolate. Hordes of skiers decked out in their colorful ski clothes crowded the chalet's hot beverage bar. I pushed and shoved with the best of them, finally walking away with my coveted steaming mug, looking for a quiet spot. The sun was gone, the sky having taken on that overcast grayness that portended imminent snowfall. I had no sooner tucked into an isolated area of the high terrace overlooking the converging lower slopes when a light snow began to fall. I drank the rich, dark chocolate as the snowflakes swirled around me.

"I wish you had mercy on me," Dumpling's whispers seemed to emanate from the veil of falling snow.

I became perfectly still. I was slowly looking around to see if she had been reincarnated on the ski slopes of Breckenridge, Colorado. Dumpling had a very distinctive voice. I'm not sure I ever heard her whisper in real life, but it was *her* voice. I did a quick reality check, scanning the outlines of other skiers on the terrace as well as small figures coming down the ski runs to make sure I had not been transported into the middle of Charles Dickens's *A Christmas Carol*, with the Spirit of Christmas Past. I have never felt crazy in my life, even in the presence of psychotic schizophrenics, excluding a few times with my ex or where hopelessly locked into the alternate reality of teenagers. I have categorically *never* heard voices of the dead.

Over and over in recent months, unusual experiences had been happening. So, what was going on? It made me feel uneasy.

"Is mercy just for other people to give, not something you dispense?" Unmistakably Dumpling's voice. The snow was falling so hard, I lost all visual cues, like a mountain climber caught in a white-out. I felt encapsulated, isolated from the world around me, caught in a waking dream state, or even worse, hallucinating. Out of the snow, Dumpling materialized. Not the broken, stroke-ravaged old woman from the nursing home or the waxy, lifeless shell left behind in the sunroom of her house. This was the beautiful, young Dumpling of the wedding picture, the fifteen-year-old bride. She stood several feet away with a wistful smile on her face.

"I am so sorry for the pain I caused you in our life together," Dumpling spoke with kindness in her eyes.

I knew the manic-depressive grandmother when she raged or took to bed; this one I did not know. My old, defensive anger rescued me from the initial surprise. I was being drawn into this surreal dialogue. Then, I lashed out, "You were so mean to me and my mother. God knows I tried to understand you. You needed help; I know that now. No one ever helped you."

As I spoke, I realized that, over the years, I had experienced a shift from being Dumpling's victim to seeing her as a victim. Predator/prey, indeed. I did not want to become her predator now, but my anger was still there.

"Will you forgive me, Kai? I need your forgiveness and your mercy. Even now, I need your mercy," she entreated.

"Do you *deserve* to be forgiven?" I flung the words sanctimoniously.

"Of course not, I simply long for it. I long to be free just as you long to be free."

"I hope you don't believe that I will ever forget what you did. Forgiveness doesn't mean forgetting." My ego was still not ready to surrender on behalf of my own humanity. Justification this time.

"Can you imagine memory without the scald of pain?" She did not rise to the lure of my anger. Dumpling's voice seemed to be fading, or was it the howl of the wind increasing?

I wanted to cry. A part of me felt five years old. I didn't know how to forgive her. Was forgiveness an act of will? Was it authentic feeling that I needed? Could I forgive her? Would I dare?

"I want to forgive you. I *want* to," I shouted.

"Neither one of us will ever be free until you forgive me, release me." Faint whispers on the wind.

Suddenly, I knew what to do. I chose to do it. It was so simple really. I stood up into the tumbling, swirling storm of flakes and threw the remnants of my warmed drink upwards, as if it was the final remnants of old fear and anger that had caged me in as surely as it kept Dumpling out.

"I forgive you, Grandmother! As best as I possibly can, I

forgive you," I cast the words forth to join the maelstrom of snow and wind. Dumpling seemed to take on a glow and then she blew her breath towards me. It seemed to transform the snowflakes into tiny creative sparks which fell upon me like fairy dust. And then she disappeared.

"Mom, Mom, is that you?" Gracen's voice was calling me out of the snow. I felt her arm around me, hugging tight. "We couldn't find you, Mom. All of us have been looking for you. ZZ even went back to the lodge to see if you were there. Have you been sitting out here in this snow storm? You must be freezing. We've been so worried, Mom, so worried," her voice was full of emotion as she held me at arm's length and gave me a piercing onceover.

"I am so very okay, love." I flashed her a smile full of light and great peace. To myself I added, "and so very free."

"Can I have some of what you're drinking?" she said it like she needed a good, stiff drink of alcohol. I looked down at my empty cup. How much had I actually drunk? Had I really thrown it? It didn't matter. I had just learned that reconciliation is possible, even after death. Forgiveness is not bound by time and space. And I was not crazy.

"Let's go get some more hot chocolate…it's heavenly."

Chapter Twenty-seven

The first weeks of the new year evolved into a blessed routine in my office. Following the frenzy of the holidays, January provides needed respite. Winter even deigned to make an early frigid appearance, setting off a predictable response: Charlestonians hibernate. Cold to us is anything under 49º F. Freezing rain and snow, which is rare, incapacitates our bridges and paralyzes the whole area. With few distractions and a natural cycle of self-reflection, hibernation is a boon to the therapeutic process. My patients work harder this time of the year than any other. I was lulled into complacency and paid little attention to the record full moon that was waxing.

It is not just old wives' tales that the moon affects human behavior. Werewolves excepted, there is an uptick in crazy, erratic behavior in ordinary human beings during the week of the full moon. It is amazing to me that there have been a handful of federal grants studying this repetitive phenomenon. Speaking from my own subjective observations over the years, my psychiatric population has borne out the federal studies.

Routine gave way to the moon. Monday of full moon week started with a seemingly homeless man sitting on the front porch steps of our office. He may have been there all night and it had been really cold. I couldn't find out because he only talked in numbers, albeit carrying on an incoherent conversation with himself. He appeared to be psychotic, out of touch with any semblance of reality. How in the world did he end up here at a psychiatric office?

"Can you tell me your name?" I asked as I sat down on the steps beside him.

"Seven, four, eight, eight," he said clearly, but with no eye contact.

I really looked at him. His torn and dirty clothes hung on his bony frame. He was gaunt. Was he hungry? The jacket was an old army camouflage. Was he a veteran? Vietnam? Right age. I remembered something I had just read a few days ago: "Be kind, for everyone you meet is fighting a great battle". Philo of Alexandria wrote these words before Christ.

Who are you, I wondered, *whose father or son or husband? What kindness do you need?*

"Is there someone I can call for you? Your parents? A child? Your wife?" He must belong to someone.

"Three, six, ten, four, ten!" he spoke emphatically with good eye contact.

This went on for some time. I could not decipher his code, I could get him to safety and to treatment. That was all I could do. I had Sarah call the mobile crisis unit which operated out of MUSC Emergency Room. He would be a candidate for their indigent care. He went quietly with them, which was a big relief. I wondered what the numbers for "take care of yourself" were in his language. It was what I wished for him.

Early afternoon on Tuesday, Willa had to interrupt me for help with one of her patients who was in a screaming match with his wife in the front parking lot. I had recently prescribed Prozac to treat his vicious temper. It was effective in low doses to help people control reactive anger. The drug had not had time to work. He and his wife had just finished a couple's session. Unfortunately, like many couples, they saved the real stuff for the "after session." Willa and I both went out to mediate. I ran behind the rest of the day.

The moon crescendoed into a huge, bright yellow orb that night. We should have closed the office for the rest of the week. On Wednesday, Mattie went missing.

I had been seeing Mattie for five years and she had *never* missed an appointment. Mattie was like clockwork, coming once a month to touch the talisman of her therapy and garner enough hope and support to make it another month. She would drive two hours to start her session promptly at nine o'clock; she went straight home afterwards so she wouldn't miss her favorite soap opera, *The Young and the Restless*, which she had been watching every day for almost thirty years. It was her other talisman. I had never been able to accurately diagnose Mattie. She had a little bit of everything wrong, almost an adult version of "failure to thrive" syndrome, which is not in our diagnostic manual, the DSM-IV. She did not fit neatly into any of our diagnostic boxes. For insurance purposes, I used Borderline Personality Syndrome. This drove her husband to distraction.

"What the hell does borderline personality mean?" he thundered over the phone to me one day after wading through insurance papers for hours. "That she almost has a personality?"

"It means, Mr. Simms, that your wife's core self is not well developed; her identity and functional sense of who she is, is defective."

"Well, who the hell knows *who* they are, doctor?"

I had used too much psychiatric jargon and failed to really communicate. I was speaking insurance company language. "Joe," I tried again, "Mattie is mentally ill. She is barely able to function. It is sad and frustrating."

I understood his frustration. I knew it was hard for him to live with Mattie. He had told me several times that he couldn't leave her. She was like one of his children now.

I glanced at the clock again; it was 9:25. Just as I decided to call Mattie's husband to see if something had happened, Sarah buzzed me on the intercom. "There's a Corporal Will Richards of the South Carolina Highway Patrol on the phone calling about Matilda Simms."

My heart skipped a beat as I answered the phone. It seemed Mattie had been going 75 in a 50 mile per hour speed zone in a notorious speed trap an hour west of Charleston. When she was stopped, she had a panic attack. The patrolman called EMS. Mattie was trying to take Xanax to calm down. That, plus her bizarre behavior, made Corporal Richards think she was a druggie. Thank God, when EMS arrived, the tech read the medicine bottle and got my name off it. I talked to him, to Mattie twice, and to Corporal Richards again, all in Mattie's remaining session time. The highway patrol got Mattie back on the road headed home. She missed seeing me, but hopefully could catch her soap opera. On a routine day, Mattie required great patience. I was not born with patience. It had taken me years to learn. Repeatedly, my intense temperament had gotten me in trouble as a child. My mother helped me the most with it. It still amazes me that I landed in the one field of medicine that requires immense patience. Today, I was drawing on reserves and it was only 10 a.m.!

I had a phone session scheduled with Stephanie after lunch. It was her first of the new year. The full moon had never affected Stephanie...before. She didn't call. Twenty minutes after the hour, Sarah finally reached her on her cell phone.

"I'm so sorry, Kai. I absolutely forgot that we had a phone time today."

235

Her voice was so low I could barely hear her. I did hear strange background sounds.

"Stephanie, where are you? Can you speak up?"

"I'm in Trader Joe's. I'm with somebody." Her voice was still guarded and low.

"Stephanie, can you go out to the car?"

"Kai, I'm with Henry. You know, the grad student I told you about. He still doesn't know I see a psychiatrist."

"Are you embarrassed to tell him?"

Even in the twenty-first century, there is often a mixture of shame and reluctant need that plagues psychiatry. Shame from the age of insane asylums lingers. Emotional need is often judged as weakness or inadequacy, especially in men. But Stephanie?

The rest of her words were drowned out by a loudspeaker announcing a daily special to shoppers.

"Stephanie, I can't hear you."

Scuffling sounds.

"Okay. I'm in the restroom. I'm so sorry I forgot to call. I needed to move this hour anyway and I forgot to call and tell you. I am doing great, Kai. I feel super and I am having the most wonderful time with Henry. He was home in California most of December, but we've been inseparable since he got back. He's waiting for me at fresh produce; he's going to cook dinner tonight at his place. I don't really have time to talk. My next scheduled time is in two weeks. I swear I will not forget it again."

"It's a full moon, Steph. No howling and running amok." I smiled to myself as the cover of the book *Women Who Run With Wolves* flashed in my mind.

That made her laugh.

"Okay, Steph, you get one free pass in therapy for unforeseen circumstances. The next time will cost you."

"I hear you loud and clear. Before I go, did you get that brochure I sent you about Dr. Halvorsen being in Charleston next month?"

The brochure had arrived with Dr. Halvorsen's picture outlined in purple Magic Marker with arrows pointing to it from all four sides. I glanced down at it laying on my desk. He was coming to Charleston to present a paper on "Innovative Research and Treatment of Stem Cell Transplants" at a symposium on cancer of the blood cosponsored by MUSC Cancer Center and the National Leukemia and Lymphoma Society.

"I got it, Stephanie. Loved the Magic Marker decorations."

"You better go ahead and sign up now to make sure you get a place. You have to meet this guy."

"Why is this so important to you, Stephanie?" I wondered if this was becoming some sort of magical thinking about linking the idealized mother and father? Did she feel it was up to her to get them together?

"He's just special, Kai."

"Guess I better not miss my big chance, huh?"

"Do not procrastinate! Also, Henry read online about a new drug in research trials at Stanford involving select leukemia patients. Get this: it's showing promise to potentially replace stem cell transplants. This could be the magic bullet, Kai!" she spoke breathlessly.

"It could, Stephanie. This must be a second stage research trial or they would have never published a paper. They are always double-blind studies. That concerns me. It means you would have a fifty percent chance of not getting the drug at all." I needed to stay positive and be realistic with her as well. This was the eternal struggle when hope for a cure was concerned.

"Well, then I would just go forward with stem cell transplant as planned," she seemed undaunted. "I want you to call Dr. H and ask him about it, doctor-to-doctor."

"Me? You know more about all this than I do! Why do you want me to call him?" She didn't know how my first call to him had gone and it was not for her to know. Regardless, I did not want to call him again.

"I send him a lot of stuff, but he blows me off. Don't get me wrong, Kai. I really, really like him. He is a brilliant doctor. But…," she trailed off, "he can be dismissive. Please call him for me. Use your authority."

"God's teeth", I grumbled as I covered the phone. "I'll call him Steph. Send me the research information, ASAP."

"As soon as we leave Trader Joe's. Oh, before I forget, Alexis has typed positive to be a stem cell donor! Cool, huh? Bye now," Stephanie said just as I was congratulating her about Alexis. She was moving on.

I picked up the brochure. Halvorsen was most definitely attractive in a rugged sort of way. Good hair, longish for a professional picture. Obviously never used sun block. Lots of wrinkles around his eyes and brow. Open collared shirt under a dark jacket. Could be an outdoors man. His picture suggested someone more laid back than his conversations did. He was probably complex like most males I knew. As a widower-doctor, he probably had every available nurse in New York City after him. I had forgotten how many years ago his wife had died. I think Stephanie said his daughter was about Andrew's age. I sighed and picked up the chart on top of the diminishing stack on my desk. I put the brochure on my to-do list with a note to call him. I felt mildly annoyed like I had just been manipulated, but shrugged it off as I went to get my next patient.

Just after lunch, Sarah pointed to the phone at her ear and mouthed, "Dr. Gellmans' on the line."

I hesitated, then mouthed back, "Referral?" I mimicked slitting my throat.

She shook her head, "Personal."

I pointed back to my office and nodded my head. Why were we using sign language? The man was on hold. I hit blinking line one. "Robert Gellman, I hope you stopped for lunch."

"Making rounds on 8 East. Lucy asked me to call you today and I just remembered. Have to complete my honey-do list before I get home. It's been a crazy day."

"Full moon, Rob."

"Lucy and I want to invite you to join us for dinner February twenty-seventh, that's a Friday night. Peter Halvorsen from Sloan Kettering is coming down to lead a symposium at Hollings the next day. You remember, he's Stephanie's transplant doctor? Halvorsen and I did our residencies together. Lucy and I thought you might enjoy getting to know each other. Can you come?"

This was just weird after Stephanie's phone call this morning.

"I will be in town that weekend, Rob. Sounds interesting. I'd probably come just for Lucy's gourmet cooking alone." I didn't tell him I had checked my Day-Timer when the brochure arrived to make sure I was potentially available to go to the symposium.

"She'll call you with the details. What's the best way for her to reach you?"

I gave him my cell number and hung up. It dawned on me that I had kept this number away from Rob in the past so he wouldn't call me for referrals on it. Doctors used buffers with each other, too.

Moon or no moon, this was conspiratorial. Had Stephanie and Gellman talked? Did she suggest the idea of a dinner to him? I had one more working day of moon week and then maybe life could get back to normal. I went ahead and placed a call to Peter Halvorsen before my first afternoon patient arrived.

Surprisingly, Peter Halvorsen was available but asked if he could call back directly from his cell to mine. I fished my iPhone out of my purse to make sure it was charged. I had made the contacts list on his cell, wonder of wonders. I answered on the first ring and quickly explained what Stephanie had discovered about the experimental drug. I asked if the research study was a possible treatment avenue for her.

"Nope." That was all he said. I waited for more that didn't come.

"I'm afraid Stephanie will never settle for that, Dr. Halvorsen. Can you give me more information?" I felt he was dismissing *me* now.

"Acute myelotrophic leukemia is too aggressive for Leucotaxin. Early evidence indicates that its use reduces the success rate of a later stem cell transplant. It is showing more efficacy for other kinds of leukemia."

"What if she's willing to try it?" I plowed on.

"Do you want me to put her in a research study that's double-blind and would preclude a stem cell transplant for the next two years?" he sounded angry. "Those trials are going on at Stanford. That was in California last time I checked. Sloan-Kettering is doing its own research and is on the East Coast."

For God's sake, I said to myself. What did I just step in? Last time I checked, Chicago, where Stephanie went to school, was in the Midwest with access to both coasts! Is medical competition between Stanford Medical and Sloan-Kettering the Super Bowl of male doctor egos? Doctors had personality issues with each other, just like anybody else. Specialists competed with each other. Ophthalmologists now performed eye lifts much to the chagrin of plastic surgeons. Anesthesiologists did more cortisone injections than back surgeons. Surgeons and psychiatrists had a longstanding mistrust of each other. They practice at opposite ends of the healing spectrum: one cuts and one listens. (In all honesty, I know a handful of surgeons who do both.) Halvorsen and I were in that group at this very moment. Sidestep this, Kai, I admonished myself and tried to change the subject.

"On another note, you might find it helpful to know that Stephanie believes strongly that meditation and acupuncture are helping tremendously. She is much more at peace with her illness and hopeful." I said it sweetly with a knife's edge.

"She's in remission," he retorted.

"May I call you Peter?" I asked, barely able to control my anger.

"If I can call you Katherine."

"My name is Kai."

"Your medical license says Katherine."

He Googled me? Absolutely amazing!

"Making sure I'm a real doctor?" I knew that was a low blow as soon as it came out of my mouth. It was childish and unprofessional. What was wrong with *me*?

"Okay, Kai. I don't profess to understand psychiatry, yoga or acupuncture. I've never read any research that is able to measure the benefits of any alternative treatments. Results are subjective at best. I'll stick to proven medical protocols for AML and leave the rest to you people."

You people. I am now officially one of *you people*? Don't react, Kai.

"What about spirituality? Don't you think a patient's belief system and faith impact their healing?" I was like a bulldog now. I wanted some kind of affirmation from him. He had now stepped on my stuff.

"Faith didn't save my wife." The words were smoldering.

"She...she died?" I stammered. Stephanie had told me months ago that he was a widower, but he didn't know I had that information, did he?

"She was killed after church one Sunday in a car wreck. Our daughter was with her. She had a lot of faith. A very spiritual person. Didn't save her."

"I'm so sorry. Really sorry to hear you lost your wife like that." *Be kind, every person is fighting a great battle*, Philo again. First a homeless man…now a surgeon.

He continued, "So don't talk to me about faith. My faith is in what I can do with my hands and technology to help the body be healed. Ciao." He hung up.

I was dazed. Did he just hang up on me? First, I evoke competition in him, then some kind of wound with his dead wife. Was he funneling all the energy generated from her death into saving women with leukemia and lymphoma? Help! I was really lost here. I needed time to process what we had just said to each other. I might even need to talk to a supervisor about this for my own personal reasons. I felt pretty sure I owed him an apology. I would see if Steph had an email address for him so I could email an apology. Dealing with Peter Halvorsen had completely thrown me.

I sent Stephanie a text that said, "Dr. H says 'nope'. Kai."

I didn't get a reply.

Chapter Twenty-eight

February had only two things to make it worth being on the calendar: Valentine's Day and the upcoming dinner at the Gellmans'. I woke up the morning of the dinner with a kind of free-floating anxiety/anticipation. I was looking forward to meeting the good Doctor H, but felt cautious. Stephanie wasn't helping matters at all. She somehow knew that I was meeting Halvorsen for dinner, which supported my conspiracy theory. She sent me eight text messages, one after the other, on my cell phone yesterday. Together, they were a "Helpful Hints" list that was reminiscent of the original contract she had brought to our first therapy session. I didn't know whether to laugh or cry when I read it. After the briefest of salutations, she had written in bold, all caps:

KAI, DON'T BLOW THIS. She then proceeded to list a version of "Dating for Dummies".

1—Don't dress like a doctor. I vote for a leg-showing basic dress, not black!

2—Keep jewelry to a minimum. Silver earrings. The amethyst firefly pendant I gave you.

I started to wonder if Stephanie was the multiple reincarnation of Coco Chanel and the matchmaker from *Fiddler on the Roof*. Honestly, she just didn't give up.

3—Wear your hair down. Your 'doctor hairdo' pulled straight back is too severe for a date.

"This is NOT a date," I retorted to the text message. Stephanie had never seen me outside of our professional relationship. I usually did wear my hair down in my not-doctor life. Jeans and flip flops, too.

4—Sling backs, open-toe sandals with real heels. Dr. H is tall!

5—Flirt.

6—Listen with your beautiful eyes, like you do in therapy.

7—Music. Dr. H likes jazz, Beyoncé, Springsteen and Josh Groban, according to his iPod I swiped. (I did return it!)

Well, that was one strike. I love music, but I'm lukewarm about jazz. To be honest, I don't like it.

8—Drink a little. Just sip it, don't get drunk.

That struck me as funny. It was hilarious, really. I remembered her telling me that during chemo, even a little alcohol seemed to wipe her out. I had mentioned that I was a one-drink wonder. My ex used to be amused by my low alcohol tolerance and always tried to goad me into drinking more. It was like a personal affront to him if I didn't drink. In reality, if I had more than two drinks, I felt like I had the flu. A biochemist once told me I probably had an allergy to the metabolic breakdown of alcohol. Made sense.

Stephanie must keep a computer profile on everyone in her life. How else could she remember such details?

9—Relax and have fun. I have a feeling about this, Kai.

"Monkey mind", that master of criticism and doubt, began to whisper in my ear, "He can be a jerk. Remember Trey? Most men are jerks." Monkey mind started playing the record of my old wounds. I knew that he also guarded the deep self and its great gifts of self-value, self-love, and self-respect. Access to that treasure meant shutting up the criticism and doubt that gave monkey mind his power.

"Stop this right now!" I shouted out loud to the monkey mind voice inside me. Abruptly, I dismissed the thoughts he tantalized me with, refusing to feed them fear or fruitless speculation. I had done that for too long. Something was changing. The woman in me, with all of her amazing feminine potential, wanted out. I would visit the Gellmans, savor Lucy's gourmet cooking and hopefully enjoy the company of Stephanie's transplant doctor. At the very least, I could get up to speed on the specifics of stem cell transplants. I did think it was interesting that Peter Halvorsen was coming to Charleston just as I was opening my personal clam shell. Very interesting. As was both our connections to Stephanie.

I decided to pamper myself before my big night out. It had taken me years to allow myself such frivolous wastes of time as massages or pedicures. I had finally conquered that nonsense. Massage was now part of my own therapy. Touch is so healing and I needed touch. I started thinking about the last time I had been touched by a man. Really, romantically touched. There had been a few men since Trey, but nothing serious. I knew for the first few years after my divorce that I had a "no vacancy" sign hanging on my heart. It was a natural phenomenon after divorce. Some people rebounded into quick second relationships that were usually disasters, but divorce was a grief process like any other loss. It took time to heal and risk love again. It had taken me years to get over my divorce. The prevailing question now was, "Am I able to choose a different kind of man?"

During my massage, I relaxed into the beauty of touch. Early on, I wasn't comfortable with having my face touched. It felt too vulnerable. Now I loved it. With a lover, such touch is the essence of intimacy. I felt ready for a lover's touch. I felt ready to risk something new. Ready to meet Peter Halvorsen in the flesh.

Chapter Twenty-nine

I arrived at Rob and Lucy's house on the Charleston battery at 7 p.m. sharp. It was one of those beautifully restored antebellum structures Charleston is famous, with light beige stucco and cream colored trim. The double-sided brick steps curved to spill on to the columned front porch. I loved the black-painted railings that met to form a Philip Simmons wrought iron creation. Simmons had just died several years ago at nearly a hundred. He worked his singular art form until the end. The unobstructed view of Charleston Harbor from the front porch was breathtaking. It was unseasonably warm for February, and Lucy led me through the house to the back veranda where a tall man was standing with Rob. An infinity pool, its water shimmering above the soft underwater lighting, formed a tranquil backdrop to these forty-something year-old men. Lucy and I paused at the open back door and watched them for a few minutes. Stephanie was right, Halvorsen was tall, well over six feet. He was dressed casually in a long sleeved blue shirt. His hair was still unfashionably long and had sun streaks through the dark blond. He had a tan. Manhattan in late winter did not a tan give. Maybe he decamped to the Caribbean, too. Maybe he was a boater.

Lucy's voice interrupted my perusal, "They've both gotten better with age." I heard affection in her voice. If Lucy was fond of the great Dr. H, he couldn't be all bad.

Lucy started out with a tray of hors d'oeuvres, with me following.

I felt self-conscious like a teenager as I followed her. I had worn a simple blue dress and sweater with the amber and amethyst firefly pendant Stephanie had given me. Some of her suggestions were good.

I gave Rob a hug and turned to face Peter. His blue eyes were icy. I felt he could see straight through the mask that I had so artfully created with makeup. I blushed, which I never do.

"So, you are Kai." He was not smiling.

"Dr. H, I presume," calling him by Stephanie's moniker. I gave him my most radiant smile.

Rob Gellman stared from one of us to the other. "You haven't met before, have you?"

"Only on the phone when she calls to manage Stephanie Edinger's drug regimen." His eyes never left mine.

"Did you get my email apology?" I tried to stare him down.

"You apologized to him before you met him?" Rob was flummoxed. "What's going on, Kai?"

"Long story, Rob." I managed just as Peter turned away to follow Lucy inside.

As Rob and I trailed behind them, I heard Stephanie's words in my head, "Don't blow this, Kai." I'm afraid it had been blown weeks ago.

Dinner was delectable. Rob and Peter talked about their residencies together at John Hopkins, old friends with a patina from years of weathering together. Lucy was as warm as ever, and started talking about music, which broke the tension between Peter and me. When the topic of jazz came up, I confessed ignorance and listened while Peter shared his passion of the musical art form. I'd had a glass of pinot grigio by the pool and with dinner. It helped me relax. After sherried lobster and asparagus au gratin, Lucy's *coup de grâce* was her dessert flan served with cordials.

Eventually, conversation turned toward Stephanie.

"Well, I find it downright intriguing that we are all sitting here together tonight because of Stephanie Edinger," Rob said. "Not totally surprising, though. As my old grandfather would say, she's a whippersnapper."

We all laughed.

"If that means one helluva woman, your grandfather is right on," Peter replied.

He had definitely loosened up. He liked Rob's Scotch.

"Peter, how did you make the decision to specialize in oncology?" I asked intrepidly.

He hesitated a moment, glanced at Rob, and then answered.

"I'm a researcher at heart. In medical school at Cornell, I had the opportunity to work with Karl Zuiderman, a world renowned Dutch immunologist. He was working jointly on a research project with Cornell and Sloan Kettering."

"What he's *not* telling you, Kai, is that he did a joint PhD and MD program," Rob interjected.

Peter actually looked abashed. "Believe it or not, it was fun. Either program alone would have been a little dry. Together, they were dynamic." He spoke passionately.

"Peter's reputation preceded him to residency," Rob pitched in another comment. "It was fun tormenting him, but he won us over."

"I still don't hear the link to oncology," I persisted.

"Immunology. How our bodies fight virus and cancer are distinctly parallel. Dr. Zuiderman was researching HIV which taught us how the body does or does not fight cancer. Most people don't realize that our body's immune system kills about ninety-five percent of the rogue, mutant cancer that arises on a cellular level. It's the five percent it misses or is 'blind' to that progress to the cancer we're all familiar with. Using our own immune systems to fight cancer is one of the most exciting approaches to treatment that has come directly from HIV research. It also opened up a new understanding of the roles of T-cells and stem cells in the immune system."

"Peanut gallery to earth," Gellman interrupted. "Peter's stem cell research has improved modern stem cell transplants for leukemia and lymphoma. We are in a rarified presence here, Kai."

The plot thickened. Peter was definitely a complex man.

"You are in the trenches on the front lines of cancer treatment, Rob-bo, with my utmost respect," he raised his glass towards Rob.

"You gotta love this guy," Rob said. "He could get disconnected in his ivory tower and he doesn't."

Just don't talk to me from the ivory tower, I said smugly to myself.

"Tell us about Stephanie's chances with transplant, Peter," I asked more seriously.

"She's an excellent candidate. Young, perfect preexisting health, and she had a remarkable response to her chemo. She has almost no malignant blast cells at this point, which means we probably have at least six months before transplant. The allogeneic match from her half-sister is also very promising. I am very hopeful."

"At what point do you make the final decision to proceed with transplant?" I asked.

"We will do blood work monthly and if aberrant blast cell formation begins, we'll schedule it immediately."

"Do you mind telling me the protocol?" I was aware that Lucy was clearing dishes and away from the table. We docs were already talking shop which borders on rude to someone like Lucy. I really wanted to hear this and hoped Lucy would take care of herself for a while.

"We would fly her sister to New York and prep her for stem cell extraction. Concomitantly, we would prepare Stephanie for total bone marrow and blood element ablation using mega doses of toxic chemicals. As soon as she is stable, we cultivate the sister's stem cells and inject them into Stephanie. Then, she spends thirty days in isolation while the new stem cells hopefully make themselves at home and survive Stephanie's immune system. We deliberately weaken her immunity with suppressing drugs. That necessitates an absolutely sterile environment. She will have no immunity until her white blood cells can differentiate from the transplanted stems. We may have to transfuse 'clean' red cells and platelets in the interim to sustain her."

"She could reject her sister's stem cells?" I kept on.

"She could, but she is as close a genetic match to her sister as most full siblings. We will certainly be ready to treat her with anti-rejection drugs if necessary."

Rob Gellman interjected, "If anybody can make it through stem cell transplant, Stephanie can!"

"She *is* a most unusual young woman. Her grasp of her disease and its treatment is extraordinary, especially for one so young," Peter added. "And her spirituality."

I almost fell out of my chair. I stared at him, trying to tell if he was being sarcastic. I detected none, so took a leap.

"Her work in therapy has been deep, transformative. She has faced the potential of death as consciously as any patient I've ever worked with. Her spirituality is essential to her well-being...she is full of hope," I added.

"Well, she's certainly made a big impression on all three of us," Gellman said as he stood up and ushered us to the library where Lucy was waiting with brandy and a warm fire. Apparently, Rob and Peter loved brandy, especially Remy Martin VSOP. Apparently that is an expensive brand of the stuff. If they broke out cigars, I would object. I hated cigar smoke, really hated it. Damn if they both didn't light up!

"Guys, I can't do cigars. Makes me sick. Sorry." I shrugged.

Peter stood up, "Let's go back out to the pool, Rob." They left Lucy and me by the fire.

Lucy tried to carry on. "Kai, how have you been? Lauren and Gracen get to see each other, but we never do!"

"I love practicing psychiatry, but sometimes my friendships don't get the time they should. I've missed you."

"Are you dating anyone?"

"I'm going slowly. It's been seven years now. Thanks to some good therapy and friends, I'm getting there. How have you been, Lucy?"

"Rob's working too much, but I'm happy. Being the parent of a teenage daughter is the most challenging thing I've ever done. Is Gracen being a witch yet?"

"No, not yet." I laughed and shook my head.

"I beg you for helpful hints, insight, fashion guidance." She wrung her hands in mock despair.

"This definitely calls for in depth commiseration." I really liked Lucy. We needed to stay in closer touch.

It was getting late. How many cigars were they smoking? I told Lucy I had to get home to the kids.

"You must tell Rob and Peter goodbye for me," I said as I stood up.

"Let's go get the social miscreants," she was irritated, too.

"No, no, I'll see Rob tomorrow at the symposium. Remind him to keep a seat for me!" I kissed Lucy goodnight and slipped out. Abandoned for a cigar; I was disappointed. I did have a great meal and learned the latest protocol for stem cell transplants, which is just what I said was the bottom line. I felt dejected and a little lost. Sad. Seemingly, I expected more. I don't know why I went to the symposium the next morning. The auditorium was crowded but I located Rob right away. I had sent him a text message that morning reminding him to save me a seat. He sent one back apologizing for the cigars. Apparently,

Lucy had spoken to him. Peter's lecture was spellbinding, even for an out-of-the-oncology-loop psychiatrist. I had to concede, the man was a power house in his field.

At the first coffee break, I started, "OK, Gellman, I want the scoop on this guy. I mean the *real* stuff. He's got all the makings of a 'star complex' like so many of our narcissistic medical brethren. He also radiates a kind of sexual magnetic appeal to me. Is he a womanizer? Does he have a love interest in the wings?" my voice rose in question.

Rob answered in reverse order, "No to the womanizer and reformed to the narcissism. He married Susan during our residency and he was true blue. Women would come on to him and he seemed oblivious. Susan used to complain about how brazen some of them were, even with her standing beside him. To tell you the truth, it's like his switch has been in the OFF position since Susan died. Parenting and working are about all he does. Did you know his daughter, Claire, was in the car when Susan was killed?"

"He did mention that once on the phone."

"It was bad. Took Peter down. He was pretty cocky when he came to Hopkins. I guess he did have a star complex. Hell, he *was* a star. Lucy and Susan got to be good friends, so I saw a softer, less driven side of him socially. Took them a while to have Claire. His family was his anchor in life."

Rob seemed to be struggling with his emotions as he continued.

"Peter was devastated, flattened by Susan's death. We all were. Susan was a really good person. But you and I know that goodness has nothing to do with the bad things that happen to some people."

I nodded, riveted by what he was saying.

"After her death, Peter took Claire and went on a year-long sabbatical out of the country. He came back changed, Kai. It's hard to describe. It's like he developed more humility... kindness. He deserves to be happy. He asked me a lot about you last night after you left. He seemed interested in you." Was Rob being coy with me?

"Rob, I stepped on some of his negative stuff on the phone. He was almost attacking. I feel the need to be cautious with him. His fortress is formidable."

"Trey was a long time ago, Kai. And Peter is *not* Trey. Oh, he has flaws, all right. He's a man after all," Rob smirked. "Seriously, Kai, he has a much softer side. He's a neat guy. You have more in common than you realize. Besides, you both have gone without sex for too long!"

I punched him in the arm for that. It really did feel like we were back in medical school again.

"You old lech."

"Want some advice?"

I raised my right eyebrow.

"Go with this, Kai. Find out for yourself what makes Peter tick. Trust yourself. Might be fun to have an equal in your life."

Throughout the break, Peter was mobbed. He never got away from the podium. As the seminar resumed, Peter's command of his audience was complete. His command of my attention was unsettling. This was new territory for sure.

Could I just stay open to whatever happened? Not analyze it to death or try to control it? Just let it be?

Chapter Thirty

The next few days in my office were uneventful. It is restful to have therapy hours that are predictable and manageable. Routine creates a kind of emotional safety for my patients and me. Therapy is meant to be a safe harbor from the world where patients are cloistered and undisturbed; where they can tend to their healing needs. At the end of sessions, they would often say "time to go back to the real world". I was grounded by my Andrew and Gracen. Knowing they would be home, teenage angst and all, was my beacon for normalcy.

To get from my office to them, I had to cross the abyss of six o'clock darkness. Winter's perpetual shortage of light was wearing on me. Dusk fell at five o'clock. Daylight Saving's time change was another month away.

I had just made it to my car and turned the key, when my cell phone rang. It startled me. Caller ID said Halvorsen. I answered it without hesitation.

"Dr. Ingersohn…Kai?" His voice was tenuous.

"Yes?"

"It's Peter…Halvorsen."

"Hi, Peter," my good mood prevailed.

"I just wanted to call and apologize for the cigar thing when I was in Charleston."

I was speechless for a few seconds. Then, I said, "Thank you. I really appreciate your apology."

"I remember when you sent me an email apologizing after I told you my wife had died."

He had never responded to that email. I just thought he had brought unfinished business between us to Charleston.

"I couldn't imagine going through a traumatic death like you did. It probably would have shattered me."

"Your email was kind. It disarmed me."

"Can you explain what the cigar thing was all about?" my voice was soft, almost imploring.

"I'm not sure I fully understand it myself. I'm defensive with you. Those first two phone calls, you sounded critical, as if I didn't know what I was doing in my treatment with Stephanie. At Rob and Lucy's, I didn't...expect you to be so... attractive. Stephanie said you were pretty, but she understated it."

"Thank you again, Peter. I think that's a compliment."

"I'm not great at this, Kai. I don't apologize a lot. I'm probably stingy with compliments, too."

"You're doing great so far." I wanted to pinch myself. I wasn't dreaming. I looked at the dashboard lights in my darkened car.

"Would it be alright if I call you again one evening, just to talk?"

"I would really like that, Peter."

After we hung up, I just sat still for a few minutes. Who was this guy? Full of surprises. He certainly kept me off-kilter. I really did need to talk to somebody who was out of the loop... even my office loop.

Chapter Thirty-one

Two days after Peter's phone apology, I called a colleague-friend in North Carolina who had lost a spouse to cancer. We had remained friends long after our psych residencies where deep bonds were forged. He had my utmost trust and respect and I had been there for him when his wife died prematurely. He was not only smart and highly-trained himself, but he kept his sense of humor. The Stephanie-Peter-Kai axis was personal and professional. Stephanie's therapy was intertwined with Peter and me. Whatever happened with the two of us, it was our direct responsibility to protect Stephanie.

Will listened patiently to my history of Stephanie and the entrance of Peter into the picture. I sketched as many dynamics as I could, including what I understood about myself. This was sprinkled with questions and clarifications from him. After a short pause, he started chuckling.

"Kai, Kai, Kai. I anticipated this call coming earlier. I ran into Dr. Edinger at a conference at Duke University a month ago and he asked me if I knew you. Told him I taught you everything you know! He's quite concerned about his granddaughter. He's pleased with her work with you. He also mentioned the specialist at Sloan Kettering. I know of Halverson through one of my patients."

"I felt Edinger was looking over my shoulder," I replied, "until I realized he was just as human as the rest of us. AML is no respecter of the powerful."

Will cleared his throat which I had heard him do many times when he got serious.

"Kai, all of us get a case like this if we practice long enough. It's a complicated medical illness with a complex patient and a large cast of doctors. It will demand that you know your stuff and your own self. You and Stephanie are fine. If you couldn't operate 'out of the box', as you call it, you wouldn't have been able to hold her as a patient. You already know that. Remember in your residency when you drew fire from everyone for trying to integrate spirituality with therapy. All of us were subject to the lingering effects of the old Freudian School and science/religion split. Simple Freud didn't work for either of us; we needed a more inclusive medicine of the whole person. This Dr. Halvorsen... Peter, is it?"

"Yes."

"Sounds like fate just dropped him into the picture. There is usually a wild card in cases like this. I think it's him. He's vital to Stephanie's survival, but not yours. I'm wondering what he means to you?"

"He can be arrogant and dismissing," I blurted. "But, he definitely has a tender side, especially with his patients. When he called to apologize, it really threw me."

"You're attracted to him?"

"Negatively and positively."

"Doesn't matter. He's stirring up a lot of energy in you."

"He could be catching some of my father issues. He is authoritative. He seems to affect Stephanie that way. She trusts him with her life but thinks he is dismissive of her. She's put me up to calling him twice."

"So you're taking on the powers-that-be for Stephanie?"

"I've always done that, Will. We both have, as therapists."

"You're not doing therapy with him, Kai."

"Should I just not deal with him anymore...to protect Stephanie?"

"You tell me. Is that in Stephanie's best interest?"

I hesitated, "No. Maybe mine." I didn't want to admit it.

"Kai, she *has* both of you. She told you up front that she wanted a team to help her. It sounds like Stephanie is simply a catalyst for you and Peter. The rest is up to the two of you. You will have to deal with your own personal issues now. Might need to consider therapy if this is tapping deeply. You have my permission to get *real* help."

"Physician heal thyself?" I sighed.

"Over and over, my friend. It is one of the perks of being a therapist. It is also one of the downsides."

Chapter Thirty-two

Gracen was the first one to sense something different going on with me. The child had an internal radar system that had always read nuances of my behavior. Could be hereditary...I had it with my mother. I always thought mine was a learned, vigilant survival thing. Maybe it's just specific to mothers and daughters.

Saturday morning, some weeks after Peter and I began talking on the phone at night, Gracen crawled in the bed with me. She was propped on one elbow behind me when I rolled over to face her.

"Okay, Mom, who's the mystery caller?" she asked. "And why do you hide in the bedroom when you talk?"

"Justin Bieber. I didn't want to tell you I was robbing the cradle," I teased her about her current rock star heart throb.

"Moth...er," she pinned me with her best disgusted look.

"I've met someone."

"Someone...?"

"A doctor from New York City."

"New York City!" She seemed genuinely surprised.

"He's a friend of the Gellmans'."

"You met him while Andrew and I were with Dad? At that dinner party you went to at the Gellmans'?"

"Yes, we met at the Gellmans'."

"What was he doing in Charleston?"

"He's a cancer doctor at Sloan Kettering Medical Center in New York. He was down here giving a seminar at MUSC."

"How old is he?"

"Forty-eight."

"He must like you if he calls so much." It was more of a question than a statement.

"We like each other."

"You're not falling in love, are you?"

"Way too early for that."

"Mom, I can't live in New York. You wouldn't leave Andrew and me to go live up there, would you?"

Gracen was worried. For seven years she and her brother had been the sole focus of my love and attention. That was beginning to shift. I scooted closer to her and pulled her into the crook of my arm.

"Listen, Gracie," I reverted to her old pet name from babydom, "ain't nobody going to leave nobody. I like this guy and I've only known him a short time, so try not to launch too far ahead of that."

"Does he have kids?"

"As a matter of fact, he has a daughter who is a little younger than Andrew. Her name is Claire. Her mother was killed in a car accident."

"That's terrible, Mom. I can't imagine losing you like that. How long ago did it happen?"

"Three years."

"Will I get to meet Claire?"

"Probably...sometime in the future. He's asked me to come to New York next weekend. You'll be with Dad again. I think I'm going up."

"You do like this guy. What's his name?"

"Peter Halvorsen."

"Mom, you've been really happy the last couple of weeks. Kind of goofy."

"Goofy?"

"I don't know...just different. I can feel it. It's like when I have a crush on somebody."

"Like Justin Bieber?"

"Or Alex Collins," I heard a smile as she spoke the name of her latest seventh grade crush. "Mom, no big surprises, okay?"

She was definitely feeling insecure.

"Honey, you and Andrew are my eternal loves. Never doubt that." I leaned over and gathered her in my arms. We hugged, hard. God, I loved her. Her well-being was so important to me.

"Okay. I'm happy for you, Mutti, I really am." She flashed a big smile full of braces. "How about some French toast?"

I flew to New York City the next Thursday evening after work. Peter met me at LaGuardia and we drove to the Hamptons on Long Island in his old, racing green MGB convertible with the top up. He inherited this prize possession from his father, an auto mechanic who had completely restored it. He had periodic access to a beach cottage in Quogue, Southampton from his accountant whose son he had treated five years before. The boy was a teenager now and flourishing. It was still quite cool in New York in early spring.

During the flight up, I started obsessing about how to handle the issue of sex. It was a very vulnerable arena for me. I didn't want to get in over my head in this relationship and getting physical would do just that. Marvin Gaye started playing over and over in my head: "Let's get it on...." Get a grip, Kai. My generation might have been the last to believe that love and commitment mattered. Sexual mores had changed since I married Trey twenty years ago. Here I was, a forty-six year old psychiatrist, caught in the ageless sexual throes of all women of all time.

"So, talk to him about it, dummy." Ho! monkey mind was trying to help? It sounded like a plan to me.

When Peter and I drove up to the beach house, there was a full moon that beamed a lighted pathway from the ocean to the beach. When we entered the house, its back rooms were diffusely illuminated. Without stopping, I headed straight out onto the back deck to stand under the reflected light and absorb its beauty.

Peter brought up our luggage and some groceries, then joined me on the deck, pulling me into the circle of his arms.

"I scheduled that moon just for you," he murmured.

"Good work," I leaned back into him. It was the first real hug of our lives.

"Being the consummate gentleman that I am, I put your bags in the guest bedroom suite."

"Peter, I had decided to talk to you about sex when we got here. It's a loaded issue for me. I need to go slowly." I turned to face him, staying in the circle of his arms. "Lots of desire going on in me in case you're wondering." I quit obsessing about the sleeping arrangements, relaxed and enjoyed the feel of his body behind me.

"Probably only a fraction of what's going on in me. I've been a little nervous about this weekend, too," he confessed. I loved his admission. It felt real to me.

I looked up into his face. The ambient light of the moon gave it a soft glow. Beautiful man, wrinkles and all.

"Let's get a foundation under us, Peter. Time and trust go a long way. Besides, Stephanie told me not to 'blow this relationship'."

He laughed out loud, "Ah, 'she who must be obeyed'." He kissed me lightly on the lips. "I'll start a fire and pop a bottle of Santa Margherita Pinot Grigio."

The smells of coffee and frying bacon lured me out of sleep the next morning. I guess I would have to tell Peter about the weirdo coffee thing. I always traveled with tea bags. The man cooked a mean breakfast. The pancakes were as good as Andrew's. He had already been for a long jog before I got up. I was not a morning person. He clearly was. I also didn't jog any more. I walked. I hoped he could slow down some.

The weekend unfolded smoothly. We rode bikes all over the nearby village and down the beach as I acclimated myself to its different feel from the barrier islands of the South. The air was deliciously cool. After lunch, we took a nap cuddled together on the oversized couch. Fireplaces get big points with me, even gas logs controlled with a hand-held clicker.

We leisurely drove all over Southampton and Easthampton the next day, stopping for lunch on the waterfront. This was Peter's sanctuary. He was so relaxed out here. We grilled lobster and corn and I made key lime pie for dinner.

We lay on the soft, thick rug in front of the fireplace sipping wine. Gradually, Peter began to tell me about Susan's death and its aftermath.

"A drunk man ran a stop light and t-boned the car on Susan's side. He was driving so fast, the rear end of the van flipped up and came down on top of her Volvo. She was brain-dead by the time they got her to an ER. Claire was trapped in the passenger seat and had to be cut out. She knew her mother was gone. It was a nightmare. She was so traumatized; I was afraid she would never get over it. She was treated for months for post-traumatic stress disorder which I think will always be with her to some extent. I went with her to some sessions. That summer I took a sabbatical. Claire and I headed out west to visit friends in Santa Fe. Spent two more weeks in San Diego with Susan's old college roommate and her husband. I thought we both just needed to get away. Four weeks later, I still couldn't go back. I asked for a year's sabbatical; Sloan Kettering gave it to me. I didn't care what it cost. I used up my savings and took penalties to get over half my retirement."

He took a sip of the smooth white Pinot. His eyes were dark. Haunted.

"Claire and I traveled north through the Napa Valley in California, then flew to the big island of Hawaii. Next, we spent three months bumming around New Zealand retracing the scenes from Lord of the Rings trilogy shot there. I loved the wild, primordial, untouched places. Claire kept up with her lessons on a laptop. We did kind of a quasi-home schooling together. The Internet is an amazing tool for that and the travel added a whole new dimension to her education." He paused and caught my eyes. "Is this too long-winded?"

"Please go on, Peter." I was too moved to say much more.

"We spent time in Singapore, but not long. Too many people. We made our way to Prague, drove through Western

Europe, and ended up staying with my relatives in Sweden. My grandfather grew up on Gotland, an island off Sweden's eastern coast. It was blessedly remote. Claire loved exploring her roots. We spent a few quiet months there."

"Was your grandmother Swedish, too?"

"Yes and she was from Stockholm. They immigrated to Minnesota in the 1920s. His sister still lives on the island. She doesn't speak much English. One of my cousins, a psychiatrist in Stockholm, came over to help translate. He also told me about a healing center in Aberdeen, on the east coast of Scotland. Claire and I went there next and stayed two months. That's where I really faced Susan's loss, as did Claire." His pain now was just a distant echo of that which had seared his soul so long ago.

His shields were down and I laid mine down too. I shared the pain and humiliation of my failed marriage and what I had learned from it. As I spoke, I realized that I was ready to claim my own remission-pardon and release from that wound.

With the deep touching of our inner selves, something shifted. God fire came. Passion sparked, manifesting in Peter's eyes. The bright blue irises began to darken to the almost opaque azure of lapis…lovely, dark and deep. He kissed me. He kissed my lips, my eyelids, trailing down to my neck. I kissed back wantonly and then I began to cry. I didn't mean to…I didn't want to, but I couldn't seem to help it. I had been so deeply touched by this man that a river of tears broke loose. He held me and let me cry. He didn't tell me to hush or show any particular concern.

Tonight, we both knew we had crossed a threshold of trust and vulnerability that could only take us forward.

The firelight was diminishing and we were both sleepy. Peter's dark eyes began to lighten, as we both relaxed. We spent the night on the soft rug by the fire nestled in soft pillows and blankets. There was no doubt in me that we would become physical lovers in time.

As I drifted into sleep, the words from Calvin Miller's book, *The Singer,* came, "*What do you want to be when you grow up, little girl?*"

"*Alive,*" she said. "Alive," I repeated to myself.

Chapter Thirty-three

Over the ensuing months, Peter and I met in Washington, D.C., Philadelphia and Key West. What had begun as infatuation slowly and surely developed into love. We sent each other cards and flowers. Memorial Day, I lured him to my sanctuary, Daufuskie Island. He loved Daufuskie on first sight. I loved that he loved my barrier islands. It was there that we finally had a serious fight. Let me be clear, equals can do battle with words and emotions. Being evenly matched means no one ever wins, but both can lose. I can't even remember how the fight started. Somewhere in the middle of that idyllic weekend, something deadlocked. We had a meltdown.

"Damn it, Kai, you're overreacting," he said loudly.

"Don't yell at me!" I yelled at him.

"Let's just calm down and take some time out," as he reached for reason.

"I want to finish this now!" I wouldn't be reasonable.

"Stop it, Kai. You're getting carried away and I don't like it," he sounded very authoritative, like my father or a transplant surgeon.

"You want a time out, you got it," I barked as I stomped out of the cottage.

How many times have I told patients at this juncture in their love affairs that they would have "the fight"? They would passionately and authentically disagree. The key to long term commitment was to see if they could resolve it. Even if they needed to call a timeout and retreat for a while, they needed to come back together, hash it out, understand the underlying issues and finish it. By the time I agreed to a timeout, I was ready to flee the island and leave Peter in the dust. I dredged up a lot of old, negative "men experiences" and threw Peter into them. I felt self-righteous and put upon. I stormed down to the beach and plotted my escape. Major, major regression on my part. Fortunately, most of it happened inside me. This had the feel of self-sabotage. I was so good at running away, but could I stay and work this out? Deep inside, I think I knew that I had to go back to this man that I loved and reconcile our differences. I crept back to the cottage. I wondered if he had left, too. But he was waiting for me.

The screen door to the back porch squeaked like a dying chicken waiting to be plucked. So much for stealthy entrance. Peter was sitting in a wicker rocking chair on the side deck off the master bedroom. He was serenely reading a medical journal. He looked up as I came across the wide-slatted wooden floor with its light wash of white. He smiled. I softened...a little.

"Want to come sit on my lap?" Obviously, he wasn't as good at holding grudges as I was.

I sat down on a wicker cassock covered in green and yellow chintz...ten feet away. It was hard for me to look into his eyes.

"Tell me what just happened between us," he started. How could he be so calm – was he sitting on his feelings? He had been mad when he yelled at me.

"I'm not sure. Sometimes you sound very authoritarian... almost like my father."

"I'm not your father, Kai. Have no interest in coming off that way. I'm sorry if I did. Just tell me if I do it again."

"It annoys me when you do that, but I'm not sure that's what upset me."

"Then what did?" He was calm and composed.

I felt vulnerable and confused. I looked at him, caught his eyes.

"You just seem so, so perfect and powerful. I think you're used to all the nurses and staff at the hospital catering to your whim. It's like you don't want to be questioned. I can't be subservient to you, Peter. If I'm genuinely emotional, it's so unfair for you to tell me I'm overreacting or getting carried away." I sounded petulant to myself. It was hard to tell him what felt wrong.

"Honey, I live with a sixteen-year old girl who invented extreme emotion and thinks I don't do anything right. You need to ask her if I'm perfect. At the hospital, we all work as a team. Each person has their job to do. They are *not* subservient to me. That's just unfair. If you feel I'm treating you without respect, I need to get in touch with that. I don't feel I am. I have the utmost respect for you. As professionals, I see us as equals with different specialties. As parents, I see us on parallel tracks, able to help each other. As lovers and emotional partners, we are very compatible. I know I'm more rational than you are…I love your passion and expression."

He was being very honest. The truth was that I felt *very* vulnerable. Our lovemaking seemed to lower my defenses. I had fallen in love with Peter and, truth be told, I feared rejection… betrayal…abandonment. There it was again – the big three. This man met me on every level of my being and it was scaring the hell out of me. I had always felt I was capable of intimacy, but the men I had chosen in life weren't. So, here was intimacy with all the attendant ups and downs. Maybe it was me, after all, who wasn't capable of trust.

"I'm afraid of you, Peter. Maybe I'm not your equal after all. I just feel vulnerable. I've always run away when I feel like this. I *want* to stay and work this out with you." My eyes filled with tears, I felt I was close to doing what Stephanie had warned me about – blowing it!

"Will you come and sit on my lap and let me hold you?" Peter's voice was soft, inviting. Those were the longest ten feet of my life. I settled into his arms and laid my head on his chest. The tears came. Why was I crying again? It was definitely not rational.

When I quieted, he spoke, "You know that I love you deeply. I've only been in love once before and it lasted until she died. It will always be there in a way. I now have a second chance to love again. I am here, Kai. I'm not going to give up on us because of a fight or two or however many it takes for us to learn each other."

Peter never faltered. He had no intention of running or quitting our relationship. All that ideation had been mine.

In the end, we came to a mutual resolution that we loved each other, that we were committed to make the relationship work. It felt good. To seal it, we made love with the same fervor that had fueled our fight. We were definitely passionate equals and the time was spontaneously right. We reached a new plateau that weekend. We began to discuss how our children could meet.

Chapter Thirty-four

Steph was making up for lost time, romantically and academically. She had missed one whole semester of course work. Trying to keep me in the loop, she recommended that I read her religion course books, *Great Religions of the World* by Huston Smith and Karen Armstrong's *The History of God*. I started both of them and made it through Buddhism, Hinduism, Judaism, Islam and Christianity before I burned out. I read less than half of each. It reminded me why young people did graduate work, including medical school. At my age, I could barely comprehend the work she was doing. Stephanie was also taking a course based on Joseph Campbell's work and I did know about him. Campbell was famous for *The Power of Myth*, a series of videotaped interviews done by the television journalist, Bill Moyers. I had the complete set which was among my prized possessions. It had taken me years of weekend conferences and independent study to assimilate some of the knowledge Stephanie was getting in a few years. Age related wisdom was my only edge with her. Still, she inspired me to keep learning.

Stephanie brought Henry home to Charleston at spring break in mid-March. She called me to see if she could bring him to her next session. I was delighted and told her so. It was an important step for her to bring Henry into her therapy. Since she had a full week in Charleston, she scheduled a second hour to come alone as well.

I stepped into the waiting room to meet Henry for the first time and almost stumbled into him. Stephanie was standing by the bookshelf while Henry was exiting the restroom. We both opened our respective door simultaneously. He came through the door looking like a tall, quite thin Little Orphan Annie! The red curly mop of hair could have been Annie's wig. I remembered that Stephanie had chosen to wear a beautiful long red wig after her chemo. When Stephanie started grinning, I thought it was a joke. Henry must have been used to all manner of looks because he strode towards me with his hand out, totally nonplussed.

"Hi, Dr. Kai. I'm Henry," and shook my hand.

"And his hair is real," added Stephanie.

"Henry, so glad to meet you. Stephanie never mentioned your hair," I smiled.

"It's a great ice breaker," his brown eyes flashed behind rimless glasses. He looked much younger than his twenty-nine years. He also looked kind of like Steve Jobs with brown hair at his same age. There was an aura about both of them that exuded quirky intelligence. I knew he had a full fellowship for his doctoral work. I liked him immediately. On the way back to my office, we talked about the red hair in his very Irish family. They had moved from Boston to California when he was a child. The red hair gene had come from his mother's line, he told me like a true geneticist. His older brother was a motorcycle mechanic. The younger was backpacking across Europe. Stephanie welcomed Henry to sit beside her, so unlike what she had done with her father.

With no warning whatsoever, Henry said, "Stephanie and I are getting married."

Marriage? They had only known each other since last September when she returned to school. My head swiveled towards Stephanie. She looked like the Cheshire Cat. I hadn't seen Stephanie in the flesh since Christmas. The quiet interlude had lulled me into complacency.

"Carpe diem." She raised her hands palms upward and shrugged her shoulders.

"Okayyy," I stalled for time to process.

"So, what do you think?" she asked.

"It seems like you are moving at the speed of light," I said, looking from one to the other. My protective antennae were fully operational.

"Dr. Kai, I hope you don't mind me calling you that?" Henry raised his thick chestnut-colored eyebrows questioningly.

"It's quite all right," I smiled.

"I feel I have known Stephanie all my life. Even before

this life, maybe. She is my soul mate. I want her to be my wife. I have never loved a woman the way I love her." He was unconsciously speaking with his hands as he touched his heart.

I glanced at Stephanie. She was looking at him, in profile to me, completely absorbed in the moment and in him.

I knew that Stephanie and Henry had come for my affirmation of their plans to marry. It was usually important to patients that their therapists be supportive of important life decisions. At times, we couldn't be because there was a terrible lack of balance in them. Or a decision was a replay of some old, destructive pattern. There was none of that now. They were not asking permission, just respecting my relationship with Stephanie. Intuitively, it felt right, but I was off balance. I could never anticipate the swings in her life.

I remained silent, savoring the peacefulness as Stephanie and Henry stayed in their own world for a few more minutes. Stephanie turned back to me.

"Can you give us your blessing, Kai?"

Before I could answer, Stephanie continued with no hint of self-pity, "We know that we might not have that long together. Whatever time we have, six months, a year, five years - it is important for us to spend it together, committed." The unspoken had now been said. Stephanie's illness was definitely part of the timing.

"It will not be easy, Henry, if you have to see her suffer," I said, trying hard not to take away from their happiness.

"I know," he spoke softly.

"Have you talked to your parents yet, Steph?"

"Tonight. Two-Pop and Nana are coming to Mom and Dad's house for supper. They already feel like they know Henry. I just wanted to have you with me on this."

I could think of other issues, but Stephanie had spoken to my main concern. I was relieved that nothing need stand in the way of what they wanted from me.

"Thank you for honoring our work together, Stephanie. I am with you. May you be blessed with peace and joy."

After that, we just chatted superficially for a while and stopped early. They had done what they came to do.

Stephanie returned for her second session three days later. She stood in front of her favorite painting for a long time, the one of the antique tea set with flowers. When she turned toward me, she seemed exceptionally subdued. With a quiet depth in her voice, she said, "I am pregnant, Kai."

A perfect stillness filled the room. I closed my eyes, trying to hide the truth in those windows of my soul. A deep, visceral pang of fear swept through me. Stephanie pregnant? I was holding my breath as I tried to stay calm. The roller coaster ride was moving again. The "car" was swooping down into a trough and I prayed it wouldn't run off the rails.

"How far along are you?" I blurted out, in spite of my attempts not to.

"I think about fourteen weeks."

My thoughts leapt ahead. What did AML do to a developing baby? Did she still have time for a safe abortion? Was that even an option? I remembered the session we had about sex. She knew that Gellman and Halvorsen wanted her to use birth control. She hated how "the pill" made her feel. I had heard from a number of patients over the years that excess estrogen and progesterone created a mental fog for them. Fluid retention and bloating were other side effects. Stephanie and I had discussed condoms. Good, expensive condoms. It appeared that the good, expensive condoms had failed.

Therapeutic hypotheses were flooding my mind. Did Steph and Henry subliminally want to have a baby to create a legacy? Something that would survive the leukemia? Would Stephanie have sabotaged a condom to set it up? Force a marriage? I discarded that one right away. The rule of thumb in psychiatric exploration is to examine *all* possibilities, even the ones you don't like or may be blinded to by your own prejudice. Was Stephanie replaying her mother's tapes? Were the two of them just careless? I remember Steph flipping off a comment in a session after she found out about her mother's decision to carry her pregnancy: "I probably would have had an abortion." This situation was different. Her mother didn't have leukemia when she was pregnant with Stephanie or her sister, Alexis. What would pregnancy do to her leukemia presently in remission? I needed to talk to Peter ASAP. It was possible that Steph would qualify for medical abortion. My mind felt like a runaway train. All these thoughts had taken only a few seconds. I needed to bring some of my questions into dialogue.

"How long have you known you were pregnant, Steph?"

"Ever since the chemo my periods have been erratic. I had some spotting six weeks ago. My body had been feeling different though, especially my breasts. They were tender. When I finally did one of those drugstore stick tests, it was positive. I told Henry; he was shocked. I'll tell you about that in a minute. At first, I was afraid. I didn't know how pregnancy hormones would affect my remission. What if it caused a recurrence of my leukemia? Then what?" She trailed off. So, she had been thinking about all the ramifications.

"Then what, Stephanie?"

She sat quietly. There was palpable tension between us.

"I will not take my baby's life to save my own, Kai. Don't you go there, too. I've already had to fight this battle with Henry and my dad."

"Tell me what battles you have fought," I leaned towards her slightly.

"Henry really freaked out when I first told him. I've never seen him react like that about anything. He's been so cool about the leukemia. I mean he freaked. He wanted me to have an abortion when we came to Charleston. We got into a big fight."

"He betrayed none of that conflict when he was here."

"He promised to let me tell you about the baby when I came back to see you."

"So, you deliberately separated the pregnancy from the marriage for my benefit?"

"No…yes…I was afraid you might not approve. I need you on my side to get through this with Henry and Dad."

Stephanie visibly drooped at this point, like she was tired or dispirited. Then, she lifted her head and spoke again, "I told Henry what I just said to you, 'I won't take my baby's life to save my own.' We got into another fight about it the night we were home after we saw you. He stormed out. Dad and Victoria heard him slam the front door. So I told them about the baby. Believe it or not, Victoria…Mom, was the one who really came through. Dad couldn't even talk. Mom just came over and held me. I don't remember her doing that since I was a kid," Stephanie paused and closed her eyes. She was trying not to cry. She opened her eyes and went on, "Mom asked Dad to let us be alone. We sat next to each other at the kitchen table and talked, like a real mother and daughter. She understands.

She was never able to get pregnant, yet she *knows* how I feel about this baby."

I was hanging on her every word, amazed. Stephanie had come home to her mother; the one who had taken her in long years ago and had been tangled up in "the secret" Stephanie's whole life. She had put all her yearnings into the only child she would ever have. In spite of flaws, she had been steadfast through it all. Had she been here, I would have given her a standing ovation. This pregnancy had brought Stephanie full circle with her true mother work. Why was I so surprised? Her healing matrix far exceeded what I could anticipate.

She continued, "When Henry came back to the house, he and Dad talked alone for a while; then they walked into the kitchen and sat down across from Mom and me. It was like a family-style inquisition." Stephanie went on to relay the whole discussion, almost word for word.

"Henry asked if my trying to carry this baby could cost me my life and the baby's. That scared me. I asked him what he meant. He said, 'If this pregnancy forces you out of remission, or you simply come out on your own, you might not be able to have a stem cell transplant or any further chemo without harming the baby. If you become as ill as you did before, you could die and the baby would die, too.'"

"I told them all that is just a risk I will have to take! What if my mother had only thought of herself? Dad said just what you did, Kai, 'Your mother didn't have an active case of leukemia when she was pregnant with you. We don't know what she would have done. Besides, making the decision to have an abortion is never easy for any woman.'"

"Mom helped again, 'Steve, I'm not sure you are listening. Please try, honey.'"

"I know you all love me and want to protect me, but this is my decision. I will talk to Kai, Dr. Gellman and Dr. H, too. It's only fair that they know. They won't change my mind, I can tell you that."

Henry kept shaking his head, 'How could you be so sure about all this? Your mind is made up even before you talk to your doctors? If you relapse, there will be definitive medical reasons to intervene, even over your objections. It's my baby, too. And you are my wife'.

Not yet! Not 'til we figure this out. I didn't plan to get pregnant. Henry, you know we took precautions to prevent it. Our efforts failed. Maybe it was simply a failed condom or maybe it was divine intervention. Don't any of you have the least bit of faith?"

"Henry said, 'It's not about faith. It's about life and death!'"

"Then, a preternatural calmness came over me before I responded, 'How can you separate faith from life and death? Living and dying are totally connected. Faith is the foundation for both. Taking chances, living life without fear will ultimately prepare me for dying. I want to be free from the fear. Can't you understand that? Intuitively, I know there is a spiritual force inside me that I can trust. It's pointing me to life…telling me to risk it. Today, that is all I know. Tomorrow, it might say something else.'"

She stopped and looked at me as if to say, "Are you still with me?"

I was absolutely "still with her" and was in the ranks of those feeling afraid. Whatever else I wanted to do for her, she just needed me to be with her.

"I don't want this pregnancy to be the cause of your death, Stephanie. I think that is what Henry and your father are saying. That's probably selfish for all of us to say, but it's the truth. You're right that all of us are afraid. In one way or another, we are asking you to save us from the fear of losing you. I am feeling that right now. The pregnancy is an added dimension of risk to your blood cancer."

"What if pregnancy protects me? Cures me?" she retorted.

That had honestly never crossed my mind. What if it cured her? My need to talk to Peter intensified. All of a sudden, I felt better. A little surge of hope swelled up inside me.

She never took her eyes from mine. She never wavered or stumbled over her words. She had spoken her truth which was some compilation of all her studies, her experience, her beliefs, her concepts of faith.

Ostensibly, I was older and wiser than Stephanie, but who was the teacher between us now? One of the great myths of psychiatry was being detonated: that psychiatrists have all the answers. That we know the truth and that patients just have to pull in, fill'er up, and drive on by in life. A more accurate model might be that we therapists simply make a safe container for the patient while they learn to listen to the healer deep within themselves. It is this healer who truly knows what they need to be whole. It was this healer that Stephanie was listening to. Ironically, I was listening to hers as mine awoke from its slumber.

"Stephanie, I hear you. I totally honor that you have spoken your deepest truth. Whatever happens, you have my full support. I only hope that someday I will have the clarity of faith that you do. If you need to bring your whole family in here, we can do that. Or bring Henry back again. Is Henry okay now? Does he support you?"

"He wanted me to talk to you and Gellman, but it's been Victoria he has listened to the most. He seems to trust her right now more than he does me. Isn't that amazing? He loves me, Kai, and I trust that. I think his love will be greater than his fear."

There was no more for us to say. We stood and hugged. We held on to each other a long time. Neither one of us wanted to let go. I think we were afraid the other one would collapse.

With that, she left.

Chapter Thirty-five

Peter usually called me from New York when he finished rounds at the hospital, sometime between early evening and ten o'clock. His dedication to his work often concerned me. Did he have any time for his personal relationships? Tonight, I needed to talk to him about Stephanie. I'd almost called him during my lunch hour, but I didn't want us to be rushed or distracted by work. Now it was almost nine and the last vestiges of early spring light were giving way to the dark. I felt uneasy. The small ray of hope I had felt during my session with Stephanie that morning seemed to be dissipating into the encroaching dark. The kids were on spring break with Trey. I savored the aloneness but needed to hear Peter's voice. I needed some kind of reassurance. When I called, the voice mail answered. I pressed three to leave a message.

"Hi, sweetheart, it's me. Really need to talk to you as soon as you can light somewhere. Call the land line; I'm at home."

I decided to get in the tub, therapy to me. The Jacuzzi was half full when the phone rang. It was Gracen. I was glad to hear from her, but disappointed it wasn't Peter.

"Hi, Mom, wha's up?" Gracen sounded upbeat.

"Just running water for my tub bath, hon pie."

"Mom, I just read in a magazine that soaking in hot water for more than twenty minutes isn't good for your skin."

Sometimes Gracen's thirteen-year-old know-it-all take on life was grating. She believed everything she read in her myriad of magazines, with their skinny models prancing around in size two bikinis, air brushed as they were, articles on weight loss, fashion, make-up and the love lives of movie stars.

"Oh, but it's so good for my soul." I added some mango almond bath oil to the water as I spoke. The candles were already lit so I shed my clothes and slipped into the warm, soothing water.

"So, how's Amelia Island?" I took a sip of Welch's Light grape juice over ice. Next best thing to wine for phenols, and it didn't make me feel sick.

"It's okay, I guess. Dad's got a new girlfriend here with us."

"What happened to the last one...Summer, or was it Autumn?"

"Summer. I liked her. They broke up. This one's named Crystal. Mom, she's not much older than Andrew. Dad is forty-six. I think she's twenty-five. She's really ditzy. She works in Dad's company. A secretary or assistant. She also smokes, Mom. I can't believe Dad would date a woman that smokes. He's such a health fanatic. Andrew and I trounced her and Dad in tennis yesterday. Dad got really mad. You know how he likes to win. I think Andrew's got the hots for her. He's been flirting with her and blushes when she whispers in his ear. That's sick, Mom, Andrew lusting after Dad's girlfriend."

"Oedipus did it," I couldn't help myself.

"What? Mom, I'm being serious," she admonished.

"I'm sorry, Gracen. Your Dad is way off my radar these days. Maybe you better tell him how you feel about his dating a woman so young."

"It's not just that she's young, she's so...so...provocative."

I couldn't believe my thirteen-year old knew that word.

"As in?" I could tell she wanted to blow off some steam.

"As in low-cut halter tops and short shorts. Her bikinis are disgusting."

I wondered if Gracen was a little jealous, or feeling competitive for her father's attention.

"So, I am here and you are there. What about talking to your father?" I asked again.

"Maybe after we're home. I don't want to make him feel bad."

Gracen was very protective of her father since the divorce. I knew she was in the final phase of being Daddy's girl. Eventually, she would have to resolve her childlike attachments to her father and turn to the pathway of the adult woman. So much of the self-esteem and self-love she needs to bring to this initiation process stems from the value and affirmation gifted by her father. Trey had done a pretty good job of that.

"Are you having fun?" I wanted to get back to something upbeat.

"Andrew and I really like the jet skis and windsurfers, and the food. Crystal's a vegan. She won't even eat honey from bees raised in captivity. Don't you think that's a little extreme? She wants to buy Andrew a book about eating vegan. He seems really interested. It's completely crazy for a vegan to smoke. That is twisted!"

I sat up in the tub. Now, this had my full attention. Just a minute, Ms. black-widow-Crystal-Summer, you keep your extreme idealism away from *my* son.

"Where is Andrew now?"

"He's out in the pool with *her*."

"Where's your Dad?"

"Playing tennis with some guys."

"Ask Andrew to call me when he comes in."

"Okay, Mom. Just wanted to check in. I love you, Mutti-lein." She used the German form of mama she'd learned in Holland. She was a crafty little thing. She had tattled on Trey and Andrew all under the guise of checking in.

As soon as I hung up, the phone rang again. I was adding some more hot water and oil to the bath and knocked the receiver off the side of the tub. It bounced off the marble step and skidded across the dark green marble tiles. "Jeez Louise," I muttered as I launched out of the water and grabbed the phone.

"Andrew?" I wondered aloud.

"Nope, Peter."

I settled back down in the tub as the fragrance of mango wafted up with sloshing water.

"Hi, Peter. So glad to hear your voice." I had almost forgotten about Stephanie.

"I've been trying to call for the last twenty minutes." He sounded mildly annoyed.

"I'm sorry. Gracen called just after I left your message."

"I just got home, anyway. Do you mind if I eat a ham sandwich while we talk?"

"Where's Claire?" I inquired about his daughter.

"Studying upstairs. You sounded upset on the message you left. Is Stephanie okay?"

"Oh, Peter. I saw her today and she dropped a bombshell. She's pregnant."

"What! Are you sure? I mean, is she sure?"

"Absolutely sure. Fourteen weeks. She didn't tell anybody because she didn't want anyone to talk her out of staying with it. I saw her with her boyfriend, Henry, a few days ago. They're going to get married. Peter, I'm really afraid for her. Tell me what this means. What does pregnancy do for remission?"

"I've only had a few cases and they usually get an abortion."

"She clearly does *not* want that."

"I had one case, a woman in her late thirties who had tried to get pregnant for years. She finally did and developed a non-

Hodgkin's lymphoma. She insisted on carrying the pregnancy at any cost to herself. We used a low-dose chemo throughout the last two trimesters which really should have done nothing. She went into remission and had a normal, healthy little boy. I always considered it somewhat miraculous."

"Did the pregnancy cause the lymphoma?"

"We didn't think so. I think it was just coincidental. There was a family history in that patient's case."

"Does pregnancy ever protect someone in remission?"

"I'm not aware of any research on that. I need to ask around."

"It just makes sense that the high levels of hormones, estrogen and progesterone, might be protective, like a primitive defense mechanism to help the fetus survive." I was really hoping so anyway.

"Maybe it did, in that case. The baby is almost ten years old now. And the mother is perfectly fine. On the other hand, with other mothers who conceive after forty, we see lymphomas precipitate after birth. I've had three or four of those."

"Peter, what if Stephanie comes out of remission in the next two or three months? Is there any regimen you could recommend?"

"No, not without irreparably harming the baby, especially in the first two trimesters. If she relapsed like before, it could kill her without treatment."

I felt fear crawling back into my gut.

"Tell me something hopeful, Peter. Lie to me, if necessary."

"Stephanie is strong, Kai. She's responded beautifully to initial treatment which started late. She's in full remission. No abnormal proliferation of blast cells, so we didn't need the stem cell transplant. Let's try not to cross that bridge before we get to it. She's no ordinary patient for either one of us. I've listened to you for months, Kai. God's hand is all over this case."

"Some people under God's hand die, Peter."

"And some live, Kai. Until we know otherwise, let's ask for her and the baby to live. We need to have hope."

That was the most overtly religious thing Peter Halvorsen had ever said to me. He was quiet about his own spiritual beliefs, although he was very attentive and accepting when I talked about my own.

"I wish you were here to hold me right now."

"Want me to fly down tonight?"

I had to smile at his attempts to make me feel better.

"I loved being with you last weekend."

I'd flown to New York City and we'd driven to the beach house in the Hamptons again.

"Ummm," I murmured as I sunk farther down in the warm water, remembering.

"Not as much fun being in the tub alone."

"If I wasn't so dog tired, I would fly down."

"Peter, how do you do oncology every day? How do you

stay positive and hopeful?" I couldn't seem to put the Stephanie piece to rest tonight.

"Well, my war is with cancer. I do everything I can to keep up with research and treatment. I take each case, one by one, every day. I do my best. I win some, lose some, and some are still to be decided. Not always my call."

"But, don't you have a Stephanie sometimes? One that gets past your defenses and imprints your heart?"

"Most all of my patients are special to me, Kai. When we get good news, I give them a happy face sticker. With bad news, they get a hug. Hope is a gift that sustains me and my patients." He sighed. "I love you, Kai. Let go of Stephanie a while. You're just not in charge tonight."

"Is there any doubt in your mind why I love you, Dr. H?"

"My great prowess as a lover?"

"Well, there's that, too."

"I need your love, Kai. I need to love you and be loved by you. And right now, I also need sleep. I'm going to bed. Regretfully, alone." We said good night.

So, I'm not in charge tonight. What a great illusion to think I am ever in charge of what happens in life. I am loved instead. I slipped all the way under the scented water and floated in the freedom of it all.

Chapter Thirty-six

The emotional storm around Stephanie's pregnancy abated, as all storms do. She weathered it on safe, high psychological ground while protecting herself from the fear of those who loved her. Waiting on feedback from her oncology doctors was hard. She did not want to do battle with them too. Her inner judge had already ruled: the verdict was final. She hoped the rest of the jury would cast their votes for her.

Her family rallied. They all met with Rob Gellman who represented Peter Halvorsen, as well. In essence, both doctors finally agreed to honor Stephanie's wishes to continue her pregnancy. They would follow her closely over the next six months with regular bloodwork and coordinate her physical exams with her Chicago specialists. This way, she could return to school and complete her degrees. If she relapsed with AML, they would all confer on the best way to proceed. Apparently, Dr. Gellman did a masterful job of addressing her family's concerns…all of them. It was another turning point for Henry and Stephanie. They reconciled their original intent to live life as fully as possible, as long as they could. They set their wedding date for the summer solstice the third week in June. Fittingly, it would be the day of longest light in the year.

I found myself longing for Peter. I don't think it had anything to do with Stephanie. Peter and I talked on the phone every night but I needed his touch, to see his eyes, bask in his smile. I also needed to be seen and touched by him. To complicate matters, our children's winter and spring breaks were not the same. He was coming for Stephanie's wedding in June but that was months away. The reality of having a long distance relationship was becoming more and more clear. I could not or would not go to New York because Andrew's upcoming spring break was his last one in high school. I was shocked that he wanted to spend it with Gracen and me! We decided to go to Disney World, Sea World and Legoland. Graduation would follow in May.

It seemed unreal that after eighteen years of nurturing, protecting and guiding that it was time for Andrew to leave home. He was ready to go to college and stay for the best part of a year. His red jeep, given to him by his father when he got his driver's license, would be his transportation to a whole new world.

Somewhere, amidst all the talk about roommates, dorms, and spending money, Andrew started talking about finding brothers in college.

"Here's the thing, Mom, I've never had a brother. There would be brothers for me in college, maybe in a fraternity. I'm going to check it out. I really want some brothers."

Andrew and I had never talked about him not having a biological brother. Not once. It was sobering to hear him speak so earnestly about his need to belong to a brotherhood. At that moment, I was so full of love and hope and excitement for him. He knew what he needed and he was ready to go get it.

Still, there was a niggling sense of dread. Andrew, Gracen and I had been a family unit for years. How would Gracen and I do without him? How had I done when my brother Mark left for college?

I was almost Gracen's age when, early one morning, our father drove him to The Citadel. Jamey, Mom and I hovered around them in the kitchen as they choked down cinnamon rolls and coffee. It was still dark outside, adding to the emotional pall in the house. No one showed any emotion, especially Mark. I did *not* want him to leave me. I wanted to cry, but we all jointly put up a good front as the two of them loaded up the car and drove off. Deep inside, I was bereft. I knew that our family had irrevocably changed. Little did I know that except for holiday visits, he would never live at home again.

This time my son was leaving me. I was about to join a long line of mothers throughout the ages, whose job being done, released their sons. How bittersweet it must have been for them, as it was for me now. But, this I was coming to know: mothers cannot make their sons into men; brothers, fathers, male mentors and friends do that. It was to them that Andrew, as Mark before him, would turn.

This time, if I needed to cry, I would. So would Gracen.

Chapter Thirty-seven

Peter was taking a commercial flight down to attend the wedding and I was late picking him up at the airport. Thankfully, the plane was behind schedule. He was standing outside baggage claim with his iPhone to his ear. I had left my phone recharging at home. He could get annoyed with people who were late...just like my father used to do. But, my father he was not! I flashed my lights as I pulled up to the curb.

"Want a ride, stranger?" I spoke through the open passenger side window. He broke into a grin. If I could just disconnect him from all his electronic devices and whisk him to Middleton Place Gardens, we could have an hour alone before Stephanie and Henry's wedding at 6:00 p.m.

Middleton was one of my closest outdoor sanctuaries as it was only twenty miles northwest of the Charleston peninsula. I wanted to show Peter the formal gardens which spread along the banks and graceful waters of the Ashley River. Traffic was heavy but we arrived with time to spare. We entered the gardens proper and strolled along the pathway running beside the long, rectangular reflection pool.

"White swans, huh?" he asked as he stopped and stared at the beautiful birds.

"They started a breeding program years ago with six little cygnets. These two survived alligators which marauded from the nearby marsh and wetlands."

"Alligators?" Peter looked at me in horror.

"All along the Lowcountry coast and rivers," I was looking at him askance as I continued playing amateur tour guide.

"The original plantation house and formal gardens were built in the 1740s when South Carolina was still a colony of the British crown. One of the family descendants signed the Declaration of Independence. Less than a hundred years later, his grandson signed the Ordinance of Secession from the United States. At the end of the Civil War, the Union Army looted and torched the house and gardens, leaving only the south flanker building standing. It is the Middleton museum today. Twenty-odd years after the Civil War ended, the earthquake of 1886 that hit Charleston almost destroyed the gardens. The terraces were ripped open and the Butterfly Lakes, which took lots of slaves ten years to build, were sucked dry in minutes."

"It wasn't until the 1950s that the family began the massive project of restoring the gardens to their original splendor," I continued. "I hope you get to meet my friend, Charles, the heir that established the non-profit foundation which maintains Middleton now."

I loved this place. My father had first brought my mother and me here when I was nine years old. During medical school,

I would drive out in the spring when azaleas of every color were blooming. Masses of blooms on the hillside across from the rice mill was an astonishing sight, nature's version of "the greatest show on earth". I had made it a tradition to come most every spring thereafter. Was there a more beautiful place on earth to get married?

We strolled through the huge old camellia bushes and I lured him into one of the Secret Gardens, which was carefully hidden amongst their dense foliage. Cypress, tea olive, and dogwoods ringed the hidden space, as well. I had never kissed a man in Middleton Gardens, so I made a little game out of kissing him at the major landmarks of the extensive sixty acre gardens: the Octagonal Garden, the Sundial Garden, the alabaster *Wood Nymph* statue. Finally, we approached the Middleton Oak, thought to be almost a thousand years old. Even though one of its branches had broken some years before, its broad canopy of leaves was magnificent and its huge, gnarled branches bowed to the ground overlooking the rice paddies flooded by the incoming tide. Many couples married under this grand old live oak with its long, draping swaths of Spanish moss. Stephanie would marry on the formal stepped terraces that began behind the plantation house's parterre, or ornamental garden, and cascaded down to the famed Butterfly Lakes. Perhaps, Peter and I would marry out here one day. No doubt this is the place I would choose.

After leaving the majestic live oak tree, we headed to the wedding site. Some fifty friends and family were gathering to sit on the narrow wooden benches midway down the green steppes. A lone harpist was playing Pachelbel's *Canon in D Major*. I gazed out over the beautiful vista and whispered to Peter, "*This is as good as it gets.*" My friend, Francesca, said that to me when life gave one of us a moment of unparalleled beauty and perfection. I'm not sure Peter fully understood, but he smiled and squeezed my hand.

The harpist began the classical chorus of Beethoven's *Ninth Symphony*. The resonance of plucked strings carried only the melody of the mighty piece, but it evoked the memory of the written German words even as they stirred my heart: *Freude!* Joy! *Freude!* Joy!

Henry and his father strode to the front of a small marble altar with the Reverend Pat McKenna from Grace Episcopal Church. As the music filled the air, Two-Pop and Nana, Steve and Victoria, Rebecca and Alexis and Henry's mother and sister made a human arc behind the altar.

Henry's eyes lifted and gazed beyond the attending guests. We turned as one to see Stephanie standing at the top of the first terrace, cast in silhouette by the lowering, afternoon sun behind her. When she stepped out of shadow into color, she was regal in a woodland fairy way. The simple wedding dress of soft ivory silk was accentuated by a delicate mantilla veil pinned to the back of her flowing blond hair. Victoria had worn it when she married Stephanie's father. She was barefoot. The light in her eyes shone like emeralds, even from a distance. Her left hand covered her child nestled underneath the silk and the right carried a spray of late-blooming, light pink azaleas, so like the ones in her favorite picture at my office.

Had it only been two years since Stephanie had come into my life, burst into it with her drama of life and death? Changed us both irrevocably. Today, she would marry. And then...and then.... I did not need to go there just now. Today was full of joy and Stephanie carried life within her.

Chapter Thirty-eight

There was no time for a honeymoon. Stephanie and Henry finished the second session of summer school and started the fall semester after Labor Day. She and I had continued our phone sessions every two weeks since the wedding. She kept me "up to snuff" with her growing pregnancy. Some women suffer from first trimester fatigue and morning sickness and second trimester cravings and weight gain. Many enter the third trimester with the grace of a hippopotamus. It was almost annoying that Stephanie's first two trimesters were so smooth. She did yoga and meditation, exercised and napped almost every day. This driven, overachiever became mellow, almost a poster girl for a healthy pregnancy. It seemed like she discussed her sex life with Henry every time we talked.

"Kai, did you feel voluptuous when you were pregnant?" she launched into our August phone session.

"I did grow boobs, if that's what you mean."

"Well, not just that. My whole body feels softer, rounder. It's like I'm growing into a woman."

"I do remember that, Steph. You and I were both tomboys - tall, thin, wiry/athletic types. The hormones of pregnancy and the changes to the body are pretty pronounced."

"I love it. Henry says I'm glowing. My complexion is phenomenal. And sex has been so-o-o good."

"You're lucky, Stephanie, some women feel like blimps and some men don't like sex with blimps."

"So, how are you and Dr. H doing?"

"He's a jewel, Ms. Stephanie, as you well know."

"Will you marry him? Some day in the future, I mean."

"You will be one of the first to know! Lots of logistics to work out. I really don't think I can live in New York City. I've often thought I would die if I had to leave the marsh, creeks and trees of the Lowcountry. Hollings Cancer Center right here in Charleston is a world class treatment facility now and Peter would make a great addition to their stem cell transplant team. He has almost a year left on his contract with Sloan Kettering. His daughter Claire seems to like my kids and she loves the beaches. I'm hopeful it can all work out."

"I'm coming home to Charleston to have my baby, Kai. Just have to. Due date is two days after Thanksgiving."

"What if you go into labor early?"

"At the first signs, Henry and I are 'flying low' in my Jetta. It's a twelve-hour drive at that speed."

I visualized Stephanie giving birth in a car on an interstate highway.

"Don't you have exams between Thanksgiving and Christmas?"

"No. Two of my three courses are self-study with papers. The third is a weekly symposium. I can easily finish my course work by Thanksgiving. Henry could be teaching most of the courses he's in."

"Have you found out the sex of the baby?"

"Not going to. Whatever we have is fine with us."

"Names?"

"Lots of family names to choose from. We love my birth mother's name, Alexandra, if it's a girl. Boys' names are harder. Kai, I feel so good. It just doesn't seem possible that the leukemia could come back. I only have three months to go. The baby could live on its own soon, couldn't it?"

"Give that baby as much time as you can."

"I have a feeling about this, Kai. I'm going to carry her to term."

"Her?"

"Did I say that?" she laughed.

"Stephanie, you did find out!"

"No, no, I didn't. Just a feeling."

"Will you be home before Thanksgiving so I can *see* if you are the least bit hippo-esque?"

"Driving on Wednesday before."

"You will drive *very* carefully. Thanksgiving traffic is so heavy."

"Yes, Mother-r-r."

I blushed. "Can't help myself, Steph."

As it turned out, Stephanie and Henry drove straight to the hospital in Charleston the day before Thanksgiving. Her water had broken four hours away. Still in the car, she called her grandmother, Rebecca, and sister, Alexis, and begged them to get on a plane. They did. The Edinger crowd met her at MUSC hospital OB unit. Ten hours after her arrival in the dark of Thanksgiving morning, Stephanie gave birth to an eight pound, one ounce baby girl. She phoned and told me they named her Alexandra Rebecca and were going to call her Sasha. I visited late on Thanksgiving Day. Stephanie was sleeping in her room when I got to the hospital. The baby was asleep in a white bassinette pulled close to her mother's bed while Henry dozed in a chair in the corner. I tiptoed to the baby and listened to her breathe along with her mother and father. I stood by Stephanie's bed, looking at her in peaceful repose. Instead of a sterile isolation unit recovering from chemotherapy, Stephanie had just given birth to new life.

"Let her live. Please let this be the end of her suffering," I sent out a prayer to the universe. It winged its way through the night and dissolved into the universe as I slipped away without waking any of them.

Chapter Thirty-nine

Christmas was misbehaving. After twenty years of the "Great Dichotomy" before the holidays, there wasn't one this year. No one had been hospitalized. Scrooge and the Grinch had not been invited. Aberrant as it was, I let my guard down a bit. My patients were doing exceptionally well. Several had graduated, leaving openings for me to take new patients after the new year.

To top it off, I'd had an amazing session with Julia earlier in the day. She had spent months now, sifting through the remains of her lost self. She was writing poetry, taking classes in psychology at the College of Charleston, as well as being in marriage counseling with her husband. She had revisited her marriage and found much to salvage. Julia was amazed at what she was learning about Dan...and herself.

"Honestly, Kai," she said, "I always thought he had left me for his work but, as it turns out, when I had babies, he said I had no sexual interest in him. I never realized that I left first." She had been gone from Dan for a long time. Julia's ability to look at her own behaviors instead of cementing herself in blame had allowed her to make extraordinary progress in her therapy. The anger that had brought her back to life was being channeled into learning. Even her relationship with her children had altered dramatically.

Two of them were coming home for the summer to work. When Julia stopped clinging to her children, they wanted to be with her.

"Before I leave today," said Julia, "I want to speak an intention out loud to you." This was therapy talk for setting a goal and making a commitment to attain it.

"I want to take one of my poems to the top of Kilimanjaro. I will have to find a mountain climbing group and train for it. Then travel to Tanzania. I *intend* to do it by summer, a year from now."

If she needed to actually climb a mountain to claim her new self, she could and probably would. She was soaring so high emotionally, I imagined she could fly to Kilimanjaro on the wings of her phoenix, the mythical bird that rose from the ashes to bring new life.

Being with Julia had given me a lift. I remembered her first session, when she was paralyzed with depression, and then her times of rage. Now I could see an amazing transformation taking place. The spiral of her life was turning on an ascendant arc.

Julia often thought that she trudged down her pathway only to stumble and go backwards. She had felt trapped in this linear back and forth model. She was surprised when I shared my working model of her life process as a spiral with all the points of her history and experience imprinted on it, like genes along DNA. The absolute paradox of this model to me is that after an ascendant arc, life *must* turn into a descendant phase to make way for more growth and upward movement. This is what I observed in most every patient, including Julia and Stephanie. Just as their DNA is unique, so are the spirals that make up their lives; so individual that I could no more "mix up" or forget them than I could the fables of Goldilocks and the Three Bears or Cinderella.

As I finished my day, my thoughts turned to Peter. This was my first Christmas with him. In two days Andrew, Gracen and I were flying up to the City to meet Peter and Claire. Then, we were driving to the Finger Lakes in upstate New York to meet his brother, Lars, and family at their lake house. It would give us all a few days before Christmas Eve. Snow was forecast. Trey had agreed to give us an extra day this year to make the trip. It was possible we would get snowed in. Lars and Ellie had two teens to add to the mix. God help us with five of Them and only four of us.

I was so excited. I felt like I was five again when I got an adoption doll my last year in Oklahoma and, with the help of my mother, filled out her "papers" to name her Elsa. Maybe I had spiraled to a place of true peace with all that had transpired in the intervening years with my grandmother and marriage. I remembered Stephanie's Christmas gift to me last year: mercy. This year my gift was love.

Chapter Forty

Life was good, rich and full. The earliest signs of spring, the Japanese Magnolias and crocus, had crept into bloom overnight, pushing winter away. My beloved spring was here ushering in longer hours of light and warmth. Soon outrageous beauty would intoxicate us all. And tourists would come. Conde Nast had voted Charleston the Number One destination in the U.S. (and second in the world). Word was out and I did not relish the idea of sharing my lovely, quaint city with the rest of the world.

Apart from the pull of nature, I was ensconced in the safety of my office addressing depression and anxiety in concert with patients all day. Andrew's senior year would be over soon. He had made early acceptance to the Honors College at my old alma mater, University of South Carolina. He made the decision himself. This was not my far-flung kid. Gracen was already talking about Colorado and New Mexico. Her big criteria seemed to be close-by skiing.

By the end of my day, the universe had shifted. When Stephanie had given birth, I had prayed for her suffering to end. It was not to be. There would be another spiral on her leukemia journey. For both of us, the descent on her spiral would be perilous, frightening. She came out of remission on May tenth, three days before receiving her PhD from the University of Chicago.

Stephanie had been sick the week before with a cold. That morning she woke up sick like she had been in Switzerland almost two years before. I got a call from Peter between my 11:00 and 12:00 patients. He frequently called just to say he loved me. I could hear in his voice that something was amiss.

"Hi, Kai, got some news, sweetheart."

"What's wrong, Peter? Are you all right? Is Claire?"

"We're all fine. It's Stephanie. She woke up yesterday feeling horrible. Gellman ordered blood work and bone marrow to be done by a colleague of his at the Medical University of Illinois at Chicago. Malignant blast cells are proliferating wildly. Her leukemia has come back. As we speak, Henry is driving her and the baby straight to New York. Dr. Edinger and the family are on the way up. As soon as Stephanie gets here, I'll do another bone marrow."

I felt faint and sat down hard in my desk chair, leaning my head down to my feet.

"Kai?" Peter called to me.

"I'm here. Just lightheaded. Tell me what happens next."

"Apparently, Steven Edinger booked a ticket for Alexis and her grandmother to take a flight out of San Francisco tonight. If further tests uphold that she is truly out of remission, we'll cultivate Alexis' bone marrow and stem cells within hours of ablating Stephanie's."

"Ablating? Killing all the cells in her bone marrow?"

"Yes. We have to eradicate all her stem cells, blasts, as well as mature reds, whites and platelets in the blood." Peter's clinical delivery was unnerving.

"Everything?" I questioned him.

"Everything. As soon as she gets here, we'll begin preparing her. Let her rest tonight and proceed with ablation tomorrow. She will have to go into sterile isolation as she stabilizes. That may take several days. Then we will implant her sister's stem cells."

"Will she be asleep? Oh, God, tell me she will be asleep."

"It's more like a transfusion, Kai."

"Please don't hurt her, Peter. Please don't."

There was silence on the phone between us.

"We will fight to save her, Kai." He had shifted into his clinical voice when I asked him to "tell me". My gentle lover was all transplant surgeon right now.

"Can I talk to Stephanie?"

"Gellman called in a sedative for the trip. She's in considerable pain now, so hopefully she's sleeping."

"What can I *do*, Peter?"

"Wait...and pray."

"Maybe I need to *be* there...with you and Stephanie," I was begging. "I could take the last plane out tonight."

The silence that followed seemed to go on forever, then, Peter spoke quietly. "You've done your part, Kai. Hold the faith. Let the rest of us do our job now."

"That's so hard for me, Peter...to wait, to let go." All my life I had sprung into action as a way to grapple with my lack of control. How could Peter ask me just to wait? Trust him. I knew he was right. I just didn't know if I could do it.

"Keep us *all* in your heart, Kai. Got to go. I'll call you later if I can. It's going to be a long night. It may be tomorrow before I can get back to you."

I hung up the phone. I felt suspended in some kind of gel. Sluggish — half speed. So this was it. Stem cell transplant: the ultimate and final treatment for acute myelogenous leukemia. Twenty percent of patients made it to the five-year mark. Some don't survive the procedure itself.

I walked over to the peach love seat. I stood in front of the painting that Stephanie loved. With my right hand, I traced the tea cup and saucer. The cascading azaleas, ones like she carried on her wedding day. I placed my palm over the center of the painting and visualized Stephanie dressed in white in her sterile room at Hollings Cancer Center; I saw her in white in her wedding dress standing on the terraces at Middleton Place. I looked to the future to imagine her at Sloan Kettering in another sterile room of white. I sent forth all the love and light available to me into that painting that somehow embodied

Stephanie. I called on Mother and Father God to channel their love and power through me. I asked the departed spirits of Mark, Dumpling, my mother, Eva, and Stephanie's mother, Alexandra, to intercede for Stephanie. I sat down in her place on the love seat to wait and surrendered to the reality of what would be.

I heard Mark tell me again, "There's nothing to be afraid of. It's so peaceful there."

Chapter Forty-one

It was deep night and I was still asleep.

Stephanie and Gracen, Stephanie's mother, Lexy, and my own mother, Eva, were all children, playing in a great meadow filled with wild bluebells and hundreds of white swans. One single black swan was somewhere near the center. All the girls were naked with bronze skin and long, tangled hair that fell abundantly down their backs, reflecting the bright sunlight streaming around their heads. Arcing through the azure sky was a perfect rainbow, each color bright and pure. The girls were running and swooping through the swans that fluttered their wings, rising softly only a few feet off the ground to avoid being bumped by the scampering girls. Their shrieks of joy were unsurpassed by those in ordinary play. I stood on a small, grassy knoll overlooking the meadow, watching. How I longed to join their play: to cast off my clothes, pull the pins from my hair, shake it loose and dash into their midst in this great dance of freedom. Before I could act, I glanced up and saw a small brown owl hovering above me. I followed it with my eyes as it grew to the size of a great horned owl and flew directly into the light gathering above the rainbow in a great ball of fire like a second sun.

I awakened and sat straight up in bed. "God," I gasped, trying to make my way through the mist of the dream to the conscious world of my real waking life. I was covered in a cold sweat and tangled in bed covers. Something had happened, really happened, and not just in my dream. My owl dreams over the last two years had always been strong. But nothing like this. I had never had a dream like this one...*ever*. I felt apprehensive, tremors moving inside me like early signs of an earthquake. In my mind's eye, I saw it again, the owl flying into that great ball of light. It was enveloped, taken into the light, like an imploding star. Then a great calm came over me. There was nothing to fear. I lay quietly and watched the light for a long time to see if the owl would come back out.

I must have drifted back to sleep. To tell the truth, I'm not sure. I just became crystal clear about so many things: Stephanie was the owl. All the *owls* of my dreams had been Stephanie. She had broken into my life and marked my hand. She had lain on my heart and looked me in the eye and dared me to move her. Now she had flown into a ball of fire. Along with her own illness and journey of healing, she had been a manifestation of the *Divine* to encourage my own healing process.

Even so, I was perplexed. What had happened to her? Had she passed through that final grid of light into death, like Mark? Or was it the Refiner's fire that had enveloped Stephanie? That powerful, healing fire that restored, made our bodies whole?

Chapter Forty-two

Stephanie was on a respirator. In the midst of her leukemia crisis, the hemoglobin in her sick red blood cells could no longer sustain her body's need for oxygen. Her breathing was labored as she slowly suffocated. Attending her throughout the night, Peter had ordered whole blood transfusions and put her on a respirator to take over and regulate her breathing. He called me at six-thirty in the morning when the worst of the crisis had passed. Sleep and the dream did not allow me to answer his first call. I was awakened by the second call, but did not want to answer…did not want to know. If I could have frozen time indefinitely, I would have done it. In reality, the spiral of time was turning and would not give me even this concession of denial.

I answered and Peter told me the truth. Stephanie had come out of remission. The amyotrophic myelogenous leukemia was attacking her body with a vengeance. This is the type of crisis that claims so many patients for death. It is what makes the survival statistics so grim, what Robert Gellman warned me about two years ago.

How can I describe what Peter's voice conveyed when he called my name?

"Kai,"…an exhausted rasp, as if he had run the eight hundred miles from his city to mine to speak to me.

"Kai,"…searching to be emotionally sustained.

A third time, "Kai, she made it through the night."

Relief, a glimmer of hope, a respite from his effort to save her life. He told me how he and Stephanie had done battle with her dragon-disease throughout the long night. Now that she was sleeping, he would lie down.

I visualized Stephanie hooked up to that machine and imagined the rhythmic clicks marking each respiration.

"What do you want to be when you grow up, little girl?" I spoke the poem to her that meant so much to me.

"Alive."

Stephanie's family held vigil all that day and the next. So did the doctors and nurses taking care of her at Sloan Kettering. As did the Goddess of owls and her novice, Kai, miles and miles away.

Stephanie slept on and on. She slept through the night and the next day. Peter's reports did not change. She was not in a coma. An ECT showed her in Delta sleep with frequent periods of REM – dream sleep. She was simply in a deep sleep.

The third day of the crisis, Stephanie was weaned from the respirator with ease, her breathing having normalized. Later on, she awakened. She could talk but was too depleted to say more than a few words. Over the ensuing days, she began to eat and get out of bed. She still didn't have much to say. Peter was encouraged with her progress and felt they could proceed with the ablation and stem cell transplant. He posted it to be done subject to repeat blood tests.

The morning of the procedure, he was in his office reviewing final blood tests done that morning. The nurse's page interrupted, telling him to come to the floor ASAP. Stephanie wanted to talk to him. When he got to her bedside, Stephanie was calm, lucid and adamant that the cancer had left her. She asked him what the most recent tests had shown. He told her he had just begun to review them when she called. She asked him to do another bone marrow after he reviewed the blood tests. Stephanie told me later that Peter listened to her very carefully; then stared at her for a long time.

"I think he was trying to decide if I had gone off the deep end. Whether he should order more blood tests or get a psychiatric consult. He did order the tests!"

Peter almost ran back to his office to review the blood work from that morning. It was shocking. He ordered more blood tests, "stat", an emergency. He performed the repeat bone marrow himself. He accompanied the marrow specimen to the lab and watched the clinical pathologists prepare it for examination under microscope. They also prepared the newly drawn blood. Together they carefully examined

Stephanie's blood and bone marrow. It was all normal. When they re-examined the slides prepared from specimens taken after her admission five days before, the difference was phenomenal. She had come in with ragingly abnormal blood elements. As an extra precaution, Peter re-examined the faxed reports from the oncologist at the Medical University of Illinois, Chicago, tests done days earlier. Those reports and specimens drawn after admission to Sloan Kettering were unequivocal evidence of acute myelogenous leukemia that had, indeed, come out of remission. The specimens just drawn and examined that morning showed no evidence of disease - *textbook normal!*

I had been waiting all morning for a call from him or Stephanie, Henry or Steve Edinger. I had instructed Sarah to interrupt if a call came from any of them, even if I was with a patient. I had just finished my first half hour med check when Peter called. He could hardly contain his excitement.

"Kai, sit down, are you sitting down?"

How many days ago had I felt faint when he called? I sat down.

"I'm sitting, Peter. I'm sitting."

"Something extraordinary has happened, Kai. Stephanie's leukemia has spontaneously remitted. It's gone. Absolutely no trace of abnormal blasts. All her blood elements are perfect and her bone marrow. Perfect!"

He told me about being called to Stephanie's bedside early that morning.

"I didn't believe her, Kai. She tried to tell me she had been healed and I didn't believe her. I was annoyed that we would have to waste time and money repeating tests. But I couldn't proceed with ablation without her written consent. I'll have to do all the tests *again* in a few days just to be on the safe side. I'm almost to Stephanie's room now. Let me tell her the results and I'll have her call you when she can. Her whole family is in there waiting to hear. We've had a spontaneous remission, Kai. Some kind of miracle!"

I didn't try to tell him about my dream or that I was waiting for some kind of call to clarify its meaning. Right now, I was burning to talk to Stephanie.

It felt like an eternity before she finally called.

"Kai, you've heard. Dr. H called you?" At the sound of her voice, I settled down.

"He did, Stephanie. Now, *you* tell me. Tell me all of it."

"I had been sleeping, Kai. Sleeping. Deep, restful sleep. I think I dreamed, but I can't remember them. I didn't have a near death experience, at least not from what I've read about them. There were no visions, no voices. The knowing came in my sleep. Wrapped in so many layers-held in time, out of body-flying in the universe but still...totally still. Then, I woke up. I have no idea what time it was. Henry was at the hotel with Sasha and all the family, so I was completely alone.

I knew. Kai, I knew I had been healed. I knew the leukemia was gone. I tell you, Kai, they can do all the tests in the world, but it's *gone*! Call it spontaneous remission, call it whatever, I don't care. I know it is a miracle! Say you believe me, Kai. Please believe me!"

A miracle. She had no doubt. There was no attempt to rationalize; no equivocation. She just called it what she knew it was.

Understanding from my own dream gave me conviction to support what she was saying. I would share that dream with Stephanie at a later time. Now, I simply said, "I believe you, Stephanie; I truly believe you."

"I want to come home, Kai, to my marsh and tides. I want to walk under the live oaks, drape Spanish moss around my shoulders, squeeze pluff mud through my toes. Gather the biggest bouquet of azaleas that I can hold and walk around with them all day!"

I took a deep breath as our conversation lightened. It needed to as I felt I could be incinerated by emotional intensity! Stephanie lightened it some more as she said, "When next I see you, you can call me Doctor Stephanie Edinger-Mainz. I missed my graduation today."

We had moved from the realm of the absolute sublime and back to the realities of everyday life.

"It will be a pleasure to call you doctor. Didn't I sign something early on in our therapy that said we were equals? Now we are doctor-to-doctor. But can Two-Pop handle the competition?"

"He's the one that reminded me that the graduation was today! He and Nana were going to surprise Henry and me by coming to the graduation. Two-Pop had talked his way into actually presenting me with my diplomas on stage. Does he have connections, or what?"

"So, Dr. Edinger-Mainz, when are you getting out of the hospital?"

"Not sure. Dr. H wants to run one more set of blood tests. Another bone marrow. It's okay. I've gotten almost immune to the pain now. My body is still recovering. I'm still tired like I've run a marathon. When Dr. H thinks I'm ready, I'll come home to Charleston.

I don't understand what happened to me, Kai. I'm blown away and happy and tired. I look like hell with respirator-hair."

I had to laugh. I had never heard of respirator-hair before.

"There should be just enough late bloomers to fill your arms for a day down here."

"I need to see you, Kai. I need to get grounded."

"Let me know when you get here. I'll work you in or stay late. We'll take as much time as we need to process all this."

"Okay, Kai. Gotta rest now. Gotta go."

And just like that, Stephanie's spiral finished its ascendant turn and left me in a time warp.

Chapter Forty-three

Peter was exhausted. He had been on an adrenalin high for days. Word about Stephanie's cure had spread through Sloan Kettering's medical community like wildfire. He had been inundated with phone calls, emails, and hall-side doctor chats. He and Stephanie were at the center of a progressively building maelstrom of controversy. Peter's early elation was gradually being replaced with exasperation. With every phone conversation, I could hear his mounting distress. Peter wasn't a needy person, but my protective instincts were firing. My beautiful besieged boyfriend needed to be rescued...by me. I worked out a plan and made a few phone calls before we talked that night. It was finally time to go to New York.

"Peter, I'm coming up there. I'll be at the Mandarin Oriental Hotel on Columbus Circle by the time you finish rounds Friday afternoon. If you're not there by six o'clock, I'm coming to the hospital to drag you out. I'll leave the room number on your voice mail after I check in. I've also talked to Claire. She's over seventeen now and is making plans to stay with a girlfriend for the weekend. She will clear it with you. I want to take you away from the world so you can rest. We might not even leave our room. We can order room service for all our meals and I'm buying."

"I'll be there, Kai." That was all he said.

Stephanie was discharged Friday morning with a clean bill of health. It had taken her a full week after the remission for her body to strengthen and adjust to the disappearance of her disease. She and Henry were driving home to South Carolina to her family. I probably flew right over her on my way to LaGuardia.

The Mandarin Oriental is the most beautiful, tranquil hotel I have ever walked through. I had seen pictures on the Internet, but they didn't do it justice. When I greeted Peter at the door to our room, I was struck by the dark circles under his eyes. He radiated fatigue. We had a simple dinner in the room and he soaked in the marble Jacuzzi, the jets pulsing water into his tight muscles. Afterwards, I put him to bed. I read and slept on the couch so I wouldn't disturb him. He slept for fourteen hours. We ate in bed late the next morning. Room service brought coffee, juice, and croissants with raspberry jam and real butter. He was such an early riser; I'd never had the opportunity to serve him breakfast in bed! We stayed in bed after we ate and talked for a long time.

"Kai, I've never really been through anything like this. Spontaneous remission is so rare that it's like doctors don't know what to think. It's as if there is no credible place for it in our scientific understanding. The more education and degrees we have, the less we can fathom the unseen. The response at S-K to what happened to Stephanie is overwhelming."

"Good or bad?"

"Both. Some of my colleagues are fascinated and very open to the idea that something extraordinary has occurred. Then there are the naysayers. The technocrats who want it proved. Some of them are already muttering that Stephanie never came out of remission. All of them want to see the clinical data, labs… everything. Head of the department called me in to see if I would present Stephanie at grand rounds in two weeks. The whole department of Internal Medicine would be present for a case conference like this."

"Sounds like an interesting opportunity."

"He wants Stephanie to be there, too."

"Wouldn't you need her permission to use her case anyway?"

"Not if we didn't name her. I don't know if I want to ask her to do that or not."

"Why don't you let her help you make that decision?"

"I feel the need to protect her from some of the curiosity-seeking stuff that is going on. *New York Times* got wind of her story and had a features reporter call me. I haven't responded yet. I even had the wife of a colleague call my secretary to ask if I would speak at their church. I don't have time for this, Kai. Especially defending my reputation from doctors who just flat don't believe that miracles and medicine have anything to do with each other."

I wondered if that was bothering him more than the other

things. I didn't get a chance to ask before he changed the subject.

"Kai, how would you feel if I took a job at Hollings Cancer Center?"

I just stared at him in disbelief. "Peter, are you serious? Tell me you're serious."

"I'm very serious. When I came to MUSC for that symposium last year, I met with David Christian, the Oncology Department Chairman. He made me an open-ended offer for a position in their transplant division if I was ever interested. Of course, I'm way more interested now than I was a year ago." Peter had a big grin on his face. He added, "Edinger and I had lunch this week in the hospital cafeteria. He really impressed me with his understanding of what had happened to Stephanie, both medically and spiritually. Rob Gellman and I talked for an hour on the phone, too. I would love to practice medicine with people like them."

"What about Claire? She will be a senior next year."

I won't leave her alone in the city if she wants to finish school with her friends. I could split my time between Sloan Kettering and MUSC for a year with Claire visiting Charleston some while I'm there. We could make it work. Claire likes Gracen and Andrew. She talked to me about Gracen being like a little sister. She always wanted a sister."

He pulled me into his arms along the length of his body and held me. From death and divorce, Peter and I were finding life together.

Chapter Forty-four

When I returned to Charleston from New York, I had a mini-meltdown. It was my turn to be exhausted. Sometimes, psychiatrists are the last ones to recognize their own neediness. If we are taking care of others, we will defer what we need until later. I had just done that in spades. Traffic on Mark Clark Expressway between the airport and my house was at a standstill. Occasionally, it would inch along and then stop again. The tip-off that I was depleted came when I made up a song with various ditties that would have made a drunk Irishman blush. After I had embarrassed myself, I tried to do a detached clinical analysis of my condition. I was saturated. I was empty. I was overloaded, but bordered on shutdown. All in all, I was human. Just like anyone else who had ridden this kind of emotional roller-coaster, I was ready for it to stop at the station so I could get off. Extremely good and/or happy experiences can be just as depleting as negative ones. Ask anyone who has had a baby, gotten a job promotion, or moved into a new house. Too much of a good thing can be bad. The human body has a limited supply of adrenal hormones and when they are used up...curtains. Rest is the only cure.

I called Sarah on my cell phone as I rode my brakes in traffic. I asked her to please pull up my coming week's schedule and read out the patient names. As she scrolled through the hours, I listened for any potential emergencies. I usually gave patients (and staff) plenty of notice before I took time off. Some patients felt anxious if they couldn't see or talk to their own therapist. None of these were on next week's schedule. I told Sarah to mark me off for the week and to call each patient. If any felt they had to be seen, they could schedule with an associate. The doctor on call needed to be notified as well. I had only one small flicker of reality: psychiatrists do not get a paid vacation unless they work for someone else. I always took two weeks of vacation, plus time at Christmas and a few extraneous days. My trips with Peter had shot my budget and I would lose income for a week. Right now, I really didn't care.

"Mind me asking what brought this on?" Sarah inquired. I had never done this in the ten years she had been with me.

"For me...just for me." She knew a bit about Stephanie, but had no idea what had transpired at Sloan Kettering. She might find out someday on the Charleston grapevine or from Stephanie herself. It would remain a confidential issue until that time. Just now, I had only enough energy to get home to my kids.

Ironically, school would officially end in three days. Andrew and Gracen had finished exams and were entering their end-of-school pseudo-hibernation states. There were six days before Andrew's graduation ceremony. He would be DONE! I had to rest before I could grapple with that! Both would spend June with their father. Andrew was actually going to be working with him for part of the summer. I would have more time with Gracen even with camps and babysitting jobs.

Passivity is an art form with post-exam teenagers. They planned to stay up late watching Netflix and OD on technology via iPhones, iPads, and iPods. Their menu would be pizza (delivered), hot dogs from Scoogie's, cookie dough ice cream from Baskin Robbins, Skittles, queso dip with nacho chips, and Diet Dr. Pepper. Personal hygiene regressed to caveman mode: sweatpants and T-shirts would be worn 24/7.

Actually, I loved it. This time, I escaped responsibility and constraint right alongside them. The one place I differed was bathing. I soaked in the tub a couple times a day.

While the kids hung out indoors all week, I took to the dirt of the earth contained in my big, faded green ceramic pots on the decks and porch. I replenished the old with bags of nutritious black dirt and fertilizer. I loaded up on zinnias, petunias, Sweet William, caladiums, coleus and ferns. Bougainvillea and hibiscus wintered in the greenhouse. I clipped them like our dogs' summer cut and manhandled them up to the first landing of the decks. I forced Andrew out into the daylight to help me lug them the rest of the way. I never wore gloves. I reveled in the feel of warm dirt on my fingers as I dug into the rich darkness. After planting new life, I retreated to my beloved Lowcountry "pluff" mud. It is the dirt of the marsh - fecund and wet. I hopped over the retaining wall that separated the lawn from the marsh, and let my feet sink into the dark, chocolate mire. With great effort, I pulled a foot out making great sucking sounds that startled the small, black spider-like fiddler crabs whose mud homes I had stepped on. I watched the tiny silver snails that crawled up and down stalks of Spartina marsh grass eating the organic debris left by the outgoing tide. I waded into the brackish sea water of Boone Hall Creek dressed in blue jean cutoffs and a T-shirt. It was not worth changing into a bathing suit. The goal was to float!

I loved to float as a child. Daddy taught me to swim in Beaver Creek, a tributary of Wateree Lake. I used to question my father about where this lake came from.

"The Catawba River," he said. "There's a system of lakes, dams, and rivers that cross South Carolina from northwest to southeast that harness energy and redirect the water. The Catawba Dam created the Wateree Lake whose dam spills into the Wateree River. It's joined by the Congaree. Their confluence makes more lakes and the Santee River which empties into the Lowcountry."

My Daddy's mind always saw topography, a view from the air. This was honed by his years as a pilot. My mind saw simplistic lines for the rivers and circles for the dams and lakes.

"Daddy, did the Indians name all these waters? Those are all Indian names."

"You're right, Kai. When the water ran through their territory, it took on the name of the tribe. That's about all we have left of the Indians now."

I floated in the Wateree and thought about those Indians. They were almost all gone now, but the water which carried their names flowed south, taking care of so many people. Cherokee blood flowed in me and I was one of their many progenies who would live on. It held me on its surface and then allowed me to dive deep. Boone Hall Creek held me the exact same way as the Wateree waters: lifting, supporting, swirling. The only difference is the tides that pushed water from the Wando River in and out between the creek and the Atlantic. Floating, I was part of that great force of nature…one with the flow that nourished, cleansed, and took me beyond myself.

My children never checked on me until they were hungry. They sauntered down to the dock and called, "What's for supper Mom?"

"Just raiding the crab trap for y'all to pick enough for crab cakes!"

Andrew countered, "Thai, delivered?"

"Pizza?" Gracen shouted over him. "Half with mushrooms and onions, half pepperoni!"

"Got it," Andrew pulled out his cell as I trudged from my muddy retreat.

Andrew and Gracen had done the impossible: talked me into seeing *The Silence of the Lambs* while we ate the pizza. I had resisted for years on the personal principle that I would not pay good money to watch a movie psychiatrist eat and make lamp shades out of his patients. I didn't care that Anthony Hopkins had won an Academy Award for playing Hannibal Lecter. However, in an effort to be with my children, I gave in. Also, it was what was on. When it was over, the kids and I were dazed, especially me. I could not believe that America had loved this movie. Gracen broke the uneasy quiet.

"Mom, I wonder what Dad will think when he meets Peter."

Earth to Gracen, I thought. What in the world does *The Silence of the Lambs* have to do with those two men? Is she changing the subject to something that matters or is equally frightening? We had finally talked yesterday as a family about the changes that were coming because of my relationship with Peter. Or, at least I talked and they listened. They did not ask a single question.

Andrew had summarized, "We are cool Mom, with whatever. If he makes you happy, that makes us happy." Now this.

Andrew answered her, "Dad will be cool. Would Peter teach me to fly?" He turned towards me.

"I'm sure he would take you up in the plane and show you the basics. Then, we could get real flying lessons," I smiled.

"He thinks Claire is hot," Gracen added.

"Shut it, big mouth," Andrew shot back.

"Well, I think she would be a great big sister," she said to him.

So this was about the possibility of my marrying Peter.

I finally realized that they were making remarks to each other and didn't expect me to say anything…just listen.

Eventually, Gracen turned to me, "Will you invite Dad to your wedding if you marry Peter? You could let Poochie-Ching and Tallulah be the ring bearer and flower dogs."

I blushed, and kept my mouth shut.

"It'll all work out, Gracen," Andrew pulled his sister up from the couch. "Let's go get ice cream before we start the *Lord of the Rings* trilogy."

They left me sitting alone in the den, feeling happy. I stood up and followed the sound of my children's laughing voices to the kitchen. I wanted a bowl of lime sherbet with Danish wedding cookies.

Chapter Forty-five

Stephanie's homecoming session was full of emotions, for both of us. In the past months, Stephanie and Henry had finished their doctorate degrees in Chicago; traveled to New York after a recurrence of AML; experienced a spontaneous remission; and had returned home to Charleston. Whether Stephanie realized it or not, she would need to pace herself as she made a therapeutic reentry. Eventually, she would need to recount her whole remission experience. We would mine it for gold. We would try to learn what it all meant as we wove the threads into her life tapestry. But not yet. Not today. Today was a celebration.

Stephanie looked amazingly well, exuding good health. She regaled me with funny stories about residents and interns creeping around her like she was the shrine at Lourdes. She wasn't sure if she was famous or infamous.

Before Stephanie left, I told her that Peter and I were getting serious. I had been vague with her about our dating. She smiled and said, "Oh, I know".

Very gradually, Stephanie edged deeper and deeper into the experience of her healing. Only she knew the way. On her third visit, she began to share the aftermath of her extraordinary healing.

"Why me, Kai? Why did I have a spontaneous remission—a miracle, when most others do not? Why did I wake up and your little Stephanie didn't?"

Psychologically, her questioning was right on schedule. She had made her way through a life-altering disease and equally life-altering return to health. In a way, her mind and emotions were still trying to "catch up" with her body and spirit. Understanding plays a vital role in mental processing. So does realizing that many things cannot be understood with the mind alone.

"It scares me to talk like this. I don't want to sound ungrateful. I...AM...SO...GRATEFUL," she said, enunciating every word. "But...what did I ever do to deserve this reprieve? It is humbling. It is confusing. I feel grateful and guilty. I do NOT feel worthy of being healed."

She hit the issue dead center. Now, this was *my brave* Stephanie, daring to question fate. I scooted to the edge of my seat and leaned towards her, keeping some space between us. I did not want a premature ending to this important inquiry.

"Are you saying you didn't deserve to be healed?" I asked. "Begs the question of whether any of us deserve a no-strings-attached gift of this magnitude. Who judges our worthiness? Are you judging yourself, Steph? Is this causing survivor guilt?"

"Survivor guilt? You mean like when one person survives a plane crash and everyone else dies? That kind of survivor guilt?"

"It's the same. It's common that lone survivors, or unique ones like you, question their worthiness to be the one destined to live. People I've treated seem to go one of two ways: they decide life is all about chance and they got the luck of the draw, or they decide some other *force* in life has found them worthy of the gift of life when they should have died."

"Does that mean everyone who isn't healed or doesn't survive a crash isn't worthy?" she asked. Damn good question I thought.

"Do you mean," I said as gently as I could, "not healed as fast as you were? If they go through one or even two stem cell transplants and are healed, is there a different worthiness involved? What about the ones who endure chemo and die, healed through death?" I paused. People spend lifetimes trying to figure this stuff out: Becker, Küng, many of the major religious figures of the world, past and present. Today, it was just Stephanie and me.

"Don't you think all cancer patients ask for what happened to me?"

"Yes, I do. I even wonder who or what defines healing anyway. If surgeons remove a tumor and stitch the body back together, do they heal the patient? The reknitting of cells cannot be seen…or hurried. The doctor goes home to sleep and healing happens miraculously on a cellular level while the patient rests and sleeps. We understand the physiology of it, but the x-factor of healing is not known. Is it a force or energy? As I understand it, our bodies are in a constant state of repair until they wear out from old age. Healing on a deep, unseen, cellular level is going on all the time."

Abruptly, I stopped. I wasn't sure if I was helping or hurting. Did I even answer her question?

"Am I helping or hurting you?" I asked Stephanie.

In answer, she mushed on.

"What can I do with all this guilt? God knows on a normal day, I drag around as much guilt as the next person. This is different. This is disabling. Too heavy. It almost feels more like an overwhelming sense of responsibility; like I need to spend the rest of my life paying this forward."

"I think you have a choice, Steph. You can respond to your gift of healing by letting yourself share with others…or spend the same energy doing battle with guilt. False guilt can eclipse the beauty and joy of what you have experienced. If you accept the free gift of your healing, maybe it will empower you to pass it on as your genuine gift back to the world. Good news is that you are free to believe anything you want and act on it or not. I don't understand all of this in absolutes. I can't prove squat. Two years ago, you learned something while you were at Lake

Tahoe during Christmas. Something profound happened to you out there: you learned about God's mercy. I feel like you passed it on to me as a gift. I don't know if I was worthy of it or not. I just accepted it and it changed me. I think that's the way it's supposed to work. I can only speak for me, though."

She gave me a Stephanie look. In the years to come, I would always call this concentrated, piercing gaze a "Stephanie look". She started to say something and then stopped.

"I learned about mercy and then I forgot. Kai, this time, it feels more like love."

"Love indeed," I said.

We stopped after that. We both knew there wasn't anything more to say. We had put this issue of healing to some kind of rest, at least until it appeared again, on one of life's spirals. Our immediate future now needed tending. Stephanie and I had one more session scheduled. It could well be the last hour between us.

Chapter Forty-six

Endings are as important to a successful therapy as beginnings. It is not a one-hour experience. Usually, the therapist and patient begin to sense when the finish line is near. Sessions get chatty and superficial. The patient's need to come diminishes. They may even "forget" to keep an appointment. Because there is a genuine bond of caring, grief can be a part of the final process of therapy. When all is said and done, a therapeutic ending is a summary, a celebration, a finale. For the patient, the main task is letting go; for the therapist, it is more of a release.

However you describe it, it is often hard to do. In the days since Stephanie's miracle, a new realization began to dawn: my time with her was drawing to a close. Our work was almost done.

Today, Stephanie had finally acknowledged that the reason she had come into therapy no longer existed.

"I mean, do well people keep coming to therapy?" she asked, only half in jest.

"Way too expensive," I smiled.

"How about periodic check-ups, like for an oil change in a car?"

"Do those occasionally. Call them tune-ups."

"So you're going to throw me out, huh?"

"No, you're going to decide when it's time to go, and do it gracefully."

Her expression became more serious. "Kai, Henry has been offered a post-doctoral year in Zurich with the Nova Foundation. He had been emailing them before I ended up in Sloan Kettering. We have decided together that he should accept it."

"Nova Foundation?" I wasn't familiar with it.

"It's a think tank and research facility for advanced genetic study with applications to medical treatment of diseases…a privately funded counterpart that has used the work of Dr. Francis Collins as its foundation."

"Francis Collins who completed the human genome project?"

"Yes, one and the same. He mapped the three billion base components of all DNA in the human body and wrote about it in his book, *The Language of God*. I think that's the name. Henry heard him speak in Chicago last year. Apparently, he sees no incompatibility between belief in God and science. He thinks God created human beings by creating the building blocks of DNA. Interesting, huh?"

"Very. When will Henry start?" I asked.

"Mid-July."

"In two weeks?"

"We've already started packing. Dr. H and Dr. Gellman are very happy with my last four weekly blood test results. Stable and holding." Her eyes smiled. "Full circle, Kai. Zurich is where I first got sick. I wonder how that sweet, old Dr. Von Orelli is doing. I'd like to tell him about the miracle. I'm sure he's seen them before."

"I know he would like to hear about what happened to you," I said as my brain moved on ahead to a proper ending. Reality was on our heels.

"Steph, we only have time for one more session. Let's do it outside, maybe at Wadmalaw or the beach at Sullivan's Island."

"You would do that? Have a session at the beach with me?"

"It would be fitting; I've had a lot happen in my own life out on Sullivan's Island."

"It's a deal. Sullivan's Island, it is." She lifted her hand for a high five.

We chose the next Friday, late afternoon, when I would be off and inked it into our calendars. Going before sunset was very symbolic. We also decided to do a little ritual to mark our ending. Read something, gather a few symbols, say some words. I had done this with very creative patients before. We stood up and Stephanie paused to gaze around the room. She would not be here again. She brushed her fingertips along the glass of the French doors and ended up standing face-to-face with my painting. This time, she only touched it with her eyes.

"Your patient who painted this...she got well, too, didn't she?" She glanced at me for affirmation.

I nodded.

"She painted this for my mother and me, too, you know."

In an unpredictable move, she leaned forward and kissed the painting. Turning, she took a step in my direction and kissed me on the cheek.

"See you at the beach next Friday," she said, and walked down the hall for the last time.

That night, I had trouble falling asleep. Well after midnight, I decided to get up and make a cup of soothing chamomile hot tea. I padded down to the kitchen in my cotton PJs and fluffy yellow "ducky" bedroom shoes. They were a gift from Gracen who liked me to wear them. She said it kept me from being too serious about life. I glanced outside. The moon was almost full. Clouds were floating over its face, casting shadows into the night.

The moon beckoned me out to the dock. As I sat sipping my tea, the clouds slowly coalesced into overcast, blotting out most of the moonlight. A foggy mist arose over the creek as the first light drops of rain began to fall. I turned my face up to catch them in my mouth, but tasted only the salt of my tears. I was grieving Stephanie. It happened that way when we therapists let ourselves love a patient. Objectivity and boundaries were there for a reason in the land of therapeutic law. Law, however, does not always govern the heart. I let my eyes and heart weep for a while.

I thought of some of my other patients. There were so many and all so different. Like in real life, they fell along a spectrum of personality needs and therapeutic response. Stephanie was one of a kind. Her timing in my life was extraordinary. She was probably the most dramatic case I had ever had; not the most important; not the most difficult; not the most troublesome. But, what I had learned from her was colossal, critical, and pivotal in my own life.

I would really miss her. Would I ever see her again after we finished? She had a lot of family in Charleston. Knowing Stephanie, she would show up in my waiting room someday, moving like a tigress come to sniff me out. I realized how very tired I felt and sleepy. As I started back to the house, I suddenly knew what to give Stephanie as a going away present.

Chapter Forty-seven

Stephanie's Jetta was parked in the public access at Station 28 ½. I pulled in beside her. That numbering was unique to Sullivan's Island, as well as the term "station" that came from the old cable car stops on the Island. Fort Moultrie was still intact on the other end. I never understood the use of ½.

She was standing with her back to me when I broke through the high dunes onto the flat, white sandy beach. She could have been a still life painting with her blond hair blowing in the breeze and the voluminous bottom of her pink sundress wrapped around her legs. Her feet were bare, so I kicked off my shoes. She had laid out a beautiful quilt high up on the beach beyond the reach of the tide. It had interlocking circles made of patchwork with a purple backing. I knew that her Grandmother Sanderson had quilted it as a gift for her marriage to Henry. It was called a "wedding ring" design. Dumpling had made one with the same design but different colors for my mother when she had married so many years ago. It was an old Southern tradition between mothers and daughters. My mother had bequeathed it to me. That and her beautiful china dishes were all I had left of my grandmother's worldly possessions.

I had left a wrapped bundle hidden in the sea oats, but put my other "stuff" down on the quilt. I went to stand by Stephanie.

"What do you spy?" I asked.

"The next horizon," she said as she encircled my waist with her arm. I did the same.

It was almost seven-thirty, but the sky was filled with muted blues and long, white cirrus clouds. Perfect weather conditions for a sunset.

"Hungry?" she asked. She had left me a message earlier the day before that she would bring cheese and wine and "crudities". Food was so symbolic in our relationship.

"Starving! Let's eat."

Cheese was Stephanie's manna. She laid out brie, gouda, and bleu. She opened a tin of duck pâté, several kinds of crackers, along with luscious grapes. She poured each of us a glass of a deep red Burgundy. We ate with gusto as the sun dropped lower and lower in the sky.

Finally, we began our ritual. We made a circle on the quilt of our favorite symbols. I started by placing the queen of swans and the amethyst firefly necklace pendant in the center of the quilt. Stephanie put in her ivory enamel swan taken some two years ago when she began her work. Next, she gently laid a delicate old linen baby cap that belonged to Nana which she and Sasha had worn to their christenings.

I added an empty French fry container from McDonald's, which made us both laugh.

She placed a blank schedule card from my office with my name, address and phone number on it and the signed contract from our first session marked COMPLETED in bold letters on the cover sheet.

I put a small stained glass angel on the edge of the card to anchor it. The sea breeze had picked up even more as the ocean cooled faster than the earth.

Lastly, she laid down her red wig.

In the middle of the circle, Stephanie placed a battery-powered candle to create a white/blue flicker-like flame. She had known that no real candle could hold up to the wind of Sullivan's Island.

We both read poems from Rilke to each other. Spontaneously, we began saying words back and forth to each other, creating a kind of liturgy. They were words that carried great meaning in the work we had done together. They were the finale.

She started.

"Leukemia."

"Hope," I responded.

"Riding a Pac-Man horse."

"Energy arcing between our hands."

"Hopscotch."

"Fireflies."

"Paralyzing fear," her voice trembled.

"A voice that led you through the night," I whispered.

"Remission."

"Wonder," I felt it again.

"Secrets."

"Understanding."

"Love with Henry."

"Love with Peter."

"Dream of a snake," Stephanie smiled.

"Owls and more owls."

"Conception."

"'Oh ye of little faith,'" I spoke Stephanie's words of long ago.

"'I will walk with you no matter what, in life or death,' you said," Stephanie quoting me.

"Black swans."

"Relapse, sick again."

"Healed through death," I murmured, thinking of Mark.

"Miracles!" Stephanie shouted.

"Stephanie, great and small," I closed.

We lay back on the quilt and rested in the shared solitude. Breaking the final silence, I said, "I have a present for you, but you have to close your eyes while I go get it. No peeking."

She closed her eyes tightly while I retrieved the bundle from the dunes. I unwound the bed sheet protecting it and carried it to the quilt.

"Now you can open."

"My painting! Oh, Kai, you brought my painting! You're giving it to me!"

"Like you said, it was painted for you, too. Take it, Stephanie, and always remember the hours between us."

She launched up off the quilt and into my arms.

"How could I ever forget?"

The lowering sun finally touched the horizon and sent great swaths of purple, pink and rose light reflecting off the clouds. Our sunset was on the way. We reveled in the beauty, releasing the sun to its journey to the other side of the earth and each other to freedom.

Acknowledgements

For many years, I talked about writing a book based on my experiences as a psychiatrist. There were sparks of creative fire that produced short stories, but no real vision for a book-length story. That came from an owl dream. Had it not been for the wisdom and guidance of my dream group, I might have missed the message (from my first owl dream). Providentially, they helped me understand and act upon the interior siren call to begin. Dream Sisters, Barbara Curry, Donna Farmer, Terry Helwig, Cindy Hope, Alice Timmons Morrisey, Lynne Ravenel, Carolyn Rivers, and Erin Passow have been with me throughout the writing of this book and several have been readers as well.

Friend, mentor and fellow writer, Fran Hawk, shared her beautiful mountain house in Tryon, North Carolina, as a place of solitude and inspiration in which to write. In addition, she and her husband, Chris, provided a second venue in Telluride, Colorado. My gratitude to Fran is boundless. This book simply could not have been written without her.

Another unflagging supporter was Jane O'Boyle, a freelance editor who had moved to Charleston after working many years for a publisher in New York. Her expertise throughout countless edits was invaluable. Only Jane could make me laugh as she redlined whole paragraphs into obscurity. She cheered me on when I lost my way. She believed in me and my story. Thank you Jane!

Tricia Davey, my New York agent, worked tirelessly to promote this book. Her help and guidance through the canyons of the publishing world sustained me as did her belief that this book should be published.

Jonathan Haupt and his fine in-house editors at USC Press provided invaluable feedback on content and character development. Thanks for telling me "that whatever happens, the Kai and Stephanie story should be told".

Readers were a continual source of insights that led to refinement and different perspectives. Beloved college roommate, Zan Young Bramley, endured repeated readings. Settie Jones, Terry and Jim Helwig, Susan Dickson, Sue Monk Kidd, Rose Tomlin, Pat Mckinney, Donna Farmer, Annie Edwards and Mike Flores spent valuable time reading, marking, and adding their comments to early drafts. Pinky Bender, my grammar and punctuation editor, deserves special kudos for repeated corrections. SOPOG, Pinky.

Annie and Donna have been with me as "Dragonfly Sisters" for many years, both as best friends and colleagues. Their love has sustained me through most of the wounds and joys of my life, including the highs and lows of writing this book.

Dr. Robert Stewart, an oncologist at the Hollings Cancer Center at MUSC, was a valuable medical consultant who helped me review AML (amyotrophic leukemia) and all its vagaries. Thank you, Rob, for serving in the frontline trenches of cancer treatment and for sharing your wisdom and knowledge with me. Readers should note that in the interest of storytelling, some of my content about AML relative to Stephanie's case was fictionalized. Dr. Stewart is not responsible for anything I have written about AML.

My book club, working courageously, took on my manuscript as one of their monthly book selections, critiquing its strengths and weaknesses. Many thanks to Laura Stone, Laurie Meyers, Kelly Rose, Mary Stewart Murphy, Shannon Smith Hughes, Kim Maness, Kim McIntire, Carol Williams, Karen Ross, Mary Francis Bishop and Vickie Wheelus. Best book club ever!

My daughter, Erin, herself a talented editor, read evolving drafts and made loving and fearless critiques that only she could have done. She also guided me through the mysteries of social media. She taught me that in order to succeed, I had to overcome my own fear of failure.

My son, Christian, after reading an early draft commented on the weaving of fiction and truth into a "new story". His affirmation of my intent was heart-warming.

My "Owl Sisters", Monte Parsons Gaillard, Melanie Mauldin, Catherine Middleton, and Missy McIver attended me as we consigned my first draft to flames so the next could arise from the ashes. Sharing our owl sightings, symbols, and charitable adoption of an owl, have all inspired and encouraged me. Truly, you all have been the wisdom of the owl.

My therapists, Dr. Don Neblett and Dr. Ann Ulanov, long years ago, paved the way for my personal, interior journey to wholeness. My mentors, Dr. Layton McCurdy and Dr. Dick Sosnowski, who gave me the "keys to the Kingdom" of psychiatry and whole person medicine. I have the deepest love and respect for them all.

Julia Traw, computer whiz and translator extraordinaire, tackled many a hand written, lined yellow page, miraculously converting my words into neat, computer drafts. Forever indebted, Julia.

It is true what almost all writers say of their spouses: they are the linchpins of books becoming reality. My husband, Alex Beard, with unfailing love and patience, has been involved in every aspect of this book. Most importantly, he has understood the deep wellspring of my need and desire to tell this story. In this and many other aspects of marriage, he has taught me what partnership really means. He has faithfully carried the vision for me when I was stuck on the ninety-nine-yard line and could not see my way into the end zone. He has interfaced with the computer world and technology of publishing on my behalf. He has made a lot of spaghetti when I could not cook, and he has given me permission to quit (and restart) more than once. Your belief in me has helped me create my opus, Alex. You are my heart.

I am forever indebted to my deceased brother, Alan, for teaching me not to fear death and to his daughters, Danielle and Adrienne, courageous children who have grown into amazing young women. Love to his special wife, Linda. And thanks to Janet, lover of books, who keeps me reading and her mate, my younger brother Steve, who loves family with all his heart.

To my patients who have allowed me to learn so much as we journeyed together, I am eternally grateful. To the late artist who immortalized our work together in the "painting that Stephanie loved", I thank for the constant visual reminder that love and courage can conquer the dark. Her painting is one of my personal treasures and has a place of honor in my home.